Praise for the Bissonet & Cruz Investigations series by SCOTTY CADE

The Royal Street Heist

"Step aside Sherlock and Watson, Bissonet and Cruz are in the house… and they rock!"

—MM Good Book Reviews

"All in all I enjoyed this book and I highly recommend it."

—The Kimi-chan Experience

"Stellar writing, strong men and sticky romance… I'd say, give it a go!"

—Boys in Our Books

Veiled Loyalties

"I think that if you like mysteries with a romantic bent—this is your story/series…"

—The Blogger Girls

"The writing was flawless and the story well thought out. The characters were just absolutely amazing and the story was one I just could not put down."

—Inked Rainbow Reads

By Scotty Cade

Acting Out
Forever for Now
Knobs
Losing Faith
The Mystery of Ruby Lode
Sunrise Over Savannah • Chasing the Horizon
An Unconventional Courtship • An Unconventional Union

BISSONET & CRUZ INVESTIGATIONS
The Royal Street Heist
Veiled Loyalties
A Lethal Mistake

FINAL ENCORE
Before the Final Encore
Final Encore
After the Final Encore

LOVE SERIES
Wings of Love
Treasure of Love
Bounty of Love
With Z.B. Marshall: Foundation of Love

Published by DREAMSPINNER PRESS
www.dreamspinnerpress.com

A LETHAL MISTAKE

Bissonet & Cruz Investigations

SCOTTY CADE

DREAMSPINNER PRESS

Published by
DREAMSPINNER PRESS

5032 Capital Circle SW, Suite 2, PMB# 279, Tallahassee, FL 32305-7886 USA
www.dreamspinnerpress.com

A Lethal Mistake
© 2016 Scotty Cade.

Cover Art
© 2016 Reese Dante.
http://www.reesedante.com
Cover content is for illustrative purposes only and any person depicted on the cover is a model.

ISBN: 978-1-63477-659-2
Digital ISBN: 978-1-63477-660-8
Library of Congress Control Number: 2016909472
Published September 2016
v. 1.0

Printed in the United States of America
∞
This paper meets the requirements of
ANSI/NISO Z39.48-1992 (Permanence of Paper).

First and foremost, this book, as are all of my books, is dedicated to Kell, my husband of twenty years. Without your continued support and sacrifices, I would never find the time to write. I love you with all my heart.

Additionally—and I know I do this for every book—but seriously, the end product you see would never even pass for a novel if it weren't for these two ladies:

From the bottom of my heart, I would like to thank my editor, Andi Byassee. She takes my sometimes mixed-up words and turns them into a hopefully interesting and enjoyable read. Thank you, Andi, for your patience and endless wisdom.

And lastly, my cover artist, Reese Dante. She continues to visually bring my stories to life by designing a cover that catches your eye and holds you there. Thank you, Reese.

PROLOGUE

CLICK.

One simple move from a steady finger and the trigger engaged. The neighbor, standing in his front yard five houses down, had no idea he was scope practice for someone he'd casually shot the shit with a number of times. An image of the neighbor's face, full of shock and disbelief before he fell to the ground, appeared in the shooter's mind. He smiled. *Gotcha! Die, you pansyassed motherfucker.*

Of course the neighbor didn't fall. Unsuspecting, he gazed out over his lawn and then looked back toward the garage.

Another man joined the first, dragging a garden hose and carrying two beers. He handed one of the beers to the other, and instantly the shooter's scope focused on the left temple of the second man as he opened the nozzle and began to water his lawn.

Click.

In the shooter's mind, the second man, too, fell to the ground. "That'll teach you queers to infiltrate my neighborhood," the shooter said out loud.

In a quiet little neighborhood in South Kenner, Louisiana, the shooter lay stretched out on his belly, aiming a highly polished and well-maintained M40A1 sniper rifle through an oval window in a fake dormer of his attic. He constantly scanned the neighborhood for signs of anyone mulling about and almost always came up with at least one target. Today he got two.

The shooter shimmied back away from the window, sat up, and gently laid the rifle in an open gun case. He'd done this at least once a day, sometimes as a many as five times a day, for the last two years, taking advantage of various lighting changes, weather conditions, and distances, as well as maneuverability.

The shooter looked out of the window again and gave the neighbors the middle finger. "This is your lucky day, motherfuckers! If I had actually loaded the gun, both of you would have fallen, just like the rest of the assholes who won't see the bullet coming."

The shooter closed his eyes and imagined his future victims falling like snow on a winter's day in Aspen. "I'll teach the motherfucking queers a lesson."

A little voice in his head spoke to him softly. *I only wish there was a way to let them see who pulled the trigger.*

"No!" he said out loud. "I already told you that would be way too risky. Plan your work and work your plan." He added, "It's the only way."

The shooter smiled again as he imagined the expressions on his victims' faces, one by one, as he went over their names in his mind. He smiled at one name in particular, wishing he could be close enough to see the shock on that one's face, the disbelief when he finally realized it was all over and his lifeless body fell to the ground. But that was impossible. His plan didn't allow for it.

"They're fucking queers, and they deserve to die."

Queer? Just like you?

"No!" The shooter slammed the lid on the gun case closed and fought the nagging feelings of guilt and pain trying to make their way into his brain.

But, as usual, it didn't take long for anger and hatred to replace the other emotions. He slithered backward on his stomach, dragging the gun case with him, mumbling the entire time.

"They used you and then threw you out like yesterday's trash. All fucking queers are like that. Now let's see who gets hauled away like trash. The first Mardi Gras parade rolls in two days. It's finally time!"

ONE

"COME ON!" An impatient Montgomery Beaumont Bissonet slapped the steering wheel with both palms and then laid on his horn. "I love Mardi Gras as much as the next guy, but this is ridiculous." He looked at his watch. "Three blocks in an hour. We're gonna have to find a new route home."

"Beau! If you blow that damn horn one more time…."

"What? You're gonna take it out on my ass when we get home?"

Tollison Eduardo Braga Cruz, his business and life partner, raised one eyebrow. "Maybe."

Beau laid on the horn again and smiled defiantly. "Don't threaten me with a good time."

Tollison couldn't stifle his laugh. "Do you really think blowing the horn is gonna make the traffic move any faster?"

"No. But it makes me feel better."

Tollison met Beau's gaze. "Enough with the horn. Okay?"

"Come on, Tol. You provoked it. At least threaten me with something I hate."

"Okay. Like what?"

"Oh… I don't know. Like maybe forcing me to go into the bathroom after Iona or something."

Tollison howled. "Where did that come from?"

Iona Ball was a sweet elderly lady they'd met while solving the Royal Street heist. She'd been the administrative assistant to a questionable art dealer named Dudley Robinette. But when Mr. Robinette was found strangled to death at one of his gallery showings, she no longer had a job.

After the case was solved and Beau and Tollison resigned their positions to open their own private investigations business, they'd rented the space previously occupied by Robinette's business, and she… well, let's just say she came with the place.

Beau gave Tollison an incredulous stare. "Are you telling me you haven't noticed the foul odors, not to mention the strange noises that come out of that bathroom when Iona is dropping the kids off at the pool?"

"Jeez, Beau. Dropping the kids off at the pool? What a lovely term."

"Come on, Tol. I don't know what that woman eats, but man oh man."

"She's an old lady, Beau. And we knew she was an old lady when we hired her, but she's a damn good office manager, and more importantly she's our friend."

"Yes, she is, and I adore her, but can't she drop the kids off at her own pool?"

Beau was so bored he hoped he could get Tollison agitated enough to take him on. Secretly, Beau loved torturing Tollison with these kinds of discussions. They were always entertaining, and boy, did he need a distraction from the traffic right now. Anything to pass the time. Tollison opened his mouth. *Yes! Here comes the tirade.*

Beau knew Tollison well enough to know he would argue any point to the bitter end, even something as trivial as whether people should be able to use the bathroom whenever and wherever they needed to. But much to his dismay, Tollison closed his mouth when the traffic started moving and thereby avoided falling into one of Beau's traps.

Damn! I was so close. Beau was disappointed. He knew he was being disrespectful, not to mention an ass, to poor Iona, but he didn't really mean it. He was just trying to get a rise out of Tollison. In all honesty, being an ass was one of the things Beau did best. It was a gift! But being disrespectful was something he saved for when he was trying really hard to make a point.

When they finally crossed over St. Charles Avenue and things started to move again, Tollison sighed. "We're definitely going to have to find a new route home. Tonight is just the first of the many Uptown parades, and we've got another two weeks of this."

"Maybe we can switch up our hours, go in earlier and work from home a little more."

"That might work," Tollison agreed. "At least we could get home before all this mess starts."

"Hey! You don't get to refer to Mardi Gras traffic as a mess. That's a privilege reserved for us locals."

"Fine. But we don't have these traffic problems during Carnival in my country."

Beau smiled when he realized this might be another opportunity to get Tollison going. "That's because everyone drives donkeys in Portugal," he said.

Tollison huffed. "Come on, Beau. How many times do I have to tell you we don't use asses for transportation in Portugal? They're reserved for husbands and private investigators."

"Ha-ha." Beau chuckled. "Good one. But remember, you're a husband and a PI too."

"Yeah, well," Tollison agreed, "I can also be an ass."

"Tell me about it."

Tollison gave Beau another raised eyebrow, and Beau reached over and squeezed Tollison's knee. "Just kidding, love muffin."

"I figured as much." Tollison laid his hand on top of Beau's. "So we'll talk to Iona about changing our hours tomorrow morning."

"You do remember we own Bissonet & Cruz Investigations. Right?" Beau asked.

"I know, but Iona relies on us for certain things, and it will change her schedule as well."

"Good point."

Beau pulled into their driveway on Prytania Street at long last and put the SUV in park. "Home sweet home."

"Yeah. And it only took us two hours as opposed to our normal fifteen minutes." Tollison opened his door and walked around to the back of the SUV.

People dressed in all sorts of costumes were flooding down Prytania and heading up Broadway to St. Charles Avenue, pulling kids in wagons, hauling ladders with seats bolted to the tops, carrying lawn chairs and coolers. It was mayhem.

"Look at the people!" Tollison said.

Beau nodded. "Yep. First two Uptown parades. The Krewe of Oshun rolls at six o'clock, and immediately following is the Krewe of Cleopatra. Big night in the Garden District."

"Back to back?"

"Sure. And there are two more parades rolling in Metairie—Krewes' of Excalibur and Athena—and one in the French Quarter as well." Beau cast a questioning glance at his partner. "We're still going tonight, right?"

"Hell yeah. This is my first real Mardi Gras in New Orleans. Well, technically it's my second. I was living here last year, but remember I had to be back in Atlanta for a few weeks, packing up and trying to close on the sale of my condo. I missed the whole damn thing. But I wouldn't miss this year for the world."

"Good. And don't remind me," Beau said. "That was the three longest weeks of my life." He took Tollison by the hand and led him up the steps to the front porch, then unlocked the door and stepped inside with Tollison following.

"Hey, what's the official attire for a Mardi Gras parade anyway?" Tollison asked.

"Nothing designer, if that's what you're asking," Beau said playfully. "I'm wearing jeans and a long-sleeved T."

"Seriously?"

"Yep. And I'd bring a jacket. It might get a little chilly after dark."

"No. I meant seriously, nothing designer?"

Beau laughed, pulling Tollison into his arms and whispering into his ear. "I know, Mr. Armani. It's gonna be tough, but I think you'll survive."

Beau let his hands slip down to rest on the tight muscular globes forming Tollison's ass. He squeezed. "I'm gonna head up and shower." He kissed Tollison's neck. "I'll wash your back, if you'll wash mine."

"You go on up. I'll grab us a couple of beers and be up in a second."

"Okay." Beau stole another kiss. "But hurry." He hit the stairs, taking them two steps at a time, loosening his tie and sliding it from his collar as he climbed.

In the bedroom Beau shed his suit coat, toed off his shoes, and within minutes was naked as a jaybird, standing impatiently in front of the glass-enclosed shower. He bounced from foot to foot and wrapped his arms around himself as he waited for the water to heat up.

Seconds later he stepped into a steaming hot shower and closed the door behind him. He felt like he was being wrapped in a cocoon of warmth and basked in the sensations. Bracing his hands against the wall on each side of the showerhead, he allowed the hot water to beat down on his head, neck, and shoulders, washing away the stresses of the day. He waited with anticipation for Tollison to join him.

As the water streamed down on him, he thought back to his and Tollison's rough beginning. The Royal Street art heist was where it all started.

They had been involuntarily thrust upon each other while independently trying to solve the case, and at the outset it hadn't gone well. The lead detective and the insurance investigator had been a volatile combination at best, each fighting for control. Then, to add insult to injury, they'd been ordered to work *together* when the robbery became a high-profile case.

In the end that heist had forged a mutual respect and trust between them that turned into a steamy romance and then into something much more. Love. Something Beau had only experienced a couple of times in his life. He knew without a doubt Tollison had his back, and Beau would give his own life to save Tollison's. He loved the man that much.

Beau shivered but smiled broadly when he felt a momentary burst of cold air fill his warm space. He didn't have to open his eyes to picture Tollison's tan, long, lean, muscular body stepping into the shower and standing behind him. In his mind's eye, he saw every inch of the man from the top of his head to the tips of his toes. They had been together just under two years, and the expectation of Tollison's touch still drove Beau every bit as wild with need and desire as it had when they'd first met.

In a playful mood and wanting to toy with Tollison just a little, Beau ignored him and instead filled his hands with shower gel from the dispenser. Starting with his biceps, he ran his hands all over his body, soaping himself, taking a little extra time to spread his ass cheeks to make sure Tollison got a nice view of his bottom.

When Beau struck a strategic pose and bent over to wash his calves, he felt as much as heard Tollison growl as he stepped up behind him and slid his already hard length into the crack of Beau's ass.

Beau smiled. "Sam? What are you doing here? Tollison's downstairs!"

He let out something between a yelp and a squeal when Tollison's hand landed on his ass with a slap that echoed through the shower. Tollison pulled him close until his back was against Tollison's chest and held him there. Beau could feel the heat of Tollison's breath against his ear when he whispered. "Sam, huh?"

Before Beau could think of something clever to say, Tollison bit his earlobe, sending pulses of pleasure through his entire body.

Tollison's lips moved lower, mouthing seductively at Beau's neck, and Beau shuddered and tilted his head to give him better access.

"I meant to say Toll—" Beau mumbled. But he swallowed his voice when Tollison slipped one finger inside him and simultaneously bit down on the sensitive area between his neck and shoulder to suck on his wet skin.

"Say you're sorry," Tollison whispered, pushing a second finger inside, "or you'll need to be punished."

Beau closed his eyes and didn't respond.

"I said—"

"I know what you said, *Sam*, but I think I'd rather take my punishment."

Tollison hissed and scissored his fingers, which were already slowly moving inside of Beau's soapy opening. Beau stiffened and then relaxed as his cock filled with each of Tollison's movements. He placed his hands on the shower wall and dropped his head. Tollison nibbled and bit Beau's neck and shoulders, bringing him right to the edge of pain and then licking the sting away. He removed his fingers, and Beau was about to complain when he felt Tollison's length pressing against his opening, pushing in ever so slowly.

His heart rate and breathing doubled instantly, and he braced himself for the wonderful piercing pain he knew was soon to follow. Beau moaned and clawed at the marble wall when Tollison not only breached his opening but pushed all the way in without stopping.

Thousands of lightning bolts flashed behind Beau's eyes, jolting him with electricity and forcing him into submission. Tollison was in total control, and Beau didn't want it any other way. It wasn't often he could let go and give himself to Tollison like this—allowing him to completely overpower him. But when it did happen, he loved it.

Tollison held his position, giving Beau time to relax around him, but Beau didn't want to relax. He wanted Tollison to fuck him and fuck him hard.

"Move!" Beau hissed. "Now!"

Tollison pulled almost all the way out. "You gonna lay on the horn again the next time we're in traffic?"

"Hell yeah!"

Tollison slammed back into him, and Beau cried out again, "Hell yeah!" He craned his head around, searching for Tollison's mouth in the steamy shower, and they came together in a hungry, devouring kiss.

Tollison pulled out. "You ready for your punishment, boy?"

"Yes!" Beau screamed.

Plastering his lips against Beau's back, he plowed right back in. Beau's guts felt like they were going to explode each time Tollison's length filled him. With each thrust, the pain slowly morphed into pleasure, and then when Tollison brushed against Beau's sweet spot, Beau howled with unbridled desire. "Punish me, Sam. Please!"

Tollison now had him by the hips and was thrusting in and out feverishly, sending volts of electricity coursing through him with each plunge. Tollison reached around Beau, took him in hand, and started pumping in unison with each thrust.

Beau was suddenly on the verge of an explosion. All of his nerve endings were on fire, and with each of Tollison's moves, the sensations multiplied. He was on extrasensory overload, and he couldn't last much longer. "Oh God, Tol. Don't stop."

"What happened to Sam?" Tollison asked, not missing a beat.

"Who?" Beau asked.

"I love you," Tollison said as picked up the pace.

Tollison's hand and cock were an unstoppable team, and Beau was at his limit. He sucked in a ragged breath and released it. "Now!"

"Let go, baby," Tollison said. "I'm there too."

Beau's felt his ass tighten around Tollison as the first wave of his orgasm washed over him. He watched his release land on the marble wall in front of him, spurt after spurt. Almost instantly he felt Tollison's warm explosion deep inside his gut. Beau rode the waves of pleasure as Tollison rammed into him a few more rounds, emptied into him, and then slowed.

When they were both spent, Tollison collapsed onto Beau's back, and Beau kept them upright only because his hands were still braced on the wall. When Tollison was upright once more, Beau turned in his arms and covered his lips in a crushing kiss, sloppy tongues thrashing everywhere. Beau hoped the kiss expressed his gratitude and love for the man standing in front of him. When the kiss finally ended, Beau held Tollison's face in his hands.

"I love you."

Tollison ran his tongue over Beau's shoulder and licked up to his ear. "I love you too. Burt."

"Asshole!" Beau howled and smacked Tollison on the ass.

TWO

THE NIGHT was filled with an unmistakable energy—the sights and sounds of Mardi Gras were everywhere. The distant smell of horse shit and exhaust fumes from the tractors filled my nostrils, and damn if it didn't smell like every Mardi Gras before it.

I'd gotten so used to my solitude, the fact that I was enjoying this so much was extremely surprising to me. I had always been sort of a loner, especially after my relationship with Byron went south, but tonight my best friend had insisted on dragging me out to the parade, and he was enjoying himself so much it seemed to be contagious. Why not go out and enjoy myself? I had my best friend by my side, a cold beer in my hand, and all the Mardi Gras beads I could catch.

The marching bands were doing their thing. The clown cars were rolling. And the brightly colored floats were throwing any- and everything I could imagine. When a stuffed toy landed at my feet, I stooped to pick it up. Just then something else bounced off my head and shoulders. I realized I'd missed being out with friends, and Mardi Gras was a great coming-out party. A couple of carefree weeks in the middle of winter where people could let their hair down, dress up in any kind of getup they wanted, and act like fools. It felt good to feel alive again! Before I knew it, I was doing the Mardi Gras Mambo like no one was watching, and it seemed to be the only thing I cared about.

The next float rolled in front of me. Instinctively I raised my free hand and started screaming like a fool. "Throw me something, mister!"

A plastic ball bounced off my chest, and just before I bent down to pick it up, I felt a piercing pain in the back of my head. My first thought was that someone had thrown something hard. It hurt like hell, but it didn't feel like anything I could identify. I cupped the back of my head and felt a warm, wet sensation on my fingers. When I brought my hand to my face, I saw my own blood dripping from my fingertips. In that second my legs went numb and gave out, sending me to the pavement with a thud.

People's elongated faces were staring down at me with expressions of horror. I saw my best friend drop to my side, and I thought I heard him calling my name, but I couldn't be sure. His eyes were wide with panic, so I turned away and focused on the people standing above me. They all began to sway and swirl into one large blur of colorful hats and beads, and their mouths were open like they were screaming, but I heard no sounds. The noises of the night had begun to drift away until there was dead silence. I felt very weak, and then everything went dark.

THE ST. Charles Avenue parade route was filled with people at least ten deep. Beau had taken Tollison by the hand and dragged him through the crowds, weaving and winding with persistence, sidestepping here and plowing through there, using means just short of knocking down children and old ladies until they were at the front of the crowd.

Tollison stood in amazement at the sheer number of people lining the street in anticipation of the first Uptown parade. He could feel the electricity in the air as parade goers of all ages stood upright, packed together like sardines in a can. Some children were perched on their father's shoulders and some on ladders, while senior citizens sat in lawn chairs at the back of the crowd.

In the distance the faint sound of sirens, mixed with marching drums, cymbals, and tubas filled the air. A few minutes later, Tollison saw flashing lights as police cars worked their way slowly down the avenue, edging the sidewalks and keeping pedestrians pushed back and off of the street.

Beau looked at Tollison, his uncomplicated smile consuming his face. He winked at Tollison, and the simple gesture had Tollison's heart melting. Beau had his hands tucked in his jeans pockets, and he was bouncing up and down like a kid at Christmas. With each passing day, Tollison realized Beau was like an onion. There were so many layers to the big guy, and Beau had been slowly revealing them, layer after layer. The more Tollison saw, the more he loved.

Tollison had witnessed Beau on more than one occasion, mostly in business, being a complete intimidating asshole. But then with the flip of a switch, he became a very passionate lover and a sweet and caring man. He could go from grumpy and pouty to almost childlike with wonder and anticipation. Would he never see the end to Montgomery Beaumont Bissonet's layers? He hoped not. Beau was a complicated asshole sometimes, but he was *his* complicated asshole, and that's all that mattered.

"Here we go," Beau said, startling Tollison out of his thoughts. When he looked up, two people passed by carrying a banner that read The St. Augustine Marching Band, and the crowd went wild when they started playing the hit song "Titanium." The horns blared, the cymbals clashed, and the drums blasted as the band danced, spun, and weaved in complete unison. Tollison's mouth dropped open, but he couldn't help it. He'd never seen anything so amazing, even at the Macy's Thanksgiving Parade.

Beau beamed as he clapped and danced along to the music. Again, another layer of Beau Bissonet revealed itself.

Next up was a very small clown car with a dozen or so clowns hanging out, throwing beads and candy. The driver honked the horn as he maneuvered the car from left to right, the clowns laughing and screaming with delight.

Then a group of men appeared, and Tollison blinked twice to make sure he wasn't seeing things. The men were all wearing matching velvet smoking jackets and ascots and riding in motorized easy chairs. Tollison howled when he read the banner: The Laissez Boys.

Beau gestured to the chairs. "I think we need one of those."

"Who doesn't?" Tollison said, waggling his eyebrows. After several more marching bands, skimpily clad dancing women, and colorful Indians on horseback went by, the first float came into view. Pulled by a red tractor bearing a sign that read Krewe of Cleopatra, it was brightly painted and boasted a large asp on the front—curled, poised, and ready to strike. When the float passed in front of them, Tollison watched Beau raise his hands in the air and jump up and down, yelling at the all-female Krewe to throw him something. He looked spastic as his body contorted and swayed. Two seconds later they were bombarded with brightly colored beads, cups, and stuffed animals. Tollison caught everything that came his way, putting the beads over his head and stuffing his pockets with everything else.

By the time the third float rolled by, Tollison was sure he looked just as spastic as Beau, but he didn't care. He was having a ball. The excitement, the people, the lights, and the sounds created a circus-like atmosphere, and he, too, felt almost like a kid. When the last float crept by, neither he nor Beau could fit another thing around their neck and still be able to breathe. Their pockets were overflowing with toys and stuffed animals, they had Frisbees tucked under their arms, and each had a stack of cups two feet tall.

The crowds started to scatter, and Beau and Tollison headed for home.

"What did you think?" Beau asked.

"That was amazing."

Beau smiled. "Not like the carnival from your country?"

"Yes and no. The crowds are the same, but instead of floats with tractors pulling them—"

Beau interrupted, "You have donkeys?"

Tollison smacked Beau on his arm, and Beau's stack of cups went flying into the air.

"Oh shit!" Beau scrambled to catch them, but before he could gather them all, a couple of kids came out of the woodwork like skittering cockroaches and started scooping them up and running away. "Hey, you little shits!" Beau yelled. "Those are mine."

The kids mocked him, took everything they could grab, and scrambled away. "Now look what you've done!" Beau whined.

Tollison laughed so hard he doubled over and didn't think he could walk. "I'm sorry, but that's what you get for the donkey joke," he said between gasps. "Besides, what do we need with fifty plastic cups that say Krewe of Cleopatra?"

"Not the point!" Beau clutched what was left of his cups and, with a slight smile on his face, turned away and started walking home.

Tollison regained his composure and ran up behind Beau. He slipped his arm through Beau's and handed him his stack of cups. "Here. I want you to have mine. What's mine is yours, always."

Beau snatched the cups out of Tollison's hand and added them to his stack. "Damn straight."

Tollison felt comfortable walking arm in arm with Beau in their neighborhood. Uptown was pretty open-minded, and besides, who was gonna mess with a couple of guys their size and build. They could be two badass motherfuckers if they needed to be.

"Am I forgiven?" Tollison asked snuggling in a little closer to Beau.

"I don't know," Beau said. "What's in it for me?"

"How about a repeat performance of earlier when we get home?"

"You're forgiven," Beau said quickly. "But I'm the one driving this time, and you're gonna be the one begging for it, Sam."

"Deal."

As soon as they stepped into the foyer, they both dropped all their loot on the floor. Tollison sat on the stairs and looked at everything they'd caught, picking through the plastic like it was treasure.

"Pretty good haul, huh?" Beau remarked.

"I'll say. If we do this well for every parade, we'll have to buy a bigger house."

"That's why we have an attic, silly. Hey! Tomorrow night is Knights of Sparta at six o'clock. You wanna invite Bruce and Bastien and Auggie and Jenny over for the parade and a late dinner?"

Tollison hesitated. "I—I don't know, Beau. Auggie and Jenny are fine, but I'm still not sure how I feel about Bastien these days."

"What? We flew halfway across the world to save his ass, and now you're not sure how you feel about him?"

"That's different. I couldn't let him die because of something I did in my past. I guess I'm still pissed off about the way he dismissed me when he found out about my—" He cleared his throat. "—line of work. And I'm a little surprised you suggested it?"

"Why?"

"For starters, I didn't think you were that fond of the guy."

"Hey, I'm working out my shit with Bruce."

"Not Bruce, you lug."

"I'm not that big a lug. I knew who you were referring to."

"Sure you did."

"Look! At first I wasn't sure about Bastien, but once he convinced me he was going to respect the boundaries of our relationship, I decided to give the guy a chance. Besides, Bruce seems to really like him, and I know we still have our baggage, but I do want him to be happy. Bruce deserves that. Don't you think?"

"Of course he does. They *have* been sort of dating or skyping pretty hot and heavy since we got back from Zurich."

"I know," Beau said.

Tollison eyed Beau, recognizing something a little off in his quiet words. Bruce Jenkins, a detective with the New Orleans Police Department, happened to be Beau's ex. Their relationship came crashing down when Beau was still with the NOPD, soon after his promotion to lead investigator. Beau had thrown himself into his work and unintentionally neglected Bruce, who eventually turned to someone else for comfort. It was a one-night stand, but when Beau found out about it, they were instantly over. Tollison's presence in Beau's life had had a lot to do with Beau and Bruce coming to terms with their past, but they were still on shaky ground. They were getting past it slowly, but they weren't all the way there yet.

Beau locked eyes with Tollison and raised an eyebrow. "Are you okay with it…? I mean, them dating? Bastien is your ex too."

Sebastien "Bastien" Andros. He and Tollison had been together for some time a few years back. In his former life, Tollison had been an art retriever, a principled thief who illegally retrieved valuable art that had been stolen at some time and then returned it to the lawful owner. He'd kept his career choice a secret from Bastien, and when Bastien found out, he hadn't handled the betrayal well. They had parted ways abruptly and painfully.

Last October, to Tollison's surprise, Bastien had shown up in New Orleans looking for him. Unfortunately, he'd been followed by someone from Tollison's past and had been kidnapped and held hostage for the return of a piece of artwork Tollison had once retrieved. That had sent Beau and Tollison, as well as Bruce and Beau's former partner, August Hebert, to Zurich in search of the artwork, which was how and where Bruce and Bastien had met. And damned if they hadn't hit it off. Although Bastien had to stay in Switzerland for business reasons, he and Bruce had stayed in touch, and Bastien was finally arriving in New Orleans tomorrow for an extended stay.

Ever since Bastien had come into their lives, Beau seemed to need little reassurances here and there. Tollison took Beau's hand in his. "I'm still pissed at Bastien, but I'm really good with him and Bruce. Like you, I want Bastien to be happy, and Bruce is a good guy."

Beau raised an eyebrow.

"Jesus, Beau! We've all made mistakes. Seriously! Are you ever going to let that go?"

Beau sighed. "I'm trying."

"I know you are," Tollison said in a soft voice. "And I also want you to know there is nothing to worry about concerning Bastien and me. That is over, and I'm with you. Right where I want to be."

Beau's smile told Tollison he'd succeeded, at least for the moment. Beau leaned in and gave Tollison a gentle kiss. He stood, lifted Tollison's leg, and pulled off one of his boots, then grabbed his other leg and removed the second. He toed off his own shoes, took Tollison by the hand, and led him upstairs.

TOLLISON WAS cradled in Beau's strong arms, sated again and enjoying the closeness they always shared after sex.

"Wanna watch a little news before we turn in?" Beau asked.

"Sure."

Beau grabbed the remote and clicked on the television. The news anchor repeated the top story of the night. A shooting at the Krewe of Athena parade in Metairie. The male victim took a single high-powered rifle shot to the head and was pronounced dead on the scene. According to witnesses and bystanders, there were no altercations, everyone simply enjoying the parade until a single shot rang out and a man died.

"Jesus." Tollison raised up onto his elbow. "Rifle shot to the head."

"I think we've heard all we need to hear." Beau clicked off the television. "Sounds like a premeditated crime to me."

"And apparently the shooter got his man." Tollison laid his head back on Beau's chest. "Maybe you should call Auggie or Bruce tomorrow and see if they need our help."

Beau switched off the lamp and kissed the top of Tollison's head. "Good idea. Night, Tol. I love you."

"Love you too."

THREE

BRUCE JENKINS paced nervously back and forth outside of baggage claim at the Louis Armstrong International Airport. It had been a little over three months since he'd seen Sebastien Andros, and to say he was nervous was an understatement. He and Bastien had skyped almost every day, but it wasn't like being together. In person.

He hoped when Bastien arrived he would once again feel that jolt of electricity he'd felt in Zurich when he, Beau, Tollison, and Auggie had rescued Bastien from a ruthless art collector from Tollison's past. Seeing Bastien restrained, with a frightened expression on his handsome face, had made Bruce want to take the man into his arms and reassure him everything was going to be okay. The attraction between them had been almost instant, and in the hours following the incident and before they'd boarded their plane back to the United States, he and Bastien had spent every minute together.

Bruce was startled out of his thoughts by the sound of his cell phone. "Jenkins," he said without looking at the caller ID.

"Hey, it's me."

Hearing Beau's voice and the familiar greeting brought back a flood of memories of a time when they were happy together as a couple. But that ship had sailed, and Bruce had only himself to blame for it. Yeah, he'd been lonely. But instead of dealing with it, he'd allowed someone else to fill the void. It had been a onetime hookup, and the second it was over, he'd known he'd made a huge mistake. But to Beau that was too little too late. When Beau had found out about it, he'd gone ballistic, and just like that, their relationship was over. No ifs, ands, or buts about it.

Beau was a sweet, sensitive, and sometimes complicated guy, and above all, he treasured honesty and fidelity. For one brief moment, Bruce had failed miserably at both, and it had cost him his lover. Beau had continued to hold a grudge and treat Bruce like crap until Tollison had come into their lives. Tollison had made Beau see that both of them had been at fault, and since then they had been trying to salvage some type of friendship. In truth, they were doing an okay job so far.

"Oh hey, Beau."

"Do you have a minute?"

"Sure. What's—" Bruce stop speaking while a man's voice announced the carousel from which Delta Airlines travelers arriving on flight 656 from Detroit could retrieve their bags.

"Where are you?" Beau asked.

"I'm at the airport waiting for Bastien. Why?"

"Sounds chaotic."

"It is."

A few seconds of silence filled the connection.

"You excited?" Beau asked.

"Yeah. And extremely nervous. But I'm sure you didn't call to chat about Bastien and me. What's up?"

"A couple of things. First, Tollison and I saw the news last night about the shooting and wanted to offer our assistance if you guys need any help."

"Thanks. I'm sure you remember what a madhouse it is at the station during Mardi Gras, and this just adds another level of bullshit. But we're handling it. For now."

"I remember. Any suspects yet?"

"Not yet. Auggie is interviewing the victim's friends as we speak. We're hoping to know more later today."

"Well, if you need us, were here."

"Thanks, man."

"Oh, and on a personal note, Tol and I wanted to know if you and Bastien wanted to come over tonight for drinks before the parade and then my world-famous chili and cornbread after? We're also asking Auggie and Jenny."

"Thanks for including us." Bruce was touched Beau was even making the effort. "I'll have to check with Bastien, but it may be just what we need to break the ice a little. It has been a few months since we've seen each other, and I'm nervous as hell. Besides, he's never seen a Mardi Gras parade before, so it might be fun."

"Okay. Just let me know. And, Bruce?"

"Yeah."

"It's all going to be fine. I saw the way Bastien looked at you when we were leaving Zurich. If I were a betting man, I'd say he had it bad then and probably still does."

Bruce chuckled. "I sure hope you're right."

"Is he staying with you?"

"No. He rented the penthouse at the Lafayette Hotel for a couple months. We both thought it might be better that way."

Beau laughed a deep heartfelt laugh that Bruce hadn't heard in a while, and it warmed his heart. "Isn't that right around the corner from your new place on Church Street?"

"Yesss," Bruce whined, feeling like he'd been busted. "But in all fairness, I did buy the place before I met Bastien."

"Uh-huh!" Beau said. "Either way, my bet is that hotel is gonna be a big waste of money."

"From your mouth to God's ears." Bruce nearly dropped the phone when he saw Bastien coming down the escalator. God, the man was gorgeous. Tall—at least six two or three—and thin. Dressed in a black turtleneck and jeans. His dark hair shimmered with just the right amount of silver streaked through it. And God! Those deep blue eyes.

"Gotta go, Beau. I see Bastien."

"Okay. Good luck, and call me."

"Will do."

Bruce ended the call and waved at Bastien. When Bastien saw him, he beamed. They locked eyes, and for Bruce everyone and everything else faded away except the man who seemed to be floating toward him. Bruce walked to the bottom of the escalator and waited. When Bastien reached him, he dropped his bag on the floor and took Bruce into his arms. "Que c'est bon de te voir et de t'avoir enfin dans mes bras."

Bruce buried his face in Bastien's neck. God! The man smelled incredible. A combination of sweet-and-spicy manliness and pure strength. As Bastien tightened his grip, Bruce could feel the muscles in Bastien's back moving under his hands.

Fighting to maintain control and not melt into a big blob of detective right there in the baggage claim area, Bruce moaned. "I don't know what you just said, but I sure like the way you said it."

"I said, 'so good to see you and feel you in my arms again at last.'"

So much for worrying about a spark. There's a damn lightning storm going on in my pants.

"Told you I would like it."

Bruce released him and took both Bastien's hands in his. "Okay, I'm gonna give this a shot. I've been practicing." Bruce hesitated for a few seconds, looked up at the ceiling, and then locked eyes with Bastien. "C'est bon de te voir."

Bastien's brilliant blue eyes sparkled with excitement.

"Please tell me I got it right?" Bruce heard the hopeful tone in his own voice.

"Well. If you were asking if my mother is a horse, then yes. You got it right."

"What? Oh no. Of course I wouldn't. I'm so embarrassed."

Bastien burst out laughing. "No. No. Bruce. I couldn't resist teasing you. It was perfect. I missed you too."

Bruce punched Bastien on the arm playfully. "That was mean."

Bastien smiled warmly. "It *was* mean, and I'm sorry. Can you ever forgive me?"

Bruce smiled back. "I'll give it serious thought and let you know."

"Please don't wait too long. I don't think I could go on if I thought you were unhappy with me."

Bruce put his forefinger on his chin and looked up for a second. "Okay. You're forgiven."

Bastien howled. "We are going to get along royally, *mon chèr*. I can feel it already."

Bruce took Bastien by the hand and led him to the carousel. "How many bags do you have?"

"Too many to count, *ma puce*. One never knows what one might need for an extended vacation. How about if I just point them out?"

"Okay. Now tell me something. I know *mon chèr* means 'my darling.' But I'm not familiar with *ma puce*?" Bruce asked.

"Oh, *ma puce*? It's a widely used French pet name. Unfortunately, it translates to 'my flea.'"

Bruce roared with laughter. "I don't think I've ever been referred to as a flea before. But hey, I'll take it. It's been years since anyone has even taken the time to give me a pet name."

"I think that's all about to change. Oh, here come some of my bags."

Bruce looked up and spotted a half-dozen or so Louis Vuitton bags in various sizes rounding the carousel. *Jesus! I think he's gonna stay for a while!*

Bastien must have seen the surprise in his eyes. "It's not as bad as it looks. Well. That's not true. It actually is, but I didn't know what to bring, so I brought it all. I hope you understand."

"Hey! Who am I to judge?" Bruce asked. "As long as you're happy."

"This day keeps getting better and better," Bastien teased.

Bruce lifted all the bags off the carousel and stacked them neatly. He was about to lift two of them when Bastien raised his hand. Within seconds a porter showed up with a cart and loaded the bags one by one.

"For this poor man's sake," Bastien said, gesturing at the porter, "I hope you're parked nearby."

Bruce smiled sheepishly. "Yeah. Don't tell anyone, but I parked right outside with my Official Police Business card on the dash. And it's a good thing I brought my SUV."

"That it is," Bastien agreed.

BRUCE PULLED up in front of the Lafayette Hotel on St. Charles Avenue in the heart of the Arts and Warehouse District and put his SUV in park. The trip downtown felt like it was over before it even started. There hadn't been any awkward moments of silence, and the conversation flowed freely between them during the entire trip.

Over the last few months, he'd learned a lot about this mysterious man, but he still had so many questions. Over the course of their long-distance conversations, Bastien had modestly told Bruce he owned a small company called Andros International, which produced drilling equipment for mining operations. But when Bruce had later googled Andros International, he found a different story. Bastien's company was the world's leading provider of drilling services, drilling equipment, and performance tooling for the mining industry. The company operated in over thirty countries for a diverse mining customer base, spanning a wide range of commodities, including copper, gold, nickel, zinc, uranium, and other metals and minerals.

Bruce, to say the least, was intrigued. Bastien seemed so refined and worldly, and Bruce was in awe of him. There was still much he wanted to know.

As soon as Bruce popped the locks, the doorman opened his door and leaned in. "Bonjour, gentlemen. Welcome to the Lafayette Hotel."

The doorman took a step back and snapped his fingers. Bruce slid out of the SUV, but before he could make it to the back, a bellhop was already unloading the luggage.

Wow! This is some service.

Bastien came around from the passenger side, and the doorman stepped up again and nodded in Bastien's direction. "Mr. Andros, I presume."

"Oui. Bonjour," Bastien said.

The doorman held the door open as Bastien and Bruce entered the lobby of the hotel. It was a small and very charming historic New Orleans hotel, and the staff seemed eager to assist. A young woman greeted them immediately.

"Monsieur Andros. Please allow me to introduce myself. I'm Julia Draper, your private concierge, and I will be personally taking care of your needs during your stay at our hotel."

Bastien shook the young woman's hand. "Tout le plaisir est pour moi."

Julia flashed a faint smile.

"You must forgive me," Bastien said. "I meant to say the pleasure is all mine. I've been in Geneva too long and forget my manners sometimes. Yes. And this is my companion, Bruce Jenkins, and during my time here, he will be allowed entry to my penthouse at his request."

Julia turned to Bruce and nodded. "At your service, sir."

"My car?" Bruce asked.

"Of course. I'll have the valet park it for you."

"Thank you."

Julia turned back to Bastien. "Your penthouse is ready, and I received word just before you arrived that your rental car will be delivered within the hour."

"Splendid," Bastien said. "Now if you'll excuse us, I've been traveling for seventeen hours and would like to get a little rest before the festivities of the evening."

"Of course, sir," Julia said. "Would you like me to show you to the penthouse?"

"That won't be necessary." Bastien winked at Bruce.

Julia handed Bastien and Bruce separate keycards. "The elevator is right around the corner. Simply slide the card into the slot labeled

Penthouse, and you're all set. Your luggage will be up momentarily if it's not already there. Can I get you anything else?"

Bastien retrieved a bill from his wallet and slipped it into Julia's hand as he shook it once again. "That will be all. Merci, Julia." He turned to Bruce and took him by the hand. "Let's go, ma puce." The elevator doors closed, and Bastien slid the keycard into the slot as instructed. The Penthouse button on the panel illuminated and the car went up smoothly.

"Oh, that reminds me." Bruce squeezed Bastien's hand. "Beau and Tollison invited us to their house this evening for drinks, the parade, and then a late dinner."

"Really? I was certain Mr. Bissonet wasn't that taken with me."

Bruce laughed. "Yeah. That's most people's reaction, but that's just Beau. He takes a little while to warm up, but you'd be hard pressed to find a better man."

"Sounds grand, then."

The elevator dinged, and the doors opened into the foyer of a grand parlor with two free-standing stairways leading to a second floor. Bastien's luggage was neatly stacked at the base of one set of stairs.

"Wow!" Bruce stepped off the elevator and looked around. The floors were white Carrera marble, with colorful rugs defining separate sitting areas flanking two large fireplaces. The furnishings were formal and a bit over-the-top, but lovely just the same. The room was voluminous, with floor-to-ceiling windows at least twelve feet high. When his eyes followed the heavy brocaded draperies from the floor up, he was surprised to see a mural painted on the ceiling. It depicted several ladies in flowing gowns of pale blues, pinks, and yellows with cherubs at their feet smiling up at the ladies adoringly. The mural was framed by gilded crown molding at least a foot thick. "This is quite a place."

"Unfortunately it is." Bastien looked around with his hands on his hips. "Personally I prefer a more understated, less formal décor, but there are some, of course, who would find this rococo mess attractive."

"I'm relieved to hear that," Bruce said. "My place is probably way more understated than you would prefer. Rococo?"

"Oh, it's a style of architecture and décor originating in France in the early eighteenth century. I was never one to care for it, but it's characterized by elaborate, but graceful, light ornamentation, often containing asymmetrical motifs. Much like you see here."

Bruce laughed. "I must be the straightest homosexual in the world. Why didn't I know that?"

Bastien took Bruce into his arms and rested his forehead against Bruce's. "Because you are way more practical, ma puce. So am I."

"Who wants to live like this?" was the last thing Bruce heard Bastien say before he brought their lips together. Bruce wrapped his arms around Bastien's waist and brought his hands to rest on the globes of Bastien's firm ass. Bastien's kiss was gentle at first and then became heated and needy, his tongue seeking entry and Bruce willingly opening to him. When they finally came up for air, they were both breathless.

Bastien cupped Bruce's face in his hands. "I've wanted to do that since the moment I saw you at the airport."

"Me too," Bruce said.

"Can you stay awhile?" Bastien asked.

Damn! I hate my job right now! "I would love to, Bastien, but I've got to get back to the station. We had a shooting last night at one of the parades, and someone was killed. Things are a bit crazy right now. Besides, you need to get some rest."

"I'm sorry about the shooting. Such a barbaric and heinous world we have become. But I must admit, I am a little tired. Not too tired to...."

Bruce pressed his lips against Bastien's in a soft, gentle kiss. "I know. God, I know. But I'll be back to pick you up around four thirty. Is that okay?"

"Perfect, ma puce. Oh. What does one wear to a parade?"

Bruce chuckled. "Very casual. Jeans and a sweater. Oh, and bring a jacket. It may get a little chilly after dark."

"Consider it done."

"Okay. The sooner I get back to work; the sooner I get to leave."

"Be off, then." Bastien stole one last kiss, then shoved Bruce toward the door. "Until four thirty."

"Until four thirty, then," Bruce repeated, stepping into the elevator. When he turned around, Bastien was leaning against the banister at the base of the stairs eyeing him seductively, his arms folded across his chest and one foot crossed over the other at the ankle. He was looking every bit like a New York runway model. Then the doors closed and Bastien disappeared.

On the ride down, Bruce toyed at least three times with the idea of blowing off his job and going right back up to take the handsome Bastien

Andros right there in the foyer. But in the end he was too responsible. He knew he couldn't do that to Auggie. And besides, it was way too soon for that type of intimacy. Kissing? Hell yeah! Sex? Soon, but not yet.

En route to the station, Bruce called Beau.

"How did it go?" Beau asked without saying hello.

"It went well." Bruce blushed and cleared his throat, remembering the kiss.

"So are we on for tonight?" Beau asked.

"Yep. We'll be there around five. And, Beau?"

"Yeah?"

"*Please* behave yourself," Bruce begged. "Just... this one time?"

"What—"

"Oh Christ, Beau. Don't give me that," Bruce interrupted. "No dredging up the past. No jokes at my expense. You know what I'm talking about. Just give me this one night, and I'll never ask for another free pass."

"Fine! But I still—"

"Bye, Beau." Bruce ended the call.

FOUR

WHAT THE fuck? Why did I let Jules and our friends talk me into this? I hate Mardi Gras. Jules knows that. Why did he put me on the spot? Shit is literally flying everywhere, and it's almost impossible to dodge it. The fumes from the tractors are making me sick to my stomach, and if one more person yells, "throw me something, mister," I'm gonna jam my fist right down their throat.

"Fuck you," I yelled to a man who had just hurled a stack of plastic cups in my direction, bouncing them off my shoulder and sending them right into the arms of the woman standing behind me, who was jumping up and down and apparently screaming his name. What fucking idiots! Have these people lost all their senses?

God! Why didn't we bring our own car? I'm gonna be stuck here for at least another three hours of this shit. Why can't Jules hate this holiday as much as I do? That way we could stay at home and lock ourselves away from the crazies who come out every year and release their foolishness on our city.

Stop whining, Curt. You're here because Jules loves it and you love Jules. He would do the same if the roles were reversed. You kissed a lot of frogs to find your damn prince, and if a few Mardi Gras parades make him happy, it's the least you can do. Queer up and take it like a man.

Finally, the parade was nearing its end, and the crowds were starting to disperse. "One more float, Curt," Jules pleaded. "And then you're home free."

I smiled, of course, and nodded my head. Anything for you, dear.

With no desire at all to wait for the last float, I nudged Jules. "I'll be standing right back there when you're ready." I pointed over my shoulder to the curb.

Jules nodded. He placed a quick kiss on my cheek and smiled. His lips were warm, and suddenly seeing the joy on his face made everything I had just endured so totally worth it.

I turned and walked toward the curb, and then I felt it. Instant pain. I wanted to spin on my heels and beat the shit out of whoever threw something at me, but my legs wouldn't work. Nothing worked. My arms were dangling limp at my sides. I dropped to my knees and face planted into the cement. I was shouting for Jules, but I heard no sound. Everything was still, and then it was dark.

BEAU GAVE his self-proclaimed world's best chili one last stir and banged the spoon against the rim of the large pot. He slid the pot to the back burner and adjusted the flame to simmer. "It's gonna be good."

"World famous?" Tollison chuckled as he chopped vegetables for a salad.

"Damn straight," Beau said. "Wait! Are you questioning the honor of my chili?"

"Never! It's the best I've ever eaten. But… I don't know if that's enough criteria to constitute *world famous.*"

Beau's mouth instantly formed those pouty lips Tollison found so adorable, and then he lowered his head. It still amazed Tollison that his badass, scary man had such a sensitive heart. But he loved him all the more for it.

"I'm just teasing you. It's damn good chili. Everyone says so."

"You think I don't know that?" Beau asked, sliding his hands around Tollison's waist and laying his head on Tollison's shoulder. "It's world famous. Remember? I was just playing wounded to see if I could get a little action before our guests arrive."

Tollison put down his knife, wiped his hands, and turned around in Beau's embrace. "Since when do you have to play wounded to get action?"

He cupped Beau's face in his hands and pressed their lips together. Beau tasted of cumin, chili powder, and onions mixed with pure Beau. He moaned against Tollison's mouth, reached down to grab a handful of Tollison's crotch, and squeezed. Tollison sucked in a hurried breath and then cursed when the doorbell sounded.

"What the fuck?" Beau mumbled against Tollison's mouth.

"Shit!" Tollison groaned. "Talk about bad timing."

Beau stole another quick kiss. "You get the door, and I'll stir the chili."

"To be continued," Tollison said, looking over his shoulder as he headed for the front door.

Tollison opened the door and choked back a laugh. "Jesus, Auggie. You look like a Mardi Gras fairy."

"I guess I'll fit right in with the rest of you fairies, then," Auggie said, walking past Tollison without another word, apparently following the scent of the chili.

Tollison smiled and rolled his eyes.

"Tell me about it," Jenny said kissing Tollison on the cheek. "I told him not to wear that stupid headpiece. My God, and that boa! I told him the purple, green, and gold outfit was more than enough. But you know Auggie. When he sets his mind to something, there's no changing it."

"Just like somebody else I know." Tollison winked.

Jenny sniffed the air. "Damn it smells good in here."

"Beau and his chili." Tollison led Jenny to the kitchen. "We won't get the smell out of the house for at least three months."

"But it's so worth it," Beau yelled.

"Amen, brother," Auggie added.

While Beau was getting everyone drinks the doorbell rang again. Beau looked at Tollison with a pleading expression. "Fine. I'll go again," Tollison said.

When Tollison opened the door this time, Bruce and Bastien's handsome faces were staring back at him.

"Right on time," Tollison said, not really knowing what else to say. Bruce gave him a hug, and Tollison and Bastien stood there staring at each other.

"I'll give you two a minute." Bruce walked past them.

"It's good to see you again, Eddy," Bastien finally said. His use of the affectionate nickname from Tollison's middle name sounded warm and genuine.

But Tollison simply folded his arms across his chest, raised an eyebrow, and studied Bastien suspiciously. "Bastien."

They eyed each other for a long moment until Bastien spoke again. "Come on, Eddy. I know you're still angry at me for not responding to you after I found out about your career choice, but I was livid and hurt back then. Haven't you done something in your life you regretted?"

"After what we all went through a few months ago, do you now at least understand *why* I lied?"

"To protect me, I suppose," Bastien said, looking down at the floor.

"You suppose?" Tollison clenched his teeth, trying to keep his voice down. "Of course it was to protect you. Do you realize by simply coming here last year, you put everyone I care about in danger? Including you."

"But how was I to know, Eddy? I knew I was just as responsible for our relationship falling apart as you were, but—"

"I know. You were hurt and angry."

"I was. And I know I treated you poorly, so I came looking for you to try and make things right. To make amends."

"Poorly?" Tollison looked in the direction of the kitchen and pulled Bastien into the study, where they would have a little more privacy. "Seriously? I didn't plan on getting into this now, but since you brought it up. Poorly? The way you dismissed me without even allowing me to explain. That's what you call poorly? The way you turned your back on me without even a second thought. We spent five years together. Don't you think you at least owed me a little consideration?"

"Owed you? What did I get? Five years of lies. That's what," Bastien shot back. "How do you think that made me feel? I told you I felt betrayed. And I acted on those feelings. I'm sorry. I know I hurt you, but I was hurt as well."

"Shit!" Tollison rubbed his temples. "None of this fucking matters. It's not going to change anything."

Bastien put his hands on Tollison's shoulders and looked him in the eye. "But it does, Eddy. We have to clear the air. It of course will not undo the past, but it might help us to have a future. I adore Bruce and would like to see where this goes, but I can't pursue a relationship with him if you and I are not okay. I will not come between any of you, nor will I make Bruce choose."

"How gallant," Tollison said.

Where is this coming from? This is all water under the bridge. Why am I getting so upset?

Tollison rolled this question over and over in his mind. Why *was* he getting so upset? Had he not really dealt with these feelings after all? Was it the abandonment issue to which he still held on? He had never understood how after five years Bastien could have so easily turned his back on him.

"Bastien. There was a time after you closed the door on me—on us—that I resented the hell out of you. But I thought I had put all of it to bed. It's apparent now that I still have a few things to work on. But I'm not going to let my issues come between you and Bruce. I want you both to be happy."

"Thank you, Eddy."

"Don't thank me," Tollison said. "Thank Beau. If I hadn't fallen so head over heels in love with him, I don't think I could be so forgiving toward you. Yes, I lied to you—for good reason as you now know, and I know I hurt you, but you turned your back on me without even giving me the opportunity to explain why I lied, and that hurt me far more than anything I could have done to you."

Bastien's expression was unreadable. "And for that I'm truly sorry, Ed—"

Tollison held up his hand to silence him. "Let me be very clear so there will be no misunderstandings. Being with Beau has changed my life in too many ways to explain. But mostly he's shown me how wonderful a transparent relationship can be. No secrets. No lies. No cover-ups. To trust someone so completely has renewed my faith in love and relationships. He makes me want to be better. To do better. Beau makes me see things more clearly, and I'm so in love with him sometimes it scares me."

"Everything okay in here?" Beau asked, walking up behind Tollison, throwing his arms over Tollison's shoulders, and kissing his neck.

"We're good," Tollison said. "Just clearing the air."

"Should I leave you two alone, then?" Beau asked.

"No. I think we're done here." Tollison turned, kissed Beau, and walked out of the room.

BEAU STOOD dumbfounded, staring at Bastien. "What was that all about?"

"He loves you very much," Bastien said.

Beau felt an onslaught of pride. "I know that, but I can't believe he drug you in here to tell *you* that."

"And a few other things."

"Care to elaborate?"

Bastien hesitated for a long moment and then spoke. "He's still very angry at me for turning my back on him."

Beau contemplated his response. A few years ago, he would have sided with Bastien without a doubt. Lying was lying. But now? He realized knowing both sides of the story had made his version of a black-and-white issue extremely gray.

"I see his point, Bastien. But I also see yours."

Bastien sighed.

"Look. Tollison has taught me many things," Beau said. "But one of the most important would be that not everything is black-and-white. He lied to you. And I had a problem with that at first. But"—Beau held up a finger—"I now know he did it to protect you. And that made all the difference."

"I know that now," Bastien said. "But back then I was so angry and hurt, I couldn't bear to look at him. Not just for lying, but for his chosen career. He was an art thief."

"An art retriever, Bastien. There is a difference. The way Tollison saw it, he was righting a history of wrongs. And I happen to agree with him. So much art was stolen by Hitler during the Nazi plunder alone, and Tollison was instrumental in getting some of that artwork back to its rightful owners. That has to count for something."

"I imagine," Bastien said.

"Bastien. You should have seen him in action. He's damn good at what he did. And he put everything on the line to save you. We all did."

Bastien reached out and touched Beau on his arm. "Beau, please don't ever doubt my gratitude. If you hadn't risked your lives to save mine, I might very well still be held captive by DeMatteo and his thugs."

"So let's use a little of that gratitude and cut Tollison some slack. He's a good man, Bastien. I don't have to tell you that. He made a conscious decision to keep his true identity from you, but it was not malicious in any way. He was only trying to protect you."

Bastien looked like he was considering Beau's advice. He sighed. "You are right, Beau. Thank you."

Beau hung his arm over Bastien's shoulder. "Let's get a drink."

"I could certainly use one. And Eddy is very lucky to have you."

Beau smiled. "We are lucky to have each other."

When Beau and Bastien joined the others, Tollison eyed Beau suspiciously. Beau winked and walked over to where Tollison was standing, wrapped his arms around him, and pressed his mouth against Tollison's ear. "I'll fill you in later." He kissed him.

Bastien shook hands with Auggie, whom he hadn't seen since Zurich, and met Jenny for the first time before he joined Bruce.

"Hey, Aug!" Beau said. "Any developments on that parade shooting last night?"

"No suspects, but it turns out our vic, Jacob Chaps, was one of you people."

"He was a white man?" Beau asked.

"Very funny, asshole. No! He was gay."

"Ohhhh. Gaaaay," Tollison said.

"I interviewed his family and his best friend, who was with him at the parade, and everyone agreed he was a very quiet guy. Kept to himself most of the time. Didn't go out much. In fact, the friend said he'd had to drag him out to the parade that night. He was still pretty torn up about it. Said if he hadn't forced the vic to go to the parade, the guy would still be alive."

"Poor guy," Jenny said.

"Any boyfriends?" Tollison asked.

"A couple in the last few years, but nothing more."

"Did you find either of them?" Beau asked.

"Got the name of one. Turns out the vic had a restraining order against him. We're tracking him down now."

"And the other?" Tollison asked.

"According to the best friend, it was very short-lived. A week or so tops, and the friend hadn't even known about it until it was over."

"You need help tracking him down?" Beau asked.

Auggie shook his head. "Not yet. We're still in the preliminary stages of the investigation. But if we hit a wall, you'll be first to know about it."

Beau heard sirens in the distance and looked at his watch. "Hey! We have a parade to get to. You guys get a drink to go and grab the cooler by the front door. Tollison and I will finish up in here and meet you on the front porch."

THREE HOURS later the entire gang returned from the parade weighed down with all sorts of throws, each consuming beers and laughing and teasing as usual. As soon as they walked through the front door, Beau headed straight for the kitchen and started preparing dinner, Tollison on his heels. The others followed, and Auggie and Jenny sat at the breakfast bar. Bastien and Bruce stood gazing at each other like they were lost in their own little world.

"I've never seen anything quite like it," Bastien said at last as he adjusted the paraphernalia hanging around his neck and held up his adorned forcarms. "How do I get this stuff off?"

Bruce chuckled. "Here. Let me help."

"Thanks, ma puce."

Beau chuckled and rolled his eyes at Tollison, although he secretly thought the pet name was cute. He couldn't help but notice how attentive Bruce was being to Bastien.

Apparently the action didn't go unnoticed by Bruce. He shot a pair of dagger eyes at both of them as Bastien stared at a pile of Mardi Gras beads with an expression of disbelief.

"My flea?" Beau whispered to Tollison with an elbow to the ribs.

"I know, right? I wonder if Bastien is gonna buy Bruce a circus?"

"Or maybe a collar," Beau added with a snicker. "You know what they say, 'Lie down with dogs and wake up with fleas.'"

The one-liners were flying, and Beau and Tollison were giggling like teenagers.

"Hey! What's so funny in there?" Auggie asked.

"Nothing!" they said in unison and started giggling again.

Auggie laughed and shook his head. "You two pansies sound like a couple of hyenas."

"Soup's on!" Beau called, ignoring the jab, trying to clear his voice and keep a straight face. "Now everyone get your froggy asses in here and serve yourself. Except for Jenny. You head straight to the dining room, darling, and I'll bring you a plate."

"See, Auggie! These boys know how to treat a lady. You could take a few lessons."

"Thanks a lot, Beau," Auggie whispered.

Dinner was full of conversation, laughs, and of course burping.

"It's the chili," Auggie kept saying, and Beau was about to defend his chili when Auggie's phone rang. Auggie looked at the caller ID. "Damn," he said. "Excuse me."

He walked out of the dining room and returned a few minutes later. "Bruce and Jen, we've gotta go. There's been another shooting."

"Shit," Bruce said.

Beau stood. "What? Where?"

"Algiers. Krewe of Adonis parade."

"Vic?" Tollison asked.

"Pronounced dead five minutes ago. Bullet to the head."

Beau started pacing. "Jesus, Auggie. You know what this means?"

Auggie put both hands up. "Don't say it, Beau. Two random shootings during Mardi Gras doesn't automatically mean we have a serial killer on our hands."

"You're right, Aug, but you know the implications as well as I do. Both shootings took place at a parade. Both vics took a single bullet to the head, and there were no other casualties. Sounds suspect to me."

"Let's go, Jen. Bruce. Bastien. I'm sorry to ruin your evening."

"I understand. Duty calls," Bastien said. "Do you have time to drop me off at my hotel?"

"Of course," Bruce said. "Auggie, I'll meet you at the scene."

"Okay. Thank you, guys, for a great night. Sorry it had to end this way."

"It was great to get together," Tollison said. "Let's try and do it again before Mardi Gras is over."

"Sounds good."

Beau and Tollison walked everyone out to their cars. "Guys, you know if you need us, we're here to help. Or if you just need someone to bounce shit off of. Call anytime. We owe you guys a lot."

"Thanks, man," Auggie said. "I appreciate it. And I'll let you know."

BRUCE PUT his hand on the small of Bastien's back and guided him to the car. He liked the feel of the man's muscular back as it moved when he walked. Before he opened the door, he stopped. "I'm really sorry about this. This is certainly not what I planned for this evening."

Bastien laid his hand on Bruce's shoulder, and Bruce felt a rush of something he hadn't felt in a long time. Nerves? Anticipation? Desire? He wasn't sure, but he certainly liked the feeling.

"Nor I, ma puce. But work must come first. There will be times when my work will call me away as well, and I hope you'll understand."

"Certainly," Bruce said. "And thank *you* for understanding now."

Bastien pressed his lips against Bruce's cheek and kissed him gently. Bruce smiled sheepishly and opened the car door. They drove mostly in silence, both apparently very disappointed, but neither seeming to know what to say. When they reached the hotel, Bruce opened the driver's side door, and Bastien reached over and touched his arm. "No need. I'll show myself up. You have a crime to solve."

"Are you sure? I don't mind walking you up."

"Your chivalry is very admirable, but unnecessary tonight. If you get done sooner than you anticipate, please call. I'm a bit jet-lagged, so I'm sure I'll be up for hours. Maybe you can come back by later."

"I'd like that."

Bastien leaned over and pressed his lips gently to Bruce's. "Until the next time, ma puce."

Bruce smiled. "Until next time. Good night, Bastien."

THE DRIVE across the Crescent City Connection took longer than normal with parade goers all trying to get home. Bruce reached the Algiers crime scene in a little under an hour, a drive that should have been, in normal traffic, fifteen minutes tops.

Auggie was already there, of course, but he hadn't made the detour to the Warehouse District, which Bruce didn't regret for one minute.

As Bruce surveyed the area, he saw eight patrol cars, two EMT units, and a few unmarked black sedans. The crime scene had already been established and secured with yellow plastic tape, with one way in and one way out for the investigators. The vic was lying facedown on the curb, apparently where he'd dropped. First responders were packing up, and a team of forensic experts were milling about in their personal protective equipment—gloves, booties or shoe covers, white suits—which were commonly referred to as PPEs. Their top priority was protecting the scene so no vital evidence was lost, which Bruce appreciated even if they could sometimes be a little officious about it. Auggie was conversing with Jeffrey Rouse, the Orleans Parish Medical Examiner, who was kneeling over the body.

Most of the crowds had dissipated, but there were two guys and a girl standing next to a patrol car outside of the crime scene. One of the guys was crying hysterically, and the others were trying to console him.

Bruce passed them without stopping and joined Auggie and Jeffrey. "What do we have?"

"Hey, Bruce," Jeffrey said. "Male by the name of Curtis Borne. Thirty-six years old. A single shot to the head. My guess is he died instantly or pretty close to it. I won't know for sure until I complete the autopsy, but it appears the bullet went in at the top of the head and exited somewhere near the jaw. It was an odd angle."

Bruce looked up and around. "Plenty of rooftops with a clear shot."

"How does that compare to last night's vic?" Auggie asked.

"Almost identical." Jeffrey pulled the sheet over the vic's head and stood. "Guys, again, I won't know for certain until I complete the autopsy, but I'd venture to say last night's and tonight's vics were killed by the same person, using the same gun—or at least the same type of gun."

Bruce gave Auggie a knowing glance.

FIVE

KREWE OF Carrollton, Uptown, New Orleans. It was a sunny afternoon on the corner of Carrollton and St. Charles Avenues. But where we stood was shaded and cold as hell. As I looked around, parade goers were at least ten to fifteen deep, but the constant flow of people didn't seem to be hampering the party. The music was loud, the floats were colorful, and the marching bands seemed to be giving it all they had, maybe compensating for the cold. The parade was a little more than halfway over, and jumping up and down and screaming no longer seemed to be keeping me warm. "Pass the bourbon," I finally requested, holding my hand out. "I'm freezing over here."

I looked down the row at my friends, and they gave me a questioning glance. They already appeared to be three sheets to the wind. It was my turn to be designated driver, so over the course of the late morning, I had avoided the now almost depleted pint of Jack Daniels they had been passing back and forth between the two of them. They were both pretty big guys, and their excess weight was surely keeping them insulated without the need for so much alcohol.

"Girrll! That float looks like it's full of a bunch of drag queens on their way to a wig shop. Get a load of those getups," my best friend, Michael, said. Michael is the flamboyant one, but he's pretty harmless. I gave my other friend, John, a stern look, and he handed me the bottle. I took a big gulp and swallowed. As the burn made its way down my throat, I was almost instantly warmed. Whiskey or no whiskey. Cold or no cold. There was no way I was leaving the parade. I waited all year for Mardi Gras, and it was finally here. I'd be damned if I was going to pass up a parade for a little cold weather.

As I stuck my head out into the street and saw the last float about a block away, I was suddenly overcome with sadness. I knew the parades were an outlet for me. A way to distract myself from my otherwise lonely existence. Going out to the bars to meet people over the years had turned into more of a nightmare than a good time. And don't get me started on online dating. The last guy I met online turned out to be such a jerk, it soured me on the entire process. He was a shut-in or something. Said he never left his house. That should have been my first clue, but I went there anyway. He was freaky as hell. The entire time we were fucking, the guy jumped at every noise, and he would hardly even let me touch him. That had done it for me with the online thing. And then Grindr came around and, in the beginning, shown great promise, but what a disappointment it turned out to be as well. Nothing but a dead end. No one was ever who they appeared to be, and the insincerity of it all was just too much to handle. I hooked up with one guy, and we saw each other for about a week. Notice I didn't say dated. Because we couldn't go anywhere. It was all a big secret. And in the end, all he wanted was a quick fuck or a blowjob. No more than a booty call, and I was not down for that. I swallowed hard, remembering the pain of that crazy short-lived affair but quickly tried to wipe it from my memory yet again.

As I watched the last float approach, I waited with happy anticipation for the moment when the masked riders would bombard me with beads and trinkets. One moment I was giddy with delight, and then I was suddenly on my knees and falling forward. The next thing I knew, my face was plastered to the cold cement, and I couldn't move. Before I could scream for help, everything went black.

TOLLISON WAS surprised to see Iona at her desk on a Sunday morning. He recognized the frustrated expression on her face as she looked up when the little bell on the front door jingled, announcing his and Beau's arrival.

Krewe of Carrollton rolled at noon, and they'd come to the office before the traffic to get some paperwork done so they could work at home later today and tomorrow.

"What are you doing here on a Sunday morning?" Tollison asked Iona.

"Thank God you're here," Iona said, ignoring his question. "This computer is going to be the death of me. Mercy! Why can't we go back to using typewriters?"

Beau elbowed Tollison in the ribs. "I'll let you handle this one. Morning, Iona." He smiled as he passed her desk and headed for his and Tollison's office.

"Thanks a lot." Tollison chuckled. "Okay, Iona. What's wrong, and more importantly, why are you here?"

"I wanted to catch up on my accounting without interruptions. And this damn spreadsheet just won't act right. I copied the formulas like you showed me, but they're not calculating properly. And what are *you* doing here?"

"We wanted to pick up some paperwork so we could work from home after the parade today, and all day tomorrow, to avoid some of the traffic." Tollison looked at the computer screen. "Isn't this the same problem I fixed yesterday?"

"Yes! But apparently you didn't fix it, or I wouldn't be having the same problem today."

"It's not the computer, Iona," Tollison said. "See. It's operator error." Tollison moved the mouse and clicked a few times and then tapped the keyboard. "There. Remember when I told you sometimes you have to manually adjust the formula depending on the type of calculations?"

"Ohhhh!" Iona said. "Now I remember."

"Iona. What am I gonna do with you?"

"You think I'm bad?" Iona laughed. "Get this! My ninety-year-old friend Martha Cook was sitting next to me at the church's singles Bible study class, and while we waited for the pastor to start the class, the subject of computers came up. Well, Bubba Simon was sitting on the other side of Martha—and just between you and me, he's been wanting to ask her out on a date, but we keep telling him Martha has a ninety-two-year-old husband at home. Bubba has Alzheimer's, and he forgets. So we just keep reminding him."

"Wait?" Tollison held up a finger. "Singles Bible study? Iona Ball? Are you using the Lord to hook up with men?"

Iona's blush slowly crept up her face, and she giggled. "I never thought of it that way, but I guess I am."

"And why is Martha going to a singles class if she's married?"

"I know, right?" Iona patted his arm. "I asked her that *very* question, and she said everyone in the seniors Bible study are just too old, and she'd rather hang out with the younger people."

"Okay. Just checking. I guess it makes sense. Go on."

"So anyway," Iona continued, "they were still talking about computers, and Bubba asked Martha if she did Windows. Martha thought for a moment and then said, 'Of course I do windows.'

"Bubba said he was just learning but wasn't doing too well.

"Martha looked so surprised you could have knocked her over with a feather. She said, 'Really?'

"Bubba then asked her how long she'd been doing Windows, and she said ever since her mother had taught her. Bubba looked confused and replied in a surprised tone that he didn't think Windows had been around that long. Well, Martha gave me a funny look and rolled her eyes, but she finally said windows have been around for a very long time."

Tollison mentally pleaded for a break. Why couldn't Beau call him or the office phone ring? Anything to break up this little chat session. He knew Iona's stories carried on and on and never really went anywhere. But he had to admit, this one had him a little intrigued. "So?" he asked skeptically.

"Bubba told her he just thought he was too old to do Windows because he just wasn't getting it. And then Martha said…." Iona slapped her knee and started laughing hysterically. "She said she didn't think it was that hard once you got the hang of it. Her secret was vinegar and newspaper. The combination eliminated the streaks and everything sparkled and smelled clean and fresh. You get it?" Iona asked, still howling. "Martha thought he was talking about cleaning windows, and he was talking about the computer program *Windows*."

"I get it," Tollison said not able to stifle his chuckle. "That *is* pretty funny."

"I swear we never really get to much Bible study with all the stories that go around class, but it sure is fun."

Tollison heard Beau's cell phone ringing and looked up. He was relieved when he saw Beau motioning for him to join him in their office. "Gotta go. Beau needs me. Yell if you get stuck again."

"Oh, I will." Iona smiled.

"HERE'S TOLLISON," Beau said. "Let me put you on speaker, Auggie."

Beau laid his cell phone on his desk and tapped the speakerphone icon. "Okay, go ahead."

"Hey, Aug," Tollison said.

"Morning, Tollison."

"So what do we—I mean—*you* have?" Beau asked, old habits apparently dying hard.

"Coroner's report came back a few minutes ago and confirmed our suspicions. Two vics, one perpetrator," Auggie said.

"Serial?" Beau asked.

"I'm holding off on using that term—not enough vics yet—but it looks like it's going that way. One shot to the head. Same type bullet. Same angle. Same gun."

"Shit!" Beau cursed.

"What's the plan?" Tollison asked.

"I think we need to do a press conference to alert the public, but the mayor is asking us to hold off. He's afraid once we do that, Mardi Gras will be over, and the entire city will be in an uproar."

"They just don't give a crap about the public's safety." Beau shook his head. "It's all about the tourism and the money."

"Yeah, well, I'm sure you remember how that goes," Auggie went on. "Look! I'm reinforcing security along all the parade routes, but beyond that there's nothing else I can do until we get the perpetrator. You still have that badge?"

Beau looked at Tollison, and Tollison nodded. "Hell yeah!" Beau answered.

"Consider yourself sworn in. I'll fax over the coroner's reports, the names of the vics, and the witnesses for both murders in a couple."

"We're on it," Beau said.

Auggie cleared his throat. "Oh, and Beau, just as an FYI, I know the investigation is flying under the radar right now, but if we have one more murder, we're going public. Mayor or no mayor."

"Understood," Beau said.

TOLLISON TAPPED his fingers on the steering wheel impatiently. Traffic on I-10 was moving at a snail's pace in both directions. "It figures the vic's old boyfriend would live in Old Metairie. Now we have to fight the Uptown parade traffic and the Metairie parade traffic."

"Now who's impatient?" Beau grinned in the passenger seat, where he sat looking down at his notes. "The guy's address is an apartment complex on Cleary Avenue between Airline and Jefferson. If you take the Airline Highway exit, we can take the back way."

"Airline Highway is still another five miles ahead. That could take us two hours at this rate."

"It helps if you blow the horn," Beau teased.

"Very funny."

BEAU AND Tollison stood in front of a third-floor apartment, listening to the *thump, thump, thump* of techno music vibrating the door knocker. Out of habit Tollison's hand was resting on his shoulder holster as Beau knocked continuously on the apartment door.

The music stopped abruptly, and a voice called from the other side of the door. "Yeah!"

Beau looked down at a piece of paper and a photograph. "Byron Barrios?"

"Who's asking?"

Beau held his badge up to the peephole. "NOPD. Open the door, please. We need to talk to you."

"About what?"

"Jacob Chaps," Beau said. "Please open the door, sir."

Tollison glanced at Beau and then turned to the door when he heard the sound of the dead bolt. The door opened about a foot, and good-looking guy with blond hair and green eyes stuck his head out. The guy was sweating profusely.

"Byron Barrios?" Beau asked.

"Yes."

"I'm Detective Bissonet, and this is Investigator Cruz. We need to ask you a few questions about Jacob Chaps."

Byron opened the door, stepped back, and motioned them in.

The extremely muscular guy was wearing a tank top and shorts, with a towel thrown loosely over his shoulder. Tollison looked around. The apartment was neat and clean, and there was a home gym and a rack of free weights set up where the dining room table would normally be.

Byron must have seen Tollison studying the equipment. "I was just finishing up my workout," he offered, tossing the towel haphazardly onto the weight bench. "I'm sorry. I'm still really shaken up about Jacob. What do you want to ask me?"

"For starters," Tollison said, "where were you last Monday night between the hours of five o'clock and midnight?"

"I was in the French Quarter with a friend," Byron said.

"Where in the Quarter?" Beau asked.

"The Bourbon Pub. Why?"

Beau flipped open his small notepad. "Friend's name?"

"Will…. Will Falcon."

"Can Mr. Falcon verify this?"

"I guess—I mean, yeah. Sure."

"Is there anyone else who can put you at the bar that night?"

"Chuck the bartender waited on us all night. I'm sure he'll remember us. We're sort of regulars there."

"When is the last time you saw Jacob Chaps?" Tollison asked.

Byron's expression turned solemn. "It's been well over a year now."

"How did you find out about his murder?"

Byron stared at the wall behind his sofa. A single tear ran down his cheek, and he wiped it away. "I saw it on the news. I mean… at first I didn't believe it. So I called his best friend, Jared, and he told me it was true."

"It's our understanding you and Jacob dated for a period of time," Tollison said.

"That's right."

Tollison nodded. "May I ask how long?"

Byron ran his hands through his short-cropped hair. "About seven months, give or take."

"Give or take?" Beau questioned.

"Yeah. That last couple of months were kind of rough."

"How so?"

"Is this really necessary?" Byron asked.

"I'm afraid it is," Beau said.

Byron sighed. "I cheated on him, okay. And… he found out about it."

Tollison immediately looked over at Beau, and Beau's expression went sour.

Byron locked eyes with Beau. "It only happened once. I swear it," he clarified. "It didn't mean anything. But he broke it off with me. Just like that. Without even letting me explain."

"What is there to explain?" Beau asked. "If it didn't mean anything, why did you do it?"

"I know. It was stupid, but I was drunk and—"

Tollison cut him off. "Is that when you started stalking him?"

Byron's expression turned to one of surprise. "Stalking? No!"

"We know he took out a restraining order against you." Beau looked at his notes. "The order says you followed him around constantly. You showed up at his place of employment almost daily, sat in your car outside his apartment for hours at a time, and eventually even threatened to kill him if he didn't take you back."

Byron sat down and covered his face with his hands. "I gave him space at first. I figured he'd come around and eventually forgive me. But two months after he broke it off with me, he started seeing another guy, and I… I panicked. I was in love with him. I didn't want to lose him."

"So you stalked and threatened him."

"No. God! That sounds horrible! I just wanted him to see that I cared about him. I wanted to get his attention is all." Byron stood again and looked between Tollison and Beau. "Wait! You don't think *I* killed him?"

"Did you?" Tollison asked.

"No! I could never—I loved him."

Tears were now flowing readily down Byron's cheeks.

"Do you own a gun, Mr. Barrios?" Tollison asked.

"No! I hate guns. You've got to believe me. I didn't kill him." Byron's shoulders started to shake, and he once again covered his face with his hands as he cried, "I loved him! I swear it!"

Tollison and Beau stood. Tollison put a hand on Byron's shoulder. "I'm very sorry for your loss. We'll show ourselves out. Oh, and Mr. Barrios, please don't leave town until we've been able to verify your alibi. We'll be in touch."

Tollison gestured for Beau to walk out, and he followed and closed the door behind them. Tollison waited. He knew Beau well enough to know what was coming next. As soon as their feet hit the stairs, Beau let loose. "If he loved him so damn much, why did he cheat on the poor guy?"

And there it is!

"I know, Beau. I know."

Beau was quiet for a minute, and Tollison knew he was processing what they'd just learned. But instead of commenting on the case, Beau surprised him with another observation. "Do you ever stop to think about how we inevitably set things in motion? It's almost like the six degrees of separation thing."

"How so?" Tollison asked, getting into the SUV.

"Well. If Byron hadn't cheated, Jacob and Byron might still be together. And if they were, the odds of them being at that parade in that exact spot are slim to none. And if they weren't at that parade, then Jacob might not be dead."

"I see where you're going with this," Tollison said as he pulled out of the apartment complex. "But couldn't that be applied to everything we do on a daily basis?"

"I guess."

Tollison hit the brakes when the yellow traffic light in front of him turned to red. "Okay. Perfect example. Just now I hit the brakes at this yellow light, and the guy behind me almost rear-ended us. I would imagine if I had run the yellow light, he would have kept going through the light as well. And surely by *that* time, the light would have been red. Let's say the guy was broadsided by crossing traffic. Would that have been my fault? Or should I be commended because by stopping, I possibly prevented the guy from getting into an accident? It's all cause and effect, Beau. Everything we do has a ripple effect on something else. Some good, some bad, but if we were held accountable for everything our inadvertent actions might cause, we might very well be a frozen society."

Beau looked at Tollison and smiled. "Now that's why I love you so much."

"Why?"

"Because you can take my sometimes fucked-up crap, make total sense out of it, and explain to me why it's so fucked up. That, in my book, makes you a genius."

Tollison laughed. "That we agree on."

"Asshole."

"From a genius to an asshole in five seconds. That must be a record."

Beau leaned over and kissed him on the cheek. "But you're my asshole."

"And I wouldn't have it any other way. Where next?"

"Let's track down this Will Falcon and the rest of the witnesses and friends on our list and then pay the bartender at the Bourbon Pub a little visit to see if he can verify Byron's story."

As the day came to a close, they had spoken to all the witnesses for both victims, except for Will Falcon. He'd not been home when they'd knocked on his door.

Over the course of the day, they'd learned the two victims were quiet guys who kept to themselves and dated very rarely. But they shared one thing in common. A mystery man. A guy all of the witnesses were vaguely aware of but really knew nothing about.

They had one more stop, possibly two depending on how this one went. If the bartender at the Bourbon Pub couldn't verify Barrios's story, they would go back to Falcon's place and wait until he showed up. Selfishly, they had purposely left this stop for last because they knew they would need a drink by the end of the day, and why not kill two birds with one stone. They walked into the Bourbon Pub and took a seat at the bar. A bartender walked up, nodded, and placed a bar napkin in front of each of them. "What can I get you gentleman?"

"Two Bud Lights and Chuck," Beau said.

"Excuse me?"

Beau dug into his inside coat pocket and pulled out his badge. "Are you Chuck?"

"Ah, no. I'm Timmy."

"Fine. We're looking for a bartender named Chuck."

The guy looked over his shoulder and yelled across the bar. "Chuck! Get over here."

A dark-haired guy about thirty or so walked over and slapped Timmy on the ass. He was really good-looking and exceptionally built as made obvious by the tight red tank top stretched across his pumped-up chest. "Yeah?"

"These men would like a word with you."

Chuck turned to Beau and Tollison, looked them up and down, and then glanced back at Timmy. "I guess it's my lucky day, then."

He turned to Beau and Tollison and leaned over the bar. "Now, what would two extremely handsome guys want with little ole me?"

When Beau lifted his badge off the bar and showed it to Chuck, the man's entire demeanor changed. He straightened and looked back at Timmy. "What the fuck?"

"I'm Detective Bissonet from the NOPD, and this is my partner, Investigator Cruz."

Chuck threw his hands into the air. "I'm clean, man. Been clean for over eight months now."

"Relax," Tollison said. "We just need to ask you a couple of questions."

Chuck nodded. "Okay."

Timmy disappeared and came back with two Bud Light longnecks. He placed them in front of Beau and Tollison and disappeared again. Beau took a long pull off his beer and then slid the picture of Barrios across the bar. "Recognize this man?"

Chuck studied the photograph. "Yeah. That's Byron Barrios. He's a regular around here."

"Was he here Monday night?"

"Monday night?" Chuck repeated. "As a matter of fact, he was. He was here with Will. Will Falcon."

"And you're sure it was Monday night?" Tollison asked.

"Yeah. For sure," Chuck said.

Beau took another pull off of his beer and looked at Tollison. "Were they here all night?"

"Until closing," Chuck said.

"I'm sure you wait on a lot of people. Right?" Tollison asked.

"Yeah."

"So how can you be sure of that?"

"Because it was a really slow night. I closed up around one o'clock, and they gave me a lift home."

"Okay, then," Beau said. "Thanks for your time."

"No problem. Are they in any kind of trouble?"

"Not since you verified their alibi."

"Good. They're pretty nice guys."

"Thanks, Chuck," Beau said. Then he leaned over and gave Tollison a big kiss. "You ready to go, hon?"

Chuck's eyes widened to the size of silver dollars.

"What?" Beau said. "Detectives can be gay. Right?"

Chuck smiled seductively. "Sure. Hey, man, if you guys are ever looking for a third, count me in."

"Thanks for the offer, but we're monogamous," Beau said.

Chuck looked at Tollison.

"He's right," Tollison said, looking at Beau. "I'm a one-man... man!"

"That's too bad, but I'm happy for you guys. Come back and see me sometime."

"Let's go, Tol."

"See ya, Chuck."

SIX

BRUCE OPENED his eyes and squinted against the bright sunshine filling his bedroom. He checked his watch. It was just after ten o'clock. He'd crawled into bed sometime around five this morning after a long night at the station with Auggie, and he still felt as tired as when he had fallen asleep.

He yawned, stretched, and looked up at the ceiling. It would be so easy to roll over and go back to sleep, but he had other things on his mind. He sat up, swung his legs around, and plastered his bare feet on the floor.

Normally on a Sunday morning, Bruce rose around eight, watched the morning news in bed while he had his coffee, ate his breakfast, and then leisurely read the Sunday paper. But this morning all he could think about was Bastien. He'd phoned him around eleven last night, and the poor guy was still awake, suffering from serious jetlag. Bruce told him he didn't think he was going to make it there but that he'd see him in the morning. Bastien had still sounded a little hopeful and insisted he come by no matter what the time. But it had been four thirty in the morning when he and Auggie finally finished up with the crime scene, and that was way too late to intrude on Bastien or even call him.

Now Bruce was unsure what he should do. He didn't want to *not* call and have Bastien thinking he was neglecting him, but at the same time he didn't want to wake the poor man if he'd managed to conquer his jetlag and get some real sleep. He decided to give Bastien another hour, and then he would call.

Fortunately for him, Bruce didn't have to wait that long. His cell rang, and he smiled when he saw Bastien's name on the caller ID. He slid his finger across the screen and put the phone to his ear. "Good morning."

"Good morning, ma puce," Bastien said in a cheerful voice. "I hope it is not too early? I hesitated to call because I know you must have had a late night."

"I did," Bruce said. "But I've been up for a little while. I, too, was afraid to call you in case you were able to get some quality sleep."

"I appreciate your thoughtfulness. And yes, I am well rested."

"Then how about allowing me to take you to a late brunch?"

"That would be lovely. Shall we meet somewhere?"

"How about I come by to pick you up in… say thirty minutes? That way we'll only have to worry about parking one car downtown."

"I'll be ready."

"Okay. See you in a few."

BASTIEN WAS conversing with the bellman when Bruce pulled his SUV up to the curb. He was looking gorgeous in tan chinos, a sleeveless black cashmere V-neck sweater over a long-sleeved white dress shirt, and a Burberry scarf hanging loosely around his neck.

Bruce looked down at his vintage Henley, black Lucky Jeans, and black boots and realized he was going to have to step it up a notch if he was going to keep up with Bastien Andros.

When Bruce popped the locks, the bellman made a beeline for the SUV and opened the door. Bastien hesitated. "It was a pleasure chatting with you, Charles, and I do hope everything goes well with the delivery of your new baby. Please do let me know as soon as he or she is born. I'd like to do something special for your new family."

"Certainly, Mr. Andros," Charles said. "But a gift is not necessary. The fact that you took the time and interest in my family is more than enough for me."

"Please call me Bastien. And nonsense. It will be my pleasure."

The doorman smiled warmly and nodded. "You and Mr. Jenkins enjoy your day, now."

Bastien slid into the passenger seat, looked over at Bruce, smiled, and winked. "We will do our best."

"Good morning, handsome," Bruce said as Bastien leaned over and kissed his cheek. Bruce again picked up on the sweet-and-spicy aroma of Bastien's cologne. *Does this man always smell this incredible?*

Bastien's smile was warm when he spoke. "Bonjour, *ma douce*. And what a spectacular morning it is. So where are you taking me this lovely day?"

"All in good time," Bruce said through a smile he felt would be impossible to wipe off his face, even if he tried.

"WHAT A splendid city," Bastien said as he and Bruce strolled casually in front of the St. Louis Cathedral, admiring the artwork of the street vendors lined up on the perimeter of Jackson Square. The street mimes and fortune tellers were out in full force in front of the Cabildo, as were the jugglers and unicyclist putting on their shows for the tourists.

He and Bastien had just spent the last two hours enjoying the jazz brunch at Court of Two Sisters and Bruce was feeling overly stuffed from eggs Benedict and the other rich food Bastien had ordered.

Over brunch Bastien had expressed an interest in acquiring some artwork to take home, so Bruce stood back and leaned on a lamppost, his arms crossed over his chest, and watched Bastien negotiate the price of an oil painting of Jackson Square, featuring a statue of Andrew Jackson on horseback with the St. Louis Cathedral in the background.

Bruce studied his handsome companion. Bastien's smile was broad, and his hands gestured wildly as he looked back and forth between the painting and the gentleman attempting to sell it.

It was a fairly balmy winter day, and Bruce lifted his face to the sky. He closed his eyes and soaked in the warm rays of the sun. His thoughts were only of Bastien. In fact, other than work distractions, his only thoughts these days were of Bastien. The connection he felt to him was astonishing. Almost alarming.

He'd dated a few people since Beau, but none he'd even remotely considered a possibility for a long-term relationship. But Bastien was different. Over the last few months, he'd found himself thinking about the man in just those terms. But he still didn't know how Bastien felt about him. Did he share Bruce's feelings? Did he even want a long-term relationship? Beau was a tough act to follow, but from what he knew of Bastien so far, the man was completely up to the challenge.

Something was bothering him, though. No. Not really bothering him, but nagging at him—from somewhere deep in his subconscious. The events leading up to now all seemed so bizarre. So intertwined. How

Tollison had been the one who finally helped Beau forgive Bruce for his indiscretion. How Bastien had shown up in New Orleans unannounced and then had been promptly kidnapped by someone from Tollison's past. How they had all gone to Switzerland to help save Bastien. And now, Bruce and Bastien. Together. Well, sort of together. Beau's ex and Tollison's ex.

It was like they were experiencing a parallel universe or something. He wondered again if Beau and Tollison were really okay with him and Bastien dating or being together long term. It seemed as though they were when they'd had dinner together. But in the end, did it really matter? If they weren't okay with it, would he, or could he, give Bastien up? He wasn't going to think about that. Not today.

When Bruce opened his eyes again, Bastien was handing the street vendor a wad of cash. He looked over his shoulder at Bruce, winked, and smiled broadly. Bruce returned the smile and nodded. Bastien joined him and seemingly without a second thought kissed Bruce on the cheek.

"We now have an authentic New Orleans oil painting to take back to Geneva," Bastien said.

That *we* resonated with Bruce, warming him to his core. The possibility Bastien would ask Bruce to visit him in Geneva was music to his ears. So much so, he wrapped Bastien in an encompassing embrace, tourists or no tourists. When Bruce released him, they each stared into the other's eyes, and Bruce knew instantly Bastien was experiencing at least some of what he was feeling. His expression was unmistakable.

"So what's the plan?" Bruce asked.

"Oh I have plans, ma puce. Boy, do I have plans."

"Let's get out of here, then," Bruce whispered. "I too have plans."

BACK AT the Lafayette Hotel, Bruce and Bastien walked through the lobby toward the elevators. Bruce imagined he could almost reach out and touch the anticipation and sexual tension flowing between them, and the realization made his heart race. He slipped his hands into his pants pockets to keep them from trembling as Bastien slid his keycard into the slot. The elevator doors closed behind them, and Bruce met Bastien's gaze. He was certain he recognized the look on Bastien's face. Desire. Lust. Need. He'd seen the same look on Beau's face many times.

No! Do not bring Beau into this. Beau is your past. Bastien could be your future.

Bruce felt like a silly teenager. This wasn't his first time. Not even his first time since Beau, so why did it feel this way? His already racing heart felt like it was about to pound right out of his chest, and his knees felt like noodles. This was it. *Damn, man. Get it together! What are you waiting for? A formal invitation?*

Bruce took two steps toward Bastien, grabbed his Burberry scarf, and pulled Bastien close. He leaned in and gently brought their lips together. Bastien's lips were warm and soft, and he still smelled incredible. *Note to self. Ask Bastien what kind of cologne he wears.*

As Bastien deepened the kiss, Bruce released his scarf and tentatively slipped his hands around to grip Bastien's muscular ass. Bastien must have taken this as a sign because he swung Bruce around and pinned him against the elevator doors. By the time the elevator reached the penthouse, Bastien was running his fingers through Bruce's hair and grinding his crotch against Bruce's.

Bruce pulled Bastien's sweater over his head and was busy unbuttoning his white shirt when the elevator doors opened and they both nearly fell into the suite. Bruce was struggling to keep his balance, but he needn't have worried because Bastien's strong arms caught him and held him firmly in place.

Suddenly Bastien withdrew and cleared his throat. His expression was one of surprise. Almost as if he were the kid caught with his hand stuck in the proverbial cookie jar. Instinctively Bruce turned, and he silently gasped when he saw a chambermaid in a black-and-white uniform staring at them with startled eyes. The silver-and-blue-haired woman wearing a black lace headpiece was standing in the foyer, apparently frozen, holding a mop and bucket, with a shocked expression on her elderly mocha-colored face.

Bastien, to his credit, recovered quickly. "Good afternoon, madame." He nodded his head and offered her his hand. "I am Sebastien Andros, and this is my companion, Mr. Jenkins," he said, nodding toward Bruce. "I will be staying in your lovely hotel for an extended period of time, and I think it only right that we should get to know each other."

The chambermaid's shocked expression turned into a hesitant smile.

Bastien looked around. "You are surely a master at your work. The suite looks and smells wonderful."

The chambermaid tilted her head shyly and smiled again. "Why, thank you, Mr. Andros. I do take pride in my work."

"Please call me Bastien. And it certainly shows. I think you and I are going to get along famously."

"Thank you, Mr. Bastien. Well. I'm just about finished here, so I'll let you two gentlemen get back to whatever it is you were doing when those elevator doors opened." She winked as she pressed the elevator call button.

When the elevator doors opened, she stepped inside and looked back over her shoulder. "You gentlemen have a good day, now."

"Bye-bye," Bastien said, smiling.

Bruce waved as the doors closed.

"What a delightful lady," Bastien said, taking Bruce into his arms. "Remind me to leave her a tip every day."

Bruce nodded but quickly closed his eyes when Bastien's lips started caressing his neck. "Now, where were we?" Bastien whispered breathlessly in Bruce's ear.

Before Bruce could answer, he heard dogs barking. Bastien stopped, and Bruce cursed under his breath. "Fuck!"

Bastien pulled away, looking puzzled.

"That's Auggie's ring. I'm sorry, I've got to get this."

Bastien nodded and stepped back. "Should I give you some privacy?"

"No," Bruce said, taking Bastien's hand. "I'll get rid of him."

Bruce accepted the call. "Jenkins," he said in a frustrated tone.

"Where are you?" Auggie asked.

"At Bastien's hotel."

"Jeez," Auggie said. "Do you homos do anything else but fuck?"

"As a matter of fact, we haven't—wait!" Bruce caught himself and ignored the statement. "What do you want, Auggie?"

"There's been another murder."

"Fuck! When? Where?"

"A couple of hours ago. Krewe of Carrollton. Corner of Carrollton and St. Charles, to be exact. Call Beau and Tollison, and you guys meet me there in twenty."

Bruce looked at Bastien waiting patiently. "But—"

"No buts, Bruce. We have a serial killer on our hands. Your fuck will have to wait."

"Nice, Auggie. Very nice."

"Am I mistaken?"

Bruce looked at Bastien again and sighed. "Fuck you, Auggie."

"I figured as much."

"Come on, Aug. It's just…. Oh for fuck's sake. Never mind. See you in twenty."

Auggie's voice seemed to soften. "Sorry, Bruce. I know it's your day off, but I really need you on this one."

"I know," Bruce said. "I know."

Bruce ended the call.

"Another murder?" Bastien asked.

"I'm afraid so," Bruce answered, taking Bastien into his arms. "I'm so sorry. I wanted to spend the rest of the day in bed with you."

"As did I, ma puce. But I understand. Duty must come first."

"No!" Bruce protested without thinking. "I don't want anything to come before you."

Bastien smiled. He kissed Bruce gently, led him to the elevator, and pressed the call button. "We will have plenty of time, ma puce. You go and do your job, and I'll be here when you're finished."

"I wish I… well, just thank you for understanding. I'll call you as soon as I'm free."

The elevator doors opened, and Bruce stepped inside.

"I'll be here." Bastien stepped inside the elevator and kissed Bruce gently before stepping out again. "You be safe."

On the elevator ride down to the lobby, it suddenly dawned on Bruce that this was exactly what had come between him and Beau. Work! Except now the shoe was on the other foot. Fear resonated in him as he got into his SUV and called Beau and Tollison.

SEVEN

WHEN BEAU and Tollison arrived, a young police officer tried to stop them as they approached the crime scene, which was surrounded by yellow-and-black tape.

"Save it," Beau said as he flashed his badge at the rookie. "And he's with me," he added, referring to Tollison.

"Smooth," Tollison said. "Whatever happened to a little diplomacy?"

"Don't have time for it right now. We've got a serial killer to find."

The officer smirked and handed him two sets of gloves and shoe covers.

Locard's principle. Beau knew the drill, as did Tollison. When you enter a crime scene, you bring something with you. When you exit the same scene, you take part of it with you as well—and leave some trace of yourself behind.

They slipped the booties over their shoes, snapped the gloves on, and entered the crime scene.

"I think I see Auggie." Beau pointed through the group of forensics guys working the scene. Auggie was standing over the vic, who appeared to be male and was lying facedown on the sidewalk, a pool of blood surrounding his head. Jeffrey Rouse, the ME, was kneeling over the body.

"Hey, Jeff," Beau said.

Rouse looked up and smirked. "I thought you left the force, Bissonet."

"Yeah, well. Auggie asked us for a little help on this one."

"What do we have?" Tollison asked.

"What we have is a serial killer," Jeffrey said. "The same as the others. ID says we have a thirty-three-year-old male named Stuart Cole. Single gunshot wound to the head. Similar angle of entry, and by the looks of the entry wound, the same type bullet from a high-powered rifle.

But I won't know if the bullet is from the same weapon until I do my formal examination."

Beau looked at Tollison and back at the vic. "Shit," he cursed. "Figured as much."

"Thanks for the info, Jeff," Tollison said. "Have you seen Detective Jenkins?"

Rouse gestured over his shoulder. "Last time I saw him he was interviewing a couple of witnesses over there."

Beau turned and saw Bruce standing at the entrance to the crime scene. A couple of guys were standing with him. They both looked pretty shaken up.

Beau and Tollison walked in their direction. "Hey, guys," Bruce said when they reached him. "This is John Avery and Michael Dawson. They are friends of the vic—I mean, Mr. Cole. They were at the parade with him."

"We're really sorry, guys," Beau said sincerely.

The two men nodded, but they seemed to be in some stage of shock, which was not uncommon.

"This is my partner, Investigator Cruz." Beau looked around. "Damn. There's never a uniformed officer when you need one."

"Whaddya need?" Tollison asked.

"I was gonna see if I could get these guys some coffee to warm them up."

"I'll take them to find some," Tollison said.

Beau looked at the two men. "Is that all right, gentlemen?"

The guys nodded again, and Beau gestured to Tollison. "Thanks."

Beau waited until they were out of earshot and then turned to Bruce. "Have you questioned them?"

Bruce shook his head. "No. I was just about to when I saw you guys drive up. I figure I'd let you have them, and I'll help Auggie with the bystanders. By the way, how's the questioning going on the other cases. Any new developments?"

"Not yet, but I'm working on a hunch. I'll fill you and Auggie in after I interview these guys. What they say might make or break my theory."

"Got it."

Beau made his way over to the squad car where Tollison and the vic's friends were standing, each sipping on a cup of steaming coffee. "Guys, I know this is hard for you—"

"Hard? You think this is hard?" Michael said. "I just lost my best friend. I think it's a little more than hard."

The other guy put his arm around him. "It's okay, Michael. These guys are just trying to help."

"It's not okay, and it's not going to be okay. Stuart is dead, John."

"I know, Michael. I know."

"I'm sorry, Mr. Dawson," Beau said. "You're right. I don't want to be insensitive, but I really need to ask you some questions."

Michael glared at him but didn't object.

"You both were here with Mr. Cole. Right?"

Michael didn't answer so John spoke up. "Yeah. We all came together."

Beau looked at Michael. "Was there any altercation with anyone?"

"If you asking if Stuart fought with anyone, the answer is no. Stuart would never fight. He didn't believe in violence."

"So nothing out of the ordinary happened?"

"Nothing!" Michael said. "One minute we were enjoying the parade, and the next Stuart was dead, facedown in a pool of blood. Oh God. Stuart's dead."

"Mr. Dawson?" Beau asked, his gaydar on full alert. "Were either of you romantically involved with Mr. Cole?"

"No! We were not boyfriends. Just best friends."

"But you are gay. Right?"

Michael threw his coffee cup onto the street. "What does that have to do with anything? Wait! Are you one of those homophobe cops?"

"No," Beau said. "I'm not a homophobe cop. In fact, Tollison here is my life partner as well as my business partner."

Michael looked suspiciously between Beau and Tollison. "Really?"

"Yes, really," Tollison said.

"But what does it matter if we're gay or not?"

"Because Mr. Cole is the third gay male killed in the last week, and we have reason to believe they were all killed by the same person."

Michael looked at John with a surprised expression on his face, put his hand over his mouth, and gasped, "Oh God!"

"Now, guys," Beau said, "this is really important. Did Mr. Cole have a boyfriend?"

Michael didn't respond, his hand still covering his mouth.

"No," John said. "I mean, he wanted a boyfriend, but he just hadn't met anyone yet."

"Okay, then. Had he dated anyone recently?"

John looked at Michael. "Not that I know of, Michael?"

Michael didn't seem to need much time to think. "There was only one guy in the last year, and I just fucking found out about it yesterday. Quite by mistake, I might add. I can't believe that bitch kept it from me."

"Don't speak about Stuart like that," John said.

"Do you know the guy's name or anything about him?" Beau asked ignoring the comment.

"Hell no. I told you I just found out about it."

"Michael!" John said. "These guys are just trying to help."

Michael looked up at Beau through his eyelashes. "Sorry. I still can't believe my best friend dated someone and didn't tell me."

"Can you tell us what you *do* know?" Tollison asked.

"Sure, but it's not much."

"That's okay," Tollison responded.

"From what Stuart told me, he dated the guy for about a week."

"Did he say how they met?" Beau asked.

"Online," Michael answered. "But the funny thing is, the guy wouldn't go out to a public place, and he didn't want Stuart telling anyone they were seeing each other. Said he liked his privacy."

Beau glanced at Tollison. "So what happened?"

"Stuart said the guy was weird and almost bipolar. One minute he was fine, and the next he was sort of crazy."

"Crazy how?" Tollison asked.

"Screaming about how much he hated queers. He told Stuart he'd never trust a gay guy because they were all cheaters."

"And Mr. Cole didn't tell you the guy's name?"

"No. He said it was over and to just let sleeping dogs lie."

"How long ago was this?" Beau asked.

"I don't really know. Like I said, I just found out about it yesterday."

"Okay, guys," Beau said. "I really appreciate your time. Do you need a ride home or something?"

Michael looked at John and then back at Beau and Tollison. A single tear slid down his cheek. "Stuart was the designated driver, and we've been drinking, so yeah, maybe."

"No problem. What about Stuart's car?"

"It's two blocks up on Carrollton," John said. "But we'll come back and get it later. Probably with his mom."

Michael covered his mouth again. "Miss Judy. Someone has to tell Miss Judy."

"I'm sure Detective Hebert has already notified her."

Beau looked around. "Just wait right here, and I'll arrange a ride home for you."

An hour later Beau, Tollison, Auggie, and Bruce were at the station, gathered around Auggie's desk.

"What happened with the Barrios kid?" Auggie asked.

"Alibi checks out. The bartender confirmed Barrios was at the bar until after midnight."

"Okay. So you want to tell me this angle you're pursuing?" Auggie asked.

Beau glared at Bruce. "Big mouth."

Bruce shrugged. "Just doing my job."

Beau rolled his eyes. "It's just a hunch, Aug, but from all the questioning we've done, all the vics seem to have had a one-night stand or dated a guy for a very short period time."

"So?" Auggie asked.

"What if all the vics dated the same guy, and for some reason this guy is picking them off, one by one?"

Beau watched silently as Auggie considered his theory. "I don't know. It's thin. How would the perp know the vics were going to a certain parade or would be at a certain location? The parade routes are miles long."

"Maybe he followed them," Beau said. "There's only been one vic at each parade, so it is possible."

"Maybe," Auggie said. "But that seems like a long shot to me. I mean, with traffic, parking, etcetera, that might be hard. Do we have a name?"

"No," Beau said. "None of the friends, family, or witnesses ever met the guy, which is another reason to think it might be the same guy. The last vic's best friend said the man wouldn't go out in public and didn't want anyone knowing they were dating. He said the vic told him afterward that the guy was bipolar or something and didn't trust queers."

"A gay-basher?" Bruce asked.

"Sounds more like a serial killer to me," Auggie said. "Hell, maybe he's both. Anyway, it's all we have. It ain't much, but it's a start. Bruce, I need the vics' computers and cell phones as well as all the video footage from every surveillance camera at or near each of the crime scenes. Maybe we can identify a common face or track down common telephone numbers, user profiles, e-mail addresses, etcetera."

"I'll get right on it," Bruce replied.

"I know this is probably a long shot," Tollison said. "But what about social media or dating or hookup sites like Grindr as a way to know where the vics would be?"

"What in the hell is Grindr?" Auggie asked.

Beau smiled as all three other men looked at Auggie like he had two heads.

"Whaaaat?" Auggie said. "I have no idea what you homos are into these days."

"It's a cell phone app that allows gay guys to find other gay guys within a certain radius," Tollison explained. "If you are signed on and in a certain area and another Grindr subscriber is in your area, it will alert you with a photo of some type, a bio, and the person's location."

Auggie frowned. "Sounds like stalking to me."

"Not if it's consensual," Beau added.

"Fine, let's check it out. If I have to, I'll subpoena the records of— what's it called again?"

"Grindr," Tollison said.

"Yeah. Grindr."

"It might not be that easy," Tollison said. "From what I've been told, Grindr and other similar apps use special log-ins and other masking technology to protect their users' identities. The developers don't even know their users' personal information."

"So how do users know who other users are?" Auggie asked.

"When you see someone you like, you favorite them, and if they favorite you back, you can share more information."

"So in other words the user has the right to give more personal information if they want to, but it's not readily available unless it's personally shared?" Auggie asked.

"Yep."

"Hey!" Beau asked looking at Tollison. "Is it possible to post where you are, like on the social media sites?"

"What are you looking at me for?" Tollison shot back. "I'm not on that site. Everything I know I learned from Bruce."

It was Bruce's turn to give Tollison the evil eye.

"Oh please," Tollison said. "You told me you joined after you and Beau broke up."

Beau smiled. "Call homicide, Auggie. Someone has just been thrown under a bus."

Bruce looked at Tollison with an expression of disbelief. "Yeah. Thanks a lot, Tol."

"No thanks needed, man. Just trying to do what the NOPD and the fine City of New Orleans is paying us for."

"I never said anything about pay!" Auggie snapped.

Beau rolled his eyes. "Can we get back to trying to solve this case?"

"And the answer to your question is no," Bruce said. "You cannot post where you are in an open forum like you can on other social media sites, if that's what you're asking. If someone favorites you and you accept, then you can share your profile and location with them if you want to. That's how people hook up."

"Hook up?" Auggie asked. "What a lovely term."

Beau ignored the comment. "Okay. What if a person who is on Grindr posted a general vicinity of where they were on another social media site, like 'Hey, joining friends at the Krewe of Carrollton parade and will try to park as near to Carrollton and St. Charles as we can. Come and hang out with us.' And then someone else on Grindr saw that post and went to that general vicinity? Could they find each other?"

"In theory," Bruce said. "If both of their apps are on and person A went to that general area, he would get a notification that person B is in the same area and a certain distance away."

"Could he hold his telephone and walk around until he saw the distance between them shrinking?"

"Never tried it," Bruce said. "But theoretically? Yes."

"Then that could be how our perp is tracking his victims," Beau said. "But we won't know for sure until we get our hands on their computers and cell phones."

Auggie looked at Bruce.

"I'm on it," Bruce said.

EIGHT

BRUCE WAS heading back to Auggie's office after ordering equipment warrants and ran smack into Beau as he came out of the bathroom.

"Watch where you're going," Bruce said, shoving Beau playfully out of the way.

"Fuck you," Beau said.

"In your dreams. Those days are over," Bruce teased.

"Speaking of," Beau said. "How's it going with Bastien? Have you bumped uglies yet?"

"Jeez, Beau. How romantic."

"Well?"

"If you must know, the answer is one big no."

"Why?" Beau asked.

"Because every time we get close, I get a call from Auggie that there was another murder, and I have to leave him. And it's fucking getting really old."

Beau chuckled. "I imagine so."

Bruce thought for a second and held up a hand. "Can I ask you something, Beau?"

"Sure."

"Do you believe in that 'what goes around comes around' or 'an eye for an eye' crap?"

"I don't know. Maybe. Why?"

"Because this afternoon when I told Bastien there was another murder and I would have to leave him to get to the station, I had a flash of déjà vu."

"How so?" Beau asked.

"Well, I can't quite put my finger on it, but I think I saw a little bit of me in his expression from back when you had to leave me so many times. And we all know how that turned out."

Beau frowned. "Shit, Bruce. I don't know, man. That's a tough one. All I can say is, talk to Bastien. Be honest with him about your fears. He seems like a reasonable enough guy."

Bruce looked down at the floor. "I guess."

Beau checked his watch. "It's almost eight now. Why don't you go? I'll cover for you with Auggie."

"Really?"

Beau put his hand on Bruce's shoulder and squeezed. "Yeah, go. I got your back."

"Thanks, Beau. And I mean that."

"Get out of here. Oh, and I almost forgot. Wednesday is the Krewe of Druids. Rolls at six thirty. You guys wanna join us?"

"I'll check with Bastien and let you know."

"Good enough."

BRUCE CLIMBED into his SUV and pulled out of the parking garage. Beau was right. He needed to act and act now. They were both adults. What was he waiting for? He hit the hands-free calling button on his steering wheel and spoke. "Call Bastien Andros."

After two rings Bastien answered. "I was hoping I would hear from you soon."

"I'm so sorry, Bastien. I attempted to call several times, but something always kept getting in the way."

"No need to apologize, ma puce. It's your job. I understand."

Why wasn't I that understanding when it was Beau having to leave me for work? I was such a selfish ass.

Bruce sighed. "Yeah, well. Right about now I'm totally second-guessing my career choice."

Bastien chuckled. "Nonsense. You love your job, and you're good at it. I'm living proof of that."

"*You* were a team effort, my friend. And… thank God it all went as planned."

"For both of us."

"I hope you haven't been too bored on your own?" Bruce asked.

"Not at all. I've been working as well. Also lying back in bed catching up on my jetlag as well as my reading. I've missed you terribly, but it's been quite relaxing."

"Have you eaten dinner yet?" Bruce asked, feeling hopeful he hadn't.

"No," Bastien said. "I was hoping to hear from you."

Yes!

"Good! Then don't move. I have a plan."

"Sounds intriguing."

"Glad you think so. And seriously. Don't move."

"I'll be waiting, ma puce."

Bruce disconnected the call from Bastien, scanned his mirrors, and pulled to the side of the road. He used his cell phone to look up the number for the Lafayette Hotel and called the concierge. By the time he pulled back into traffic, the difficulties of the day were washing away like water running down a drain.

Minutes later, he pulled into the hotel's valet parking lane, got out of the car, and tossed the keys to the attendant. "I'll be here all night."

"Yes, sir." The guy nodded and smiled, and Bruce smiled back. He almost skipped through the lobby, shoved his keycard into the slot, and rode the elevator to the penthouse. His nerves and anticipation built with each floor, and by the time the elevator doors opened, he knew what he was going to do.

The suite was dimly lit, and the sound of soft music was floating on the air. Bruce stood in the foyer for a long moment, gathering his nerves. And then, as if someone had flipped a switch, he removed his leather jacket and let it fall to the foyer floor. He straightened, and like a man on a mission, he started walking up the stairs to Bastien's bedroom. With each step he climbed a little faster, until he was taking two steps at a time.

When Bruce reached the doorway he stopped dead in his tracks. He'd rarely seen anything so beautiful. He crossed his arms over his chest, leaned against the doorjamb, and took in the scenery.

Bastien was handsome—without a doubt—and the bedside lamp reflected softly off of the silver streaks in his hair, creating a halo effect. But he was so much more than handsome. He had this certain sex appeal Bruce had rarely experienced. He exuded masculinity in a gentle but forceful way.

Lying against the headboard, Bastien had his arms behind his head, his socked feet crossed at the ankles, and he was smiling seductively.

Bastien was still in his chinos, and his white shirt was open almost to the waist, revealing his well-defined muscles and a hint of the silver-streaked dark hair adorning his chest.

Bruce licked his lips as he pulled his Henley over his head and dropped it to the floor. He started for the bed. Bastien slid down, and his smile turned into something hot and seductive. Bruce climbed onto the foot of the bed and knelt, staring into Bastien's beautiful blue eyes. Bastien held out his arms, and Bruce fell into them, burying his face in Bastien's neck. Jesus, he smelled great.

"I've waited for this moment ever since I left Zurich," Bruce whispered.

"I as well, ma puce. But at last, our waiting is over."

Bruce sighed. "Thank God."

He kissed Bastien's neck. Gently at first. Then he bit down and licked, drawing a moan from Bastien. When Bastien tilted his neck, giving Bruce better access, Bruce took that as a sign to continue. He could feel Bastien caressing his back, lightly running his well-manicured nails up and down Bruce's spine, coaxing goose bumps to pop up all over his skin.

Bruce straightened and straddled Bastien at the waist. He slowly finished unbuttoning Bastien's shirt, pulled it free from his chinos, and spread it open, giving him full access to Bastien's naked skin. He ran his hands over Bastien's chest, following the lines of his pectoral muscles down to his taut abs and up again, never once breaking eye contact.

He finally leaned down and covered Bastien's lips in a heated and crushing kiss. Bastien opened to him, and their tongues roamed freely—exploring, tasting, and devouring the other. Bruce finally broke the kiss and licked his way down to Bastien's chest, teasing one sensitive nipple and then the other, biting gently and then licking away the sting he knew he'd surely caused. Bruce could feel his erection pushing firmly against his jeans, getting increasingly uncomfortable as he swelled with desire.

In a surprise move, Bastien leaned up, wrapped his arms around Bruce, and flipped him onto his back. Bruce was shocked at Bastien's strength and agility. Bruce was no little guy at six foot five and two hundred twenty pounds. But Bastien had flipped him with little effort, and Bruce stared up at him in disbelief.

"You're not the only one with moves," Bastien teased. "Don't let this long, thin physique fool you. I'm quite strong, and capable of manhandling you if that's what you like."

"I'm sure I will like anything you do to me," Bruce whispered through a coy smile.

Bastien wiggled his ass on Bruce's bulging erection and smiled. He shimmied down and straddled Bruce's knees. After releasing Bruce's belt, he unfastened and unzipped his jeans. Then he slid down farther and stood at the end of the bed. He unlaced each of Bruce's boots and slipped them off.

"Have you been on your feet all day, ma puce?"

"Pretty much," Bruce answered.

Bruce moaned and almost melted into the bed when Bastien started massaging his feet. He must have taken a massage class somewhere along the line because he was a master at it. Bruce felt the stresses and anxieties of the day dissipating until they had all but faded away.

Bastien eventually finished the foot massage, leaving Bruce feeling like a limp noodle. Bastien peeled off both of Bruce's socks and then reached for the waistband of Bruce's jeans. Bruce lifted a little and tensed in anticipation as the denim slid down his legs to his ankles and finally slipped off.

Still standing at the foot of the bed, Bastien removed his already opened shirt. He released his pants and let them drop to the floor, peeled off his own socks, and then disappeared into the bathroom. When he returned he climbed back onto the bed and whispered, "Roll over, ma puce."

Bruce cocked one eye open and saw Bastien kneeling over him with a bottle of some type of oil. "I think I like where this is going," Bruce teased.

"Oh. Just wait."

Bruce rolled over and rested his head on his folded arms. He heard the click of a flip-top cap being opened, and the next thing he felt was a pair of warm oily hands on his back, kneading, rubbing, and massaging diligently. His muscles were tired and achy from being on his feet and hunched over Auggie's desk for so many hours, but Bastien's hands were like magic, dissolving more stress with each passing second. When Bastien got to his shoulders, Bruce could no longer hold back the moan that escaped his lips.

Bastien chuckled in apparent amusement. "Feel good?"

"The best." Bruce said. "I don't ever think I've had such a great massage."

"I'm glad. Just close your eyes and enjoy."

Bastien addressed every inch of Bruce's body from the top of his head to the tip of his toes. He squeezed pressure points on Bruce's feet that literally brought him back to life. Bruce could almost feel the toxins oozing from his body.

Bruce stiffened a little when Bastien hooked his fingers in his underwear and pulled them off. But Bastien quickly did the same with his own and climbed back on the bed. He once again knelt over Bruce's limp body and started massaging Bruce's lower back again, eventually moving down to his ass. As he reached around between Bruce's body and the bed, Bruce rose to give him access. Bastien wrapped his fingers around Bruce's length and positioned it so it was pointing back between Bruce's open legs.

While stroking the underside of Bruce's cock lightly with one hand, Bastien brushed his fingers across Bruce's opening ever so gently, making his cock jump and his ass twitch from the sensation.

The marvel of Bastien rubbing Bruce's cock *and* his opening simultaneously was getting him extremely aroused, and Bruce was now growing uncomfortably hard. He rose up on all fours to allow his cock to spring back into its natural position, and Bastien evidently took that as an invitation to spread Bruce's cheeks wider and run his tongue back and forth over Bruce's opening, teasing and tantalizing him with each pass of wet warmth against sensitive flesh.

Bruce moaned again, and Bastien took him in hand and began stroking up and down his length in unison with his tongue action. Bruce's nerve endings were tingling with excitement. Half of his body wanted to thrust into Bastien's hand, and the other half wanted to push back against Bastien's face.

When Bruce's reserve started to break down and his body began to tremble from the attention, Bruce forced himself up on his knees. He turned at the waist, slipped his arms under Bastien's, and pulled him close as he turned and flopped back on the bed, pinning Bastien under him.

Bastien's eyes were wide with surprise, and Bruce felt a surge of pride at the success of his maneuvers. Bastien smiled warmly. "Nice move."

"Thanks. I got more where that came from."

"I can hardly wait," Bastien said.

Bruce stretched out on top of Bastien and stared directly into his eyes. He ran a hand through Bastien's thick silver-streaked dark hair and gripped the back of his head to bring their lips together again in a heated kiss. Their erect cocks were now pinned between them, and Bruce's forward thrusts were met by Bastien's, their continual movements creating jolts of friction that caused electricity to course through Bruce's body. From the quivering of Bastien's muscles beneath him, Bruce figured it was affecting Bastien the same way.

Breaking the kiss and sliding his lips down to Bastien's neck, Bruce took a moment to inhale Bastien's spicy scent and then licked his way down to Bastien's chest, caressing and teasing perfectly shaped nipples with his tongue. He continued down Bastien's torso until his chin brushed the head of Bastien's cock.

Bruce ran his tongue over the head of Bastien's cock, catching the pearls of moisture seeping from the slit, then took him into his mouth and slid all the way down his length, not stopping until he felt Bastien's crotch hair tickle his chin and the head of his erection pressing against the back of his throat. Bruce swallowed, coaxing a whimper to escape Bastien's lips. He felt Bastien's fingers gripping and tugging at his hair, exerting just enough pressure to make the simple act feel erotic and just on the edge of pleasurable pain. As Bruce glided up and down Bastien's cock, varying his pressure and suction, he slipped a finger into his mouth to moisten it and then found Bastien's opening, circling and teasing ever so gently as Bastien wiggled beneath him. He pushed hesitantly until Bastien opened up to him, and then he slipped beyond the guardian muscle that had once held him at bay.

Bruce crooked his finger a little, brushing against that ever so sensitive spot, and Bastien stiffened immediately, threw his head back, and then relaxed again. Bruce twisted his finger back and forth, and Bastien gasped and arched his back with each stroke.

"I want you, ma puce," Bastien whispered. "Now. Please."

"Condoms and lubricant?" Bruce whispered.

Bastien gestured to the bedside table. "In the drawer."

Bruce retrieved what he needed, slid the condom on, and applied lubricant to himself and Bastien liberally.

"How would you like me?" Bruce asked.

Bastien rolled over onto his right side and brought his left knee up to his chest. Bruce stretched out behind Bastien and covered his shoulder and back with gentle kisses. Bruce then positioned himself against Bastien and pushed in slowly.

When Bastien stiffened as Bruce penetrated him, Bruce stopped to allow time for him to adjust to the intrusion. When Bastien pushed back against him, Bruce began to move again. Slowly, at first, until he was finally seated deep inside of Bastien. He pulled back a little and then pushed in again as Bastien reached around and gripped Bruce's thigh, helping to guide him.

Bastien threw his left leg over Bruce's and twisted his torso around just a little as Bruce continued to move in and out of him. They were now almost face-to-face, and Bastien's deep blue eyes bored into Bruce as if he were seeing all the way into his soul. Bastien then wrapped his left arm around Bruce's neck and pulled him so close he could feel Bastien's breath against his lips. Bruce felt his emotions waking up little by little. With Bastien so close and the sensation of Bastien's velvety warmth surrounding him, Bruce was a reborn man. But when Bastien's lips touched his, it was as though Bastien was literally breathing life back into him. Suddenly every bit of him was alive. Alive with sensations he'd thought, in Beau's wake, were dead forever. Lust. Desire. Need. These and every other conceivable emotion were now boiling to the surface, bringing with them a longing he hadn't experienced in so very long. But it was a specific longing. A longing he couldn't—no, wouldn't—ignore. Not a longing for the obvious: his pending climax. That would come regardless. It was a longing for the deeper connection he and Bastien were sharing.

Overwhelmingly close to losing all control, Bruce closed his eyes and pushed his orgasm out of his mind. Instead he focused his efforts on pleasing the man moaning into his open mouth, their tongues flowing freely amid this beautiful, earth-shattering connection. At this very moment, Bruce felt so tuned in to Bastien, it was as if they were one person. Moving as one. Breathing as one. Joined at one heart, which was propelling life through their shared veins.

Without breaking their physical or emotional connection, Bastien slowly took himself in hand and started pumping—fiercely pumping in unison with Bruce's thrusts.

Bastien tightened around Bruce, moaned, and stiffened as his body expelled the first round of his release, the evidence streaking his chest. Bastien shuddered, and another round of white milky liquid covered his abs. Again and again Bastien pumped, and Bruce picked up his speed. Bastien shifted a little under him, and the sudden repositioning sent

Bruce into a complete tailspin. He shut his eyes and gasped in Bastien's mouth as he filled the condom inside Bastien with his essence. His spasms continued until he, too, was empty and sated.

Bruce attempted to move, and Bastien gripped him even tighter. "Please, ma puce," he whispered. "Not yet. Please don't move."

Bruce tightened his grip on Bastien and buried his head in Bastien's neck until he naturally slipped free. After Bruce cleaned them both, Bastien stretched out, and Bruce snuggled in next to him, his head resting on Bastien's chest.

"It took us a while to get here," Bastien said. "But it was surely worth the wait."

Bruce looked up, and when his eyes found Bastien's, they held his gaze.

"That was—" Bruce swallowed the lump in his throat. He wanted desperately to share everything he was feeling, but he had no idea if Bastien was having the same reaction. "—incredible."

Bastien stroked Bruce's hair with one hand and rubbed his back lightly with the other, but he didn't reply. And then he sighed.

Crap! Here it comes! Bruce couldn't deny the disappointment spreading through him. *But at least you kept your fool mouth shut for once.*

Bruce closed his eyes and waited. When no explanation came, he looked up at Bastien again. Bastien's eyes were watery, and it was obvious he was trying to hold back tears.

Bruce panicked. "Bastien? What's wrong? Did I hurt you?"

Bastien shook his head but didn't speak.

"What, then?"

Bastien looked away and wiped at his eyes, and all Bruce wanted to do was make him feel better. He realized at that moment he would have to let Bastien off the hook. What else could he do? If Bastien didn't feel what he was feeling, that wasn't Bastien's fault. He was stupid to think he could find love again after Beau. Maybe you only got one shot in this world. *What was I thinking?*

"I'm just overwhelmed," Bastien said. "I didn't...."

Bruce softly brushed Bastien's cheek with the back of his hand. "Didn't what?"

Bastien locked onto Bruce's eyes, and Bruce thought Bastien's deep blue eyes were searching for something. *Maybe he's trying to find the right words to give me the brush-off.*

"Didn't expect…," Bastien said and then stopped again.

"Bastien?" Bruce raised up and rested on his elbow. "Talk to me. If you didn't feel a connection, it's okay. You can't force yourself to feel something for someone. Its either there or it's not."

Sitting up in bed very abruptly, Bastien said, "Wait! No, Bruce! You don't understand."

Bruce was now totally confused. *What in the hell is going on?*

Bastien brought his legs up, crossed them Indian style, and turned to Bruce. Bruce watched in confusion as Bastien slid a finger under Bruce's chin and gazed into his eyes. "Bruce! I've never experienced that kind of a connection with another human being. Not even with Tollison."

Bruce was stunned. *So not what I was expecting.*

"We fit together so naturally. So comfortably. And it felt so damn good." Bastien looked hopeful. "Was it okay for you, ma puce?"

Now it was Bruce's turn to get teary-eyed. He knew he couldn't speak. Wouldn't try to. All he could do was nod.

Bastien took Bruce into his arms and held him tightly. "I'm so glad. I was afraid…."

"No!" Bruce said before he could finish. "*I* was afraid. When you sighed I thought you were… well, glad it was over."

Bastien pulled back and again looked into Bruce's eyes. "No, Bruce. Not at all. The connection was so intense, I was overwhelmed and could barely speak."

Bruce smiled. "I felt it too, Bastien. Almost immediately. It felt like we were one."

Bastien took both of Bruce's hands in his. "I think I'm falling in love with you, ma puce."

"I know," Bruce said. "I feel the same way. But…."

"But what?" Bastien had concern written all over his face.

"It's so soon," Bruce said.

Bastien shook his head. "Not really. The last few months of very long conversations over Skype gave us the opportunity to get to know each other without the distraction of intimacy," Bastien said. "I think it was just what we needed."

"Maybe. But I don't care either way," Bruce said. "We're not teenagers, and we owe no one any explanations. I think I'm falling in love with you too. I think it's been happening gradually, and tonight? This confirmed it for me."

Bastien leaned in and urged Bruce onto his back. He stretched out on top of him and pressed his lips against Bruce's in a gentle kiss.

Bruce was about to take the kiss deeper and start things up all over again when they heard the ding of the elevator.

"Whoever that is better go away," Bastien said.

Bruce jumped up. "Oh shit."

"What is wrong, ma puce?"

"You said you hadn't eaten, so I ordered dinner to be delivered—" He looked at the clock. "—right about now."

Bastien chuckled. "You sweet, sweet man. Well! We can't allow dinner to get cold. Besides, we have the entire night to make love. Let's eat."

NINE

TOLLISON STUDIED Beau as Beau read silently on his side of their antique, two-sided partners desk. Beau looked very into what he was reading, but Tollison was bored out of his mind. Several days had passed, and they'd exhausted every single lead they had regarding the killer the press had dubbed the Mardi Gras Murderer. They'd interviewed every family member, friend, and witness, and there was nothing more they could do until they got the information back from IT on the victims' cell phones and computers. And that was taking time.

"It sure is quiet around here when Iona runs errands," Tollison said, looking at Beau and tapping his fingers on the surface of their highly polished desk.

Beau mumbled something that could have been agreement. Or disagreement. He couldn't be certain one way or the other.

Tollison straightened a stack of papers for a third time, repositioned his stapler and telephone—again—and tore the frayed end of the scotch tape from the dispenser, leaving a nice clean-cut piece of tape for whenever he needed it next. He gripped the edges of both sleeves of his french-cuffed Egyptian cotton dress shirt and pulled them down and then ran his hand along the front of his silk tie.

Satisfied he looked neat and together and his desk was in perfect order, Tollison glanced at Beau, who was still enthralled by whatever he was reading.

Tollison sighed and ran his fingers along the carved edge of the mahogany desk and admired the woodwork yet again. It was truly a beautiful piece of furniture, and it was the perfect size and shape for their shared office. The leather inlay was pristine, and despite a few nicks on the body of the desk, which Tollison thought added character, it was in exceptional condition. But Beau got all the credit for this find. He'd known from the beginning exactly what he wanted, and he wouldn't give up until he found it.

For weeks they'd searched every antique shop up this side of Magazine Street and down the other but hadn't found exactly what Beau had been looking for. Then one day they were driving down Royal Street, and in the middle of a conversation regarding a case, Beau pulled the SUV over onto the sidewalk and slammed on his brakes. Pedestrians were aghast, cursing and fleeing for their lives as Beau stared lovingly into the display window of one of the higher-end antique stores. When Tollison followed Beau's gaze, he saw it too and knew instantly Beau was right. It was perfect for them.

They'd paid handsomely for it, of course. The desk was a sprawling six feet wide and eight feet across with sets of drawers, as well as an opening for a desk chair, on either end. Beau's justification for the expense had been that he and Tollison could share an office without having to *share* a desk. And from the moment he'd sat across from him, Tollison had been hooked. The view was perfect.

His mind skipping from one topic to another, Tollison studied Beau once again. His eyebrows were furrowed, and his precious pouty lips were pursed tightly together like he was in deep thought.

"What time are the guys coming tonight?" Tollison asked.

Another mumble. Tollison could have sworn he heard a possible "six thirty" in the jumbled response, but he couldn't be sure.

What in the hell can he be reading? We can't leave, so what in the hell am I going to do until Iona gets back?

Tollison rested his elbows on his side of the desk and dropped his head into his hands. A smile spread across his face. He had the perfect idea.

He pushed his chair ever so slightly back, trying to avoid making any sound to alert Beau. He slid down onto his knees at the opening of the desk, squatted down farther, and looked through.

He could clearly see Beau's legs stretched out in front of him and his feet in his shiny black dress shoes and dark socks crossed at the ankles. He followed Beau's legs up and saw the prize. The bulge in Beau's crotch was prime for the picking, and he was going to do a little harvesting.

Tollison didn't think Beau had even noticed him slip from his chair to the floor, but he reached back and pulled his chair tighter against the opening just in case. He then eased his body slowly through the tunnel-like space until he was eye level with Beau's crotch. He sat cross-legged while he pondered how to proceed. Tollison knew if he simply started unzipping Beau's zipper, Beau would probably freak out in surprise and start flailing, and there was no telling what might get bruised or bloodied in that scenario. So he proceeded with caution, untying one of Beau's shoes, then the other. Beau didn't move. Then Tollison grabbed the back of Beau's heel and pulled off one of his shoes.

Beau's leg jerked, but Tollison held it securely in place. "What the fuck?"

Tollison held on for a few seconds and then started massaging the arch and ball of Beau's foot. Beau sighed, chuckled, and then relaxed into the massage. Tollison knew his plan was no longer in stealth mode. But Beau didn't seem to be minding the attention.

After removing Beau's other shoe, Tollison kneaded his foot slowly, repeating what he'd done to the first foot until both of Beau's legs were stretched out and his feet were comfortably resting in Tollison's lap. Tollison wanted to make sure Beau was relaxed before he made his next move, so he spent a little extra time on the foot rub. Beau always loved that.

Occasionally, Tollison would hear an "oh yeah" or "that feels so good" escape Beau's lips, but other than that he was silent, seemingly totally into it. The massaging was doing the trick.

It was time. Tollison placed both of Beau's feet gently on the floor, maneuvered his long body to his knees once again, and reached up and squeezed Beau's crotch. Beau was already hard, and Tollison's own cock jerked with excitement.

Beau moaned in apparent pleasure as Tollison released Beau's belt, unhooked his pants, and unzipped his fly. Even in the dim light under the desk, Tollison could see the outline of Beau's length pressing tightly against his cotton boxer briefs.

With another moan Beau shuddered as Tollison pulled the waistband of Beau's underwear down and hooked it under his balls, his length springing free and pointing north. Beau shuddered again and gasped when Tollison positioned his head between Beau's legs, pulled his erection down, and took him into his mouth. Beau's enthusiasm was evident in the taste of his excitement lingering on the tip of his cock, and Tollison licked him clean.

In one slow drawn-out gulp, Tollison took Beau to the back of his throat until he felt Beau's crotch hair tickle his upper lip and chin. When Tollison eased off and repeated the move, Beau's fists slammed down on the top of the desk, and Tollison smiled to himself. He slid his index finger into his mouth alongside Beau's cock and got it wet. Then he slipped the moistened digit between the leather seat of Beau's chair and Beau's ass until he found the right spot. Although Beau leaned back and stretched out, offering his ass, Tollison couldn't get his finger in very far, but it was enough to tease and tantalize.

Tollison was now moving his mouth steadily on Beau's shaft, and his finger poked and circled Beau's opening. Beau was all but gyrating in his chair; Tollison loved the fact he could take Beau places without ever leaving their little office.

Beau was getting increasingly harder, and Tollison knew his partner well enough to know he was getting very close to losing his shit. Tollison increased his efforts, and Beau gripped him by his shoulders. Beau stiffened. He was about to blow. But they both froze when the front door bell chimed.

"Oh shit!" Tollison mumbled without releasing Beau.

"Beau?" Iona called. "Tollison?"

Beau didn't answer, and Tollison started moving again. Beau tried to push him away, but he tightened his grip on Beau's legs as well as his suction on Beau's shaft.

"Here you are," Iona said.

Beau stiffened and sat up straight.

"I'm so sorry it took me so long, but traffic was a bear."

Beau didn't respond.

This was going to be more fun than Tollison had expected. He started moving again and heard a slight moan escape Beau's lips.

"Beau? Are you all right? And where's Tollison?"

"I'm… fine," Beau managed to say. "Must be… in the bathroom," he added. "Yeah. Bathroom."

"Are you sure you're okay?" Iona asked. "You look a little pale."

"Nope. Fine."

Beau tensed, and the first round of his release slid down the back of Tollison's throat. Tollison smiled when he heard a clawing sound, like Beau was dragging his nails across the leather inlay of their desk. *That's gonna take some work to repair.*

As Tollison increased his movements, he felt Beau tremble under him, making noises Tollison didn't quite recognize. Something between a whine, a moan, and a hiccup escaped Beau's lips, and Beau thrust up into Tollison's mouth one last time.

"If you insist you're all right," Iona said, "I guess I'll leave you to whatever it is you were doing."

The heels of Iona's sensible Easy Spirit pumps clacked against the hardwood floor as she exited the office. Tollison slid off of Beau, pulled Beau's underwear back up, hooked his pants, and refastened his belt. He shoved Beau's feet back into his shoes one after the other and tied his shoestrings. Finally, he backed out from beneath the desk and peered up over the edge.

Beau was waiting for him, and when their gazes met, Beau stared at him with narrowed eyes as if seriously pissed off. But he was smiling at the same time. "What the fuck was that?"

"You were ignoring me, and I was bored, so I thought I'd shake things up a bit," Tollison explained. "Are you complaining?"

"Hell no. But I surely would have enjoyed it more if Iona hadn't walked in on us."

"Who knew?" Tollison said. "I don't think she suspected a thing."

Beau just shook his head.

"There you are," Iona said, walking back into their office. "Beau said you were in the bathroom. How did you get past me?"

"Just walked right past," Tollison said, winking at Beau.

"I must be losing my—" Iona stopped midsentence and stared at Tollison's face.

Beau cleared his throat, and Tollison glanced in his direction to witness him rub the corner of his mouth and make a weird face. Then it hit Tollison. He slid his tongue over to the corner of his mouth and tasted Beau's release on his lip.

He instinctively brought his hand up to his mouth and wiped. By then Iona's scrutiny had fallen on Tollison's knees. When he followed her gaze, he saw two dusty spots on his suit pants. Iona looked back up, and Tollison saw the exact second her expression changed. They'd been busted.

She smiled knowingly and turned away, heading for the door. In the doorway, she paused and looked back over her shoulder. "I'm glad you boys are taking advantage of a little downtime." She winked and was gone as fast as she'd come.

Beau started chuckling, and Tollison followed suit, feeling like he was twelve again and his mother had just caught him masturbating.

Beau stood and walked over to Tollison. He pushed him onto his desk and covered his lips in a crushing kiss. When the kiss ended, Beau whispered, "I love you. Promise me you won't ever let me ignore you."

"Promise," Tollison said, meaning it.

Beau looked at his watch. "We better get a move on. Bruce and Bastien are coming at six thirty."

"Funny, I thought I asked that a little while ago."

"You did. And I answered you."

"Sort of," Tollison smirked.

TEN

"THEY'LL BE here in fifteen minutes," Beau yelled to Tollison from the bottom of the stairs. "What do you want me to do with these steaks?"

Tollison leaned his naked torso out of the bedroom door. "I'm almost ready. Just salt and pepper them and leave them on the counter to come up to room temperature."

Beau stared at Tollison, his mouth watering just a little bit. He never got tired of seeing that long, lean body. Naked or clothed. "God. You're hot."

Tollison smiled at him. "Stop teasing me."

"Come down here, and I'll show you if I'm teasing or not."

"Promises, promises," Tollison quipped.

"I still owe you one. Remember?"

"And don't think I won't cash in, but I sort of like having it hanging out there," Tollison said. "It's like a freebie whenever or wherever I want it."

Beau chuckled. "I don't think it's as free as all that, but I'm open to most anything."

"I know." Tollison winked. "If I remember correctly, I think you're partial to rooftops. Now if you don't let me finish getting ready, I'm gonna be late."

"Fucker!" Beau smirked and shook his head as he walked back to the kitchen. He knew Tollison was referring to a story he'd shared about a tryst he and Bruce had had on a Fort Lauderdale rooftop after a night of heavy drinking, which might or might not have resulted in Bruce fucking Beau silly for God and every high-rise resident on Las Olas Boulevard to see.

He also thought one day he might regret sharing that story with Tollison. On the other hand, his father had always told him if you don't want people knowing you did something, don't do it. But if you're gonna do it anyway, you better own up to it. So he was owning up to it. It had been damn fun at the time, and life was too short for regrets.

Tollison was on grill duty tonight, but Beau prepped the steaks as instructed. He was contributing his favorite baked sweet potatoes. He used his grandmother's recipe, which consisted of rolling them in honey and then in rock salt, wrapping them in foil, and baking them slowly until tender. He wrapped the last one and licked the remaining honey off his fingers just before he shoved the potatoes into a two-hundred-and-fifty-degree oven. "These should be perfect by the time we get back from the parade," he pronounced.

When Beau turned around, Tollison was standing in the doorway, looking like a million dollars. His hair was slicked back, obviously still a little damp, and his black T-shirt was stretched tightly across his chest and tucked into his low-riding jeans.

"You sure clean up nicely," Beau teased, taking Tollison into his arms and pulling him close.

"So it was worth the wait?"

"Without a doubt," Beau admitted.

Tollison looked over Beau's shoulder. "You didn't sabotage my steaks, did you?"

Beau winked. "Of course not. I wouldn't dream of doing such a thing."

"Uh-huh," Tollison said skeptically.

Tollison examined his steaks and opened the fridge just as the doorbell rang.

"Right on time," Beau said. "I'll get it."

"I'm getting a beer. You want one?"

"Sure!"

"HEY, BOYS," Beau said when he opened the door. He couldn't help but notice Bruce and Bastien were hand in hand and smiling broadly. "Come on in."

Beau shook Bastien's hand "Good to see you, Bastien." He smacked Bruce on the back of the head. "Hey, dickwad."

Bruce ducked and swiped at Beau's hand. "Watch the hair, asshole."

"You're such a princess," Beau teased.

Bruce slapped Beau on the ass. "And you're such a prick."

Bastien chuckled. "Do you two always greet each other in such a pleasant manner?"

"Not always," Beau said. "Sometime we're mean and nasty."

"Oh! I see," Bastien said through a smile.

The two men continued down the hall to the back of the house. Beau tilted his head, rested his hands on his hips, and watched them closely. Bastien and Bruce were still holding hands and gazing adoringly at the other as they strolled. Something seemed different between them. It was subtle, but it was definitely there. Then it hit Beau like a ton of bricks. *Whaddya know?* He chuckled. *I'll bet they finally did the nasty.*

When Beau joined them again, Tollison was pouring Bastien a glass of wine and Bruce was twisting the top off a longneck. Beau walked up behind Bruce, laid an arm over his shoulder, and whispered in his ear, "I think someone finally got laid."

Bruce turned to Beau with a surprised expression, and Beau watched the blush creep up his face. When the edges of Bruce's mouth curved into a smile, Beau knew instantly his assumption had been correct.

"I knew it. You dog you."

Bruce looked at Bastien and elbowed Beau in the ribs. "Stop it. He might hear you."

"Ouch." Beau grabbed his ribs in a dramatic gesture. "Whaddya mean he might hear me? Wasn't he there?"

"Of course he was there, you idiot. But he doesn't need to know we're talking about it."

Beau waved him off. "Nonsense! Well?"

"Well what?"

Beau rolled his eyes. "How was it?"

Bruce looked over at Bastien again, who was now deep in conversation with Tollison. He pulled Beau out into the hall. "If you must know, it was incredible."

Beau smiled. "You know I can't believe I'm saying this, but I'm really happy for you."

Bruce laid his hand on Beau's forearm. "I know how hard that was for you to say. And I appreciate the effort."

"Actually it wasn't that hard," Beau said. "I truly do want you to be happy."

"I am happy, Beau. For the first time in a very long time. And you and Tollison are sort of responsible."

Beau thought about Bruce's admission. In a roundabout way, he was right. If Bastien hadn't come to New Orleans unexpectedly looking for Tollison, he wouldn't have been kidnapped. They wouldn't have gone to Zurich to rescue him, and Bruce and Bastien would never have met. "The universe does work in mysterious ways. Doesn't it?"

Bruce nodded. "Whatever the force, I'm just really glad you and I are in a good place. You know how sorry I am for hurting you. I blamed myself for ruining everything for so long, I thought I would never get over it. But I've finally forgiven myself, and now I'm really ready to start a new chapter in my life. One without heartache and regrets."

Beau grabbed hold of Bruce by his shoulders and looked him in the eyes. "I'm glad, Bruce. And I truly mean that. I know I can be the biggest asshole on the planet, and we both know I have a hard time forgiving and forgetting, but it really was time for me to let go of the past and definitely time for you to move forward. It's just time. For both of us."

Beau used his thumb and wiped away a tear that had escaped Bruce's eye and rolled down his cheek.

"I never thought I'd ever hear those words leave your mouth."

"Nor did I ever think I would say them," Beau confessed. "But Tollison has made me see that our demise wasn't all your fault… and I would never get over it if I didn't let it go. And he was right. Just don't let it all be for nothing."

Bruce offered his hand to Beau and Beau accepted it, but instead of shaking, he pulled Bruce close to him and wrapped his arms around him. "Be happy, man. Just be happy."

"You too."

WHEN THE four men finally left the house, Tollison and Beau each had an end of the cooler and Bastien and Bruce were carrying the lawn chairs. St. Charles Avenue was a hustle and bustle of parade goers, all on a mission to find just the right spot from which to watch the festivities. Beau chose a spot on the corner of St. Charles and Euterpe, where they dropped the cooler and set up the chairs.

Mardi Gras was the best people-watching time of the year, next to Halloween, and tonight was no disappointment. From their front row seat, Beau and Tollison watched as female Tulane and Loyola students in skimpy outfits marched up and down the parade route, holding on to half-dressed men showing off their highly toned sports bodies. Kids were riding in wagons being pulled by grandparents dressed like clowns, and adults of all ages were reveling in the festivities.

The sounds of marching drums in the distance were getting closer, signaling the parade's approach. Beau leaned over, slid his hand in Tollison's coat pocket, and placed a kiss on his cheek. Tollison smiled and gestured with his head for Beau to look over his shoulder, and when he did, he saw Bruce and Bastien cooing and whispering as if they were the only two people left on earth.

The parade arrived on time, and the celebration began. The floats rolled one after the other, spaced between marching bands, horses, dance troupes, and Shriners, as well as other organized clubs. Before Beau knew it, he saw the last float in the distance. Tollison was on his left, lost in the fanfare, and Bruce and Bastien were to his right, doing the same.

As the last float approached, Beau threw his hands into the air, and beads began to pelt him in the head, bouncing off him and falling to the ground. Tollison was bending down to pick something up when Beau heard the sound of a gunshot ringing in his ears.

His training kicked in instantly, and he dove on top of Tollison, pinning him to the ground. He looked to his right, and Bruce was on top of Bastien, neither of them moving.

People were screaming, some frozen in place, others scattering in every direction. Parents were clutching their children, and the scene was pure pandemonium.

"Tol? Baby, are you okay?"

"Yeah, I think so."

"Oh thank God."

"You?" Tollison asked.

"I'm okay. Yeah! I'm okay."

Beau's next thought was of Bruce and Bastien. He shifted to Tollison's left and yelled to Bruce. "Bruce? Bruce?"

Bruce looked over at him. "We're okay, Beau. You and Tollison?"

"Yeah. We're okay."

Beau jumped to his feet. The parade was moving on like nothing had happened. In a flash Bruce was standing by his side. Together they began to scan every rooftop and every apartment building. Beau then looked around at the crowds. People were on their feet now, looking stunned and fearful. They were quickly gathering their things and disappearing into the Uptown streets, making their way back to their cars or their homes.

There didn't appear to be any casualties that Beau could see. The hairs stood up on the back of his neck when he saw a guy running down the street yelling at the top of his lungs. Out of habit, Beau reached for his gun, but of course that was in vain. "Shit," he cursed.

He instinctively stepped in front of Tollison and looked for anything he could use as a weapon. As the guy got closer, Beau could begin to put the guy's words together.

"It's okay, everyone," the guy called. "Don't panic. It was just a tractor backfiring. I was standing right behind it. It's okay. No one is shooting at you."

Beau felt relief wash through him. He knew Tollison didn't fit the perp's victim profile, but it had still scared the crap out of him.

What in the hell has happened to you, Bissonet? a little voice in the back of his mind chimed in. *You've gone soft. That's what. These situations never scared you before.* He looked over at Tollison, who was gathering their things. *I guess I just have too fucking much to lose.*

Shaking his head in disbelief, Beau walked over to where Tollison was standing. He was trembling just a little when he took Tollison in his arms. "Jesus, Tol!" Beau's voice cracked. "It was just a tractor backfiring. But it could have been any one of us."

"I know, baby." When Beau felt Tollison's arms return the embrace, he started to settle a little. "But we're all okay."

Beau looked over Tollison's shoulder at Bruce and Bastien, Bruce was comforting Bastien, who still looked a little shaken.

"You boys ready to go?" Beau asked with a sense of relief.

"I think so," Bruce replied.

"Then let's go. Dinner's waiting."

ELEVEN

"My compliments to the chef," Bastien said, holding up his wine glass. "My steak was cooked perfectly."

"I'm glad," Tollison said.

"And those sweet potatoes," Bruce added. "I sure wish I had gotten custody of that secret recipe in the divorce."

"Yeah, well," Beau said. "Maybe I'll share someday."

Bruce laughed. "Sure you will. Excuse me if I don't hold my breath."

Tollison was genuinely enjoying seeing the ease with which Beau and Bruce were now interacting. They'd come a long way since Tollison had come into the picture. And he really loved seeing Bruce so happy. But if he were being honest, he still had a long way to go in the forgive-and-forget department where Bastien was concerned. He knew now it had all happened for a reason. He was with Beau, and he wouldn't change that for the world, but the pain he'd endured back then was still sitting just below the surface. Each time he looked at Bastien, he was reminded of it.

Then it occurred to him. Were he and Bastien any different than Beau and Bruce? The constant reminders with which Beau had had to deal while working with Bruce day in and day out must have been intolerable sometimes. And now with Bastien so near, Tollison understood it completely.

Beau had held a grudge for the longest time and now so was Tollison. Bruce had made a mistake, but Beau was not without some blame. And the same could be said for him and Bastien. Bastien had hurt him deeply, but Tollison was not without fault either. In fact, if truth be told, Tollison had been more at fault than Bastien. The realization hit him hard, and no matter how he tried to slice or dice it, he kept coming back to the same conclusion. He needed to let it all go.

Beau had done it, and now he truly understood just what he'd asked of him. *Beau is a much bigger man than I will ever be. Am I a serious hypocrite, or what?*

Bastien cleared his throat and gave Bruce a questioning glance.

Bruce smiled and nodded.

"Beau," Bastien said. "If you are serious about sharing that recipe, you might want to do it sooner rather than later."

"Oh?" Beau asked. "Why is that?"

"We weren't going to say anything just yet," Bastien said. "But the events of this evening made us realize life is just too short and it can be taken from us at any time. So here goes." Bastien took Bruce by the hand and gazed into his eyes. "I've asked Bruce to accompany me back to Geneva when I return."

Beau looked at Tollison, and Tollison raised an eyebrow. "Seriously?" Beau asked. "For how long?"

"Indefinitely," Bastien said.

Beau smiled weakly. "What does that mean, exactly?"

"It means I'm moving to Switzerland," Bruce said.

"For how long?" Beau asked.

"Forever. Or as long as Bastien will have me."

Bastien reached over and kissed Bruce on the cheek. "Forever is good by me, ma puce."

"But you're only just now getting to know each other, and you're quitting your job and moving across the world?" Beau asked. "Isn't this a little rushed?"

"Not really," Bruce said. "At least it doesn't feel that way to us."

"Bruce is right," Bastien said. "We've been slowly getting to know each other over the last few months. Being apart and skyping every day forced us to take it slow and afforded us the opportunity and time we needed to fall in love. And being together in person has only brought us closer. Am I right, ma puce?"

"Absolutely!" Bruce agreed.

"Well," Beau said. "You are grown men, and if this is what you want, I say go for it."

"Thank you, Beau. Bastien and I appreciate your support."

"Tollison?" Bastien asked. "You haven't said anything. Do we have your support?"

Tollison chose his words carefully. "Bruce, I hope you know how fond I am of you. I still have some issues where you're concerned, Bastien, and I'm trying to work through them, but if this makes you both happy, of course you have my support." Tollison held up his wine glass. "Here's to a long and happy future together."

Beau also raised his glass. "I wish you all the happiness in the world."

"À la vie, à l'amour, et aux nouveaux commencements," Bastien said, touching his glass to the others.

"To life, love, and new beginnings," Beau repeated.

Moments later Tollison stood and started clearing the dinner dishes.

"Please allow me to help," Bastien said.

"Thank you."

TOLLISON CARRIED a load of dishes to the kitchen, and Bastien followed. When they got there, Tollison placed the dishes on the counter and turned. Bastien was eyeing him suspiciously. "What?" he asked.

"Are you really happy for us?" Bastien asked.

Tollison turned around and started rinsing the dishes and placing them in the dishwasher. "If you make Bruce happy, who am I to object?"

"And my happiness?" Bastien asked.

Tollison shrugged. "Makes no difference to me."

Bastien frowned. "As I suspected. Why is it so hard for you to understand how hurt and betrayed I felt when I found out you'd lied to me for so many years?"

Tollison gripped the plate he was holding almost hard enough to snap it in two. "Bastien, let's not do this. What's done is done. We are both happy in our new lives, so the way I see it, everything has worked out as it was meant to."

"That it has," Bastien said. "But we will never get past this if we don't at least make an attempt to forgive each other for our indiscretions."

"You think I don't know that?" Tollison sighed. "But seeing you here just reminds me of all the pain and rejection I felt so many years ago."

"You don't think seeing you does the same to me?" Bastien said. "We both had our reasons for the way we reacted, but there is no way to go back and change that now. Do I regret the way I acted? Do I regret turning my back on you without allowing you to explain? Absolutely. But what's done is done."

Tollison leaned on the counter and closed his eyes. Bastien hadn't admitted that to him before. And if he were being truthful, it felt damn good to hear. Tollison turned around and finally looked Bastien in the eyes. "And I regret lying to you as well, Bastien. I really do. We both know I had my reasons for being dishonest with you, and if I had it to do all over again, I would have handled it very differently. But knowing that now wouldn't have softened the blow back then. And for that I'm sorry."

Bastien opened his arms, and Tollison stepped into them. "We both made mistakes, Eddy."

Tollison sighed, knowing Bastien was right. "But on a good note, those mistakes brought us to where we are today," Tollison said.

"Exactly. So can we let go of the past, be grateful for what we have now, and try to move forward?"

"Yeah," Tollison said. "I believe I can."

"As do I."

Bastien released Tollison and stepped back, holding him by the shoulders. "We both have bright futures to hold on to, so I guess we did something right. Now let's get these dishes finished so we can join our men."

"SO HAVE you told Auggie?" Beau asked.

"Not yet," Bruce said. "We just decided earlier today."

"He's not gonna be happy."

"I know, but I have to follow my heart."

Beau nodded and took a sip of his wine. "Are you gonna resign completely or just take a leave of absence?"

"Resign, I think," Bruce said. "I don't think taking a leap of faith with a backup plan is truly a leap of faith."

Beau smiled weakly. "I guess not."

Bruce slid his wine glass in a circular motion and stared at the red liquid as it swirled around in the glass. "I guess I'm gonna jump in with both feet and let the chips fall where they may."

Beau studied Bruce's face and thought he detected a chink in Bruce's armor. He decided to take a chance. "I know you very well, Bruce. I may be wrong, but I don't think you're near as confident as your words make you sound."

Bruce turned and looked at the doorway to the kitchen, apparently trying to see if Bastien was in earshot. "I love him, Beau. I know it might seem quick to you, but I'm sure of that."

"Okay. You're sure you love him. But what are you unsure of?" Beau asked.

Bruce hesitated, still staring at his wine glass. When he finally spoke, his voice was low. "I'm not sure. We spent hours upon hours via Skype talking about everything under the sun and getting to know each other long distance…."

"But?"

"Every fiber of my being tells me he's a good man, but you can never know for sure until you've really lived with a person."

Beau thought about the admission. And when he spoke he chose his words carefully. "Do you respect and trust Tollison?"

"Of course I do. Hell! The fact we're even sitting here having this discussion is because of him. I truly love the guy. But what does that have to do with anything?"

"It's simple," Beau said. "Tollison loved Bastien a great deal. So if you respect and trust Tollison, you should realize he would have never stayed with or loved a man for so long if Bastien wasn't worthy of that love."

Bruce smiled. "Damn, Beau. You've turned into Yoda or something. When did you become so wise?"

"Fuck you, asshole!"

"Now that's the Beau I know and love."

Beau flipped him off just as Tollison and Bastien entered the dining room.

"I see not much has changed in here," Tollison said.

"To the contrary," Bruce said. "Beau has been very helpful."

"Really?" Tollison said. "Beau? Helpful?"

"Bastien? Do you hear this?" Beau asked. "They think I'm nothing but a pretty face. This is what I put up with day in and day out."

Bastien shook his head from side to side. "I'm afraid I do," he said. "Gentlemen, I must say I'm shocked!"

"Finally!" Beau slapped his palm down on the dining room table.

Bastien continued, "You think this man has a pretty face?"

Tollison and Bruce started laughing uncontrollably.

Beau pursed his pouty lips together. "Oh no, Bastien. Not you too!"

Bastien frowned. He walked over to Beau's chair, rested his hands on Beau's shoulders, and started massaging gently. "I'm afraid so, Beau. You see. I am but a weak man, and you are just too adorable for words. And so easy to tease."

Beau smiled halfheartedly. "It's always been a curse of mine."

"Getting teased?" Bastien asked.

"No! Being adorable," Beau said.

"Touché, my new friend," Bastien said. "It has been an absolutely wonderful evening, except for that little incident at the parade. Bruce, I say we bid our hosts adieu."

"Speaking of parades," Beau said, "tomorrow is the Knights of Babylon. Shall we do it all again?"

Bastien looked at Bruce and nodded. "I'm game, ma puce."

"Under one condition," Bruce said.

"What's that?"

"You allow us to bring dinner."

Beau looked at Tollison and shrugged. "Sure. If you like."

"We like," Bruce replied.

Beau and Tollison walked their guests to the front door. "Good night." Beau rested his hand on Bastien's shoulder. "And congratulations again. Tol and I wish you all the happiness in the world."

"And you," Tollison said, hugging Bruce. "We're gonna miss the hell out of you."

"Thank you." Bruce stepped back. "Thank you both."

Bastien bowed his head. "Merci, and au revoir, gentlemen."

TWELVE

BEAU CLOSED and locked the door and started turning out lights while Tollison silently gathered the few things left in the dining room.

They met in the kitchen and as soon as Tollison put the dishes down, Beau took him into his arms and buried his face in Tollison's neck. "Some night, huh?"

"That's putting it mildly."

"You okay with all of this?" Beau asked.

"Sure." Tollison said. "I guess. I mean… what choice do I have?"

"I feel the same way. I want them to be happy, but it's just…."

"Weird having our exes together?" Tollison asked, finishing Beau's sentence.

"Thank God. I was hoping I wasn't the only one feeling a little strange about it."

"Oh no," Tollison said.

"You guys were in the kitchen a very long time. Is everything all right between you and Bastien?"

"I think it *will* be," Tollison said. "He apologized for the way he handled our breakup, and I think he meant it. In return I apologized to him again for lying to him. I think we had some sort of breakthrough."

Bean smiled. "That's good."

"And what about you and Bruce?" Tollison asked. "You guys were awful deep in conversation when Bastien and I joined you. Anything I need to know about?"

"Bruce was feeling a little hesitant," Beau explained.

"Really? I hope he's not second-guessing his decision."

Beau rinsed and put the wine glasses in the dishwasher while he spoke. "No. I don't think it's anything like that. I believe he's definitely in love with Bastien, but I think he needed some reassurance that Bastien was a good man before he moved halfway across the world to be with him."

"And?"

"Well, I just asked him if he trusted and respected you."

"Me? How do I fit into all of this?" Tollison asked.

"It's pretty simple to me. At one time you loved Bastien very much."

"Yeah?"

"And I couldn't see you loving a man you didn't trust and respect."

Tollison stepped up behind Beau, slid his hands around Beau's waist, and thrust his crotch against Beau's ass.

Beau could feel Tollison's excitement growing with each grind of his hips.

Without saying a word, Tollison buried his face in Beau's neck. He kissed his way up to Beau's ear, bit his earlobe, and then sucked it into his mouth.

Beau tilted his head to give Tollison better access, and Tollison took advantage of the move.

When Tollison stopped and rested his head on Beau's back, Beau looked over his shoulder and turned around in Tollison's embrace. "What was that for?" he asked, gazing into Tollison's eyes.

"Because after all this time, you still continue to amaze me."

Beau smiled. "And I hope to amaze you until I take my last breath."

Tollison pressed his lips against Beau's and simultaneously began to unbutton Beau's shirt. Slowly. Deliberately. One button at a time until he yanked Beau's shirttail out of his jeans and slid the shirt over his shoulders.

The combination of exposed skin and the anticipation of what was coming next had goose bumps forming all over Beau's skin. Tollison kissed him, and his lips on Beau's and his warm hands caressing Beau's chest and torso made Beau shiver.

Without breaking the kiss, Tollison unbuckled Beau's belt and unbuttoned his jeans with the same slow, precise motions he had employed on Beau's shirt. Then Tollison pushed the denim down to Beau's thighs and used his foot to force them down to Beau's ankles.

Being shorter than Tollison rarely had its advantages, but this was one time when it definitely worked in Beau's favor. Still without breaking the kiss, Tollison reached down, gripped Beau behind the knees, and lifted him up onto the counter. He cupped Beau's face with his hands and finally broke the kiss. Tollison stooped down to Beau's feet and pulled off his boots, tossing them to the floor with a thud. Beau watched as Tollison tugged Beau's jeans over his feet and added them to the boot pile. Beau gripped Tollison under his arms and pulled him up. Tollison smiled coyly and then kissed his way down Beau's chest and torso until he stopped and nibbled lightly at Beau's erection with his mouth, a thin layer of cotton the only thing standing between lips and flesh.

Beau threw his head back and moaned as Tollison's moist heat coursed through him. Tollison buried his face in Beau's crotch, and Beau gripped him behind the neck and pulled his face closer. When Tollison's fingers hooked into the waistband of Beau's underwear, he pushed up on his hands just enough to allow Tollison to peel the briefs off and toss them to the floor. Beau sprang free, and in an instant Tollison had him, swallowing him all the way to the back of his throat. Beau fought his instinctive urge to thrust forward and simply leaned back on his hands and rode the waves of pleasure coursing through him. As Tollison slid up and down his length with just the right amount of suction, Beau felt his release building deep in his gut. When his balls began to tighten, however, he fought off the urge to give in to the orgasm fighting its way to the surface.

"I'm close," he whispered.

Tollison released him and looked up at him. "No, sir!" he whispered. "I'm nowhere near being done with you."

Beau smiled. He knew what that meant, and just the thought of Tollison taking him that way was enough to finish him off right where he sat.

In a move that would had have shamed the most talented porn star, Tollison had Beau instantly looking up at his own socked feet. Tollison's hands were behind Beau's knees, holding his legs up and giving Tollison complete access to what Beau was sure he was after.

Oh who was he kidding? What he wanted as well.

Tollison's warm, wet tongue circled Beau's opening, teasing and stroking the sensitive skin, sending pulses of joy through Beau's body. Then Tollison slid one finger inside of Beau and crooked it just enough to brush the delicate spot that always drove Beau crazy. Beau gasped, and his dick, now as hard as it had ever been, jumped and twitched with each pass of Tollison's knuckle. When Tollison slipped a second finger in and pushed against Beau's prostate, Beau's vision blurred, giving him the sense he was looking through a kaleidoscope.

After a few moments, Tollison withdrew his fingers, and Beau instantly felt empty. He raised his head to protest but smiled when he saw Tollison standing in front of him pulling his shirt over his head. Tollison toed out of his shoes, stepped out of his jeans, and pulled his underwear down, his erection springing free.

Beau pictured what was coming next, and the image had him literally dripping with excitement. Then a thought hit him. *Fuck! We don't have any lube down here!*

Before Beau could express his concern, Tollison opened the refrigerator door and removed a hunk of butter. He watched as Tollison smashed it between his hands, kneading and warming it with his fingers.

"This is a first," Beau snickered.

"Necessity is the mother of invention," Tollison said, stepping up to Beau.

Tollison slathered the butter around Beau's ass and then slipped his fingers in again. Beau once again threw his head back in pleasure. Tollison started moving them in and out, slowly at first, giving Beau the time he needed to adjust. With his other hand, Tollison coated Beau's length and then his own. He slid his fingers out of Beau, wiped his hands on a dishtowel, and tossed the towel into the sink.

"Hop down," Tollison whispered.

Beau did as he was told, and Tollison spun him around, gripped him by the neck, and forced him over. "Bend over and spread 'em, big man," Tollison ordered.

Glancing over his shoulder, Beau recognized the expression of pure lust on Tollison's face. He'd seen it many times, and each time it thrilled him to no end that *he* was the cause of such overwhelming desire.

Tollison positioned himself against Beau's opening and slowly but deliberately pushed in. Beau gripped the opposite end of the counter, bit his lip, and tried to relax as Tollison entered him. Breaching the guardian muscle, Tollison stopped momentarily for Beau to adjust, for which Beau was grateful. A long moment later, Tollison pushed the rest of the way in until he was fully seated, his hips cradling Beau's ass. Beau released the breath he was holding and enjoyed the fullness inside him.

Slowly, Tollison withdrew and pushed in again. The butter was amazingly smooth and caused little to no drag. Beau felt himself opening and welcoming Tollison's intrusion. He gripped his own length and pumped in unison with Tollison as Tollison drove into him.

Beau's body relaxed around his partner, and his initial discomfort was quickly turning to pleasure. Just as Beau was finding his rhythm, Tollison withdrew. "Turn around, Beau. I need to see your face."

Once Beau complied, Tollison again lifted him onto the counter. He rose on his tiptoes, pinned Beau's legs back, and pushed in again, sending chills down Beau's spine. But instead of holding Beau there, Tollison lifted him off the counter and carried him across the kitchen. Beau wrapped his arms around Tollison's neck and his legs around Tollison's waist and held on. Tollison backed him up against the refrigerator and covered Beau's lips in a crushing kiss. He started moving again, and Beau was lost in the eyes of the man he loved.

With each thrust, Beau heard the contents of the refrigerator rattling and thrashing about, but he couldn't care less. Tollison's strength was amazing. He was supporting Beau, kissing him passionately, and ramming his cock in and out of him all at the same time. Taking him. Marking him over and over again.

Beau's cock was pressed so tightly between his and Tollison's torsos, it was as if Tollison was jacking him off with each of his thrusts, bringing him closer and closer to his release. Unable to hold back any longer, Beau dug his nails into Tollison's back and cried out as the first wave of his orgasm coursed through him. Tollison picked up his pace, causing Beau's head to slam into the refrigerator repeatedly. He then gripped the back of Beau's head and pulled him closer, moaning into Beau's mouth, and Beau felt Tollison empty his warm seed inside him.

Together they rode the thrill of their climax until they were both spent. Beau flinched when Tollison slipped out of him, and Tollison eased him to his feet. He pressed Beau against the refrigerator again and kissed him softly.

"I love you so much," Tollison said.

"I know, baby," Beau said. "I feel your love in everything we do. Every little kiss. Every time we make love. I feel your love every minute of every day. And I love you just as much. I hope you feel it too."

"I do," Tollison said. "With every breath."

THIRTEEN

"AFTER TODAY, just five more days until Mardi Gras 2016 is officially history," Bruce said. "Think you can hold on?"

Auggie grunted. "It can't be soon enough for me. This has been a tough one."

"Any word from IT on the vics' cell phones and computers?"

"They promised they would have the information to me by ten this morning. As a matter of fact, Beau and Tollison are on their way over here now."

"Speaking of the dynamic duo," Bruce said, grinning, "we enjoyed the parade last night and had a great dinner with them. Wish you and Jenny could have made it."

"Me too, but Jenny had some charity thing last night." Auggie grimaced. "You know how I love those things. But we *are* coming tonight."

"Great. It should be fun."

"So you and Beau are doing okay these days?" Auggie asked.

Bruce thought for a moment. "Yeah. I think we are."

"And what about Bastien and Tollison?"

"I think they may have had a breakthrough as well," Bruce said. "Bastien told me last night he and Tollison had a heart-to-heart and cleared the air, so to speak. He seems to think they're in a better place."

Auggie shook his head. "The way you mos share lovers just amazes me. With all the gay men in this city, you had to go to Zurich to find Tollison's ex."

"The heart wants what it wants, Aug."

"What does the heart want?" Beau stood in Auggie's doorway with Tollison right behind him.

"Perfect timing as usual," Bruce teased. "Come in, gentlemen."

"So?" Beau asked, taking a seat.

"We were just discussing how you guys like to keep things in the family," Auggie said.

"Oh?" Beau asked, his voice laced with humor. "How so?"

"He's referring to Bastien and me being your and Tollison's exes," Bruce added.

"Really, Auggie? I seem to remember you telling me the story of how you and Jenny met, and the story didn't sound all that different from Bastien and Bruce's story."

Bruce perked up. "Now isn't that interesting."

"No need to get into all that," Auggie said.

Beau smiled. "Oh?"

"Okay. So the stories are similar, but none of us were in relationships. We were all just dating at the time."

"I wonder if that's how your best friend saw it?" Beau asked.

Auggie glared at Beau, and Beau smiled again. "Where's all this coming from, Auggie? You and I go way back, and I've never known you to be judgmental or homophobic."

"That's because I'm not," Auggie said. "I guess this case is just getting to me. I mean… a gay man killing off other gay men because of a one-night stand or because he got dumped? What the fuck?"

"But how is this case any different from heterosexual domestic violence cases?" Tollison asked. "It happens all the time to straight people."

"It's not really any different. I guess. I just expect better from you guys. Most of you seem to be level-headed and smart, and this guy is dumber than shit."

"On behalf of all homosexuals," Beau said sarcastically, "thanks for the kind words. But I don't think he's that dumb. I mean—he's still out there, getting away with multiple murders, and we are no closer to finding him than we were a week ago. Who knows when he'll strike again?"

"And I'm afraid IT is not going to be much help," a voice said from the doorway.

Everyone turned and followed the sound of the voice.

"Hey, Danny." Auggie motioned him in.

Danny Paris stood in front of Auggie's desk. "Morning, gentlemen." He turned to Beau. "Good to see you again, Bissonet."

Beau nodded. "You remember my partner, Tollison Cruz."

"Of course, Mr. Cruz."

The two men shook hands. "Tollison. Please."

Danny smiled.

"Oh jeez. Enough with the niceties," Auggie whined. "Come on, Danny. Please say you've got something for us. Anything."

"Some. But I'm sure it's not what you were hoping for."

"Okay," Auggie said. "Give us what you got, then."

"For starters, we can confirm that all the vics had active profiles on the Grindr application, and they each used various other forms of social media, such as Facebook, Twitter, and Instagram as well. Additionally, they all posted where they were going to be the night they were killed."

"We already suspected that," Beau said. "But what about the perp?"

"We assume he's on all those platforms, but we haven't been able to pinpoint him. He apparently has multiple profiles on each platform." Danny handed Auggie a folder. "Here's a list of all the 'mutual friends' the vic's shared on the three different social media sites."

Auggie flipped through the folder. "Jesus, Danny, there's gotta be at least twenty-five names on this list."

"I know it. New Orleans has a tight gay community, but we couldn't rule anyone out. The names are sorted by platform type and where they stated they live on their profile. Remember, the perp doesn't have to live in New Orleans, although all the indications you gave us, based on witness interviews, point to that."

"Were you able to verify any of that personal information?" Bruce asked.

"Some," Danny said. "We ran every name against our databases, and where the names and addresses matched, we indicated it in the file. So if I were you, that's probably where I would start. We also gathered the date they became friends or became affiliated on each different platform, and that might help you narrow it down some by the vic. But, guys," Danny said, "based on all the analysis we did, we are still looking for a needle in a haystack."

"And what about Grindr?" Bruce asked.

"Oddly enough we found no mutual profiles between the vics, which means the perp must have had a different profile, or even multiple profiles, for each vic he was involved with. Also in that file is a list of every Grindr profile from each vic's account. Some of the profiles have since been deleted, which might help lead to the perp if we can determine whether they were deleted at the same time, or relatively the same time, as the murders."

"And?" Auggie asked.

"We're still working on that. We had to subpoena the Grindr people, and they are claiming they don't store that information. Additionally, they said even if they did, they wouldn't share it, stating privacy policies as their reasoning."

"Apply all the pressure you need, and I'll back you up," Auggie said. "And let me know if I need to bring in the big guns."

Danny nodded.

"What about the surveillance video?" Auggie asked.

"We're still comparing the video from each of the crime scenes, but as you can imagine, it's pretty slow going. We have to compare scenes frame by frame on multiple screens and that takes a lot of time and resources."

"Just keep on it," Auggie instructed.

"We will," Danny said. "But to be completely truthful, the forensics reports show all the vics took the bullet at an angle from a higher vantage point, like a rooftop or balcony, and none of the surveillance cameras are aimed that high. They all record at street level."

"I figured as much," Beau said.

"Guys, I'm sure you figured this out on your own, but my team thinks the perp used the various forms of social media to keep up with the vics' movements and then Grindr to hone in on their exact location before he pulled the trigger."

"We agree, Danny," Beau said. "But it's quite possible we're wrong about Grindr and Facebook, so we're looking at other scenarios as well."

"Like?" Danny asked.

"Like maybe the perp is not working alone. If we can identify just one common face in the crowd, it might get us one step closer to the perp."

"Good point," Danny said.

Beau stood. "But thank you. It's good to have another set of eyes looking at all of this."

"No problem, Beau," Danny said. "That's about it for me. I'll push as hard as I can with the Grindr people and the surveillance video and keep you guys in the loop—if and when we make any progress."

"Thanks, Danny," Bruce said. "Nice work by the way."

"Yeah," Beau added. "You guys always do a great job."

Danny headed for the door. "I appreciate it. Thanks, guys."

"Well?" Beau said. "Where do we start?"

"I think we need to divide up these names," Auggie said. "Start with the local guys, and let's pay each one of them a visit. If we come up empty-handed, we call on local law enforcement in the other areas and see what they can come up with. As a matter of fact—" Auggie handed Bruce a piece of paper. "—why don't you go ahead and do that now, and we'll work both angles at the same time. It might pay off."

"I'm on it," Bruce said.

Auggie handed Beau a list of names and folded the other and put it in his coat pocket. "Why don't we grab a quick lunch and then hit these lists."

"Do you guys mind if I invite Bastien to join us?" Bruce asked.

"Might as well," Auggie said. "It looks like he's here to stay, so we may as well initiate him into the group."

Beau looked at Bruce with a distressed expression on his face. "Where to?"

"Mother's?" Auggie asked. "I've been craving a Ferdi Special."

Beau looked at Tollison, and Tollison nodded. "Good by us."

"See you guys there," Auggie said as he stood and left his office.

"You've got to tell him," Beau whispered. "And sooner rather than later."

Bruce nodded. "I know. I just need to find the right time."

"Well, you better find it fast."

"I FEEL honored to be part of your pack," Bastien said. "Truly, I do."

Bruce smiled and squeezed Bastien's knee under the table. "I'm glad you're here too."

"Oh jeez," Auggie said. "If we didn't have a serial killer on our hands, I'd tell you two to get a room."

"So what we do at these boys' luncheons?" Bastien asked.

"Well... let's see," Auggie said. "We eat."

"And brainstorm," Bruce added quickly, making up for Auggie's lack of diplomacy.

"How exciting," Bastien replied.

"Not really," Auggie said. "But if you're gonna be with Bruce, it's gonna be a way of life, just like for the rest of our spouses."

Bruce noted Beau's furrowed brow and the stare that came along with it. He elbowed Beau.

When Auggie buried his face in the menu, Bruce mouthed, "Soon."

Auggie looked around impatiently. "Where's our waitress? I want my Ferdi Special."

"What is a Ferdi Special?" Bastien asked.

"Only the best sandwich you'll ever eat," Auggie shared. "It's a po' boy packed with baked ham, roast beef, debris, and gravy, served dressed. Hell. My mouth waters just talking about it."

"Debris?" Bastien asked.

"That's the bits that fall off beef while it's roasting or being carved," Beau explained.

Bastien closed his menu. "Then I think I'll have one of those as well."

After everyone ordered their lunch, Auggie leaned back in his chair. "Okay. So here's what we know so far."

Bruce listened absentmindedly as Auggie recapped the case. He nodded occasionally, but his mind was elsewhere.

How am I gonna tell Auggie I'm leaving the force? He's been an advocate for me, both with Beau and the force, since I joined them. Can I really do this?

He looked over at Bastien, who was sitting at ease with his arm draped across the back of Bruce's chair and seemed to be listening intently and even enjoying the back and forth brainstorming.

Jesus, Bruce. Get over it. Of course you can do this. For him you can do anything.

By the time Auggie finished recapping, no new theories or ideas had come to light, which meant either they had covered every base, or they were all missing something.

"Ah, Auggie?" Bruce asked.

Auggie looked across the table. "Did I forget something?"

"No. You didn't forget anything. I...." He looked at Bastien. "I mean, we have something to tell you."

Auggie rolled his eyes. "Oh, please don't tell me you're getting married. I don't want to picture either one of you in a big white dress and fluffy hat."

Beau snorted his iced tea into his lap, and Tollison slapped him on the back, apparently trying to hold back his own laughter. Bastien, on the other hand, looked like he didn't know whether Auggie was teasing or not.

"Fuck you, Auggie," Bruce said as the waitress started bringing their food to the table.

Auggie started laughing. "I'm just teasing you, man," he said. "You too, Bastien. If you guys are getting married, I'll be right there cheering you on."

Before Bruce knew it, everyone had their mouths full of food and the time no longer seemed appropriate.

When Auggie was through eating, he wiped his mouth and dropped his paper napkin in his empty plate. "So, Bastien. How was your first Ferdi Special?"

Bastien wiped the corners of his mouth. "Just as you described. Excellent suggestion."

Auggie then looked at Bruce. "Jenkins? You never said. Are you guys getting married?"

"No." Bruce pushed his plate to the center of the table. "We're not getting married, but you're not too far off."

"Spill it, Jenkins," Auggie ordered.

Bruce looked at Beau and Tollison and then Bastien. They all gave him their nods of approval and encouragement.

"Well, Auggie. To be honest, Bastien has asked me to go back to Geneva with him."

"What?" Auggie smacked the table with his open palm. "I know you have vacation piling up, but we're right in the middle of a case. You can't just leave me hanging. That's just wrong."

"Not now," Bruce assured him. "Bastien is here until the end of March."

"Well, why didn't you say so? That's quite a different story," Auggie said, more calmly this time. "Of course you can go."

"But, Aug… it won't be just a vacation."

Auggie studied Bruce's face. "What are you saying, Jenkins?"

"I'm saying I'm moving to Switzerland with Bastien."

"What? Noooo." He looked at Beau. "He's pulling my leg, right?"

Beau leaned over and rested his hand on Auggie's forearm. "He's not pulling your leg, Aug. He's serious. Aren't you happy for them?"

Surprise along with something else like hurt, abandonment, or maybe even betrayal was evident on Auggie's face. "Ah, yeah, sure. I'm really happy for you guys," Auggie said. "Congratulations."

"Aug. You know I love you like a brother, right?"

"Yeah. Sure. Me too, man."

"You know I won't leave you hanging?"

"Sure. I know that, and I appreciate it." Auggie turned to Beau. "Looks like someone will be in the market for a new partner."

"I've got some great suggestions," Beau said. "We can talk about it tonight."

"Oh yeah. About tonight," Auggie said. "Something's come up, and Jenny and I can't join you. But you guys go ahead and have a great time without us."

Auggie dropped a twenty on the table. "Hey, I've got to hit the john before we leave. I'll meet you guys at the front door." And in a flash he was gone.

Bruce wadded his napkin into a ball and dropped it on the table. "That went well," he said as he reached for his wallet.

Bastien reached for his wallet too, but Bruce stopped him. "It's on me."

"Give him a little time," Beau said. "He'll come around. You'll see."

Bruce smirked. "I wish I had your confidence. And you know nothing came up. He just doesn't want to be around me tonight."

"We don't know that," Tollison said. "Maybe something really did come up."

"Bullshit."

"Bastien?" Tollison asked. "You're not saying much."

"I don't think it's my place. After all, I'm the bad guy here. The one taking Bruce away."

"Nonsense," Beau said. "You guys have a right to live your lives."

"Beau's right," Tollison said. "You're not leaving Auggie in a jam. You've given him two months' notice. That's more than Beau did."

"He's right!" Beau said. "I gave him a month's notice, which is more than gracious. Two months is way beyond that."

"Yes, ma puce," Bastien said. "They are right. He's just surprised. He will come around."

Bruce shook his head. "I'm not so sure. You guys don't understand."

"Understand what?" Beau asked.

"Auggie was the only one of our friends who didn't take sides when you and I broke up. And Beau, please don't make this about you."

"Make what about me?" Beau asked.

Bruce sighed. "God knows you told everyone what I'd done, and every one of our friends, except Auggie and Jenny, sided with you. They didn't judge me, and Auggie held my hand many nights after you kicked me out."

"I didn't kick you out," Beau said.

"Okay," Bruce said. "If you want to split hairs. After you told me to leave."

"And yeah, I told all of our friends, but I was devastated. Damn it. I had a right."

"I asked you not to make this about you, so calm down. I'm not blaming you for anything. You had a right to do whatever you wanted to do. I'm just...."

"Just what?" Beau asked.

"Just trying to explain why Auggie is so hurt. That's all. He was my best friend. Hell, my only friend for a few years. But even more important, since you left the force, I think I was his best friend."

Bruce turned to Bastien. "I love you, and I want to be with you. But I love him too, and I have to find a way to make this right before we leave."

Bastien nodded and smiled warmly. "I understand completely."

Bruce looked at Beau, who appeared to be still steaming. Bruce shook his head. *Ever the righteous asshole!*

But the next words out of Beau's mouth surprised him. "I get it, and I'll help," Beau said. "And Bruce?"

"Yeah?"

"I'm sorry everyone turned their backs on you. I never meant for that to happen."

"Let's be honest, Beau. I think you did. You wanted to punish me, and I deserved everything I got. But I'm through beating myself up. I made a mistake. A mistake that cost me dearly, but at the same time, that mistake has brought us to where we all are today."

Beau looked at Tollison and smiled.

"Well put, ma puce," Bastien said. "Well put."

Bruce looked at the door. Auggie was standing there watching them. "Auggie is at the door. I need to go." He squeezed Bastien's leg under the table. "I'll call you later."

Bastien nodded.

Bruce stood and nodded at Beau and Tollison. "Thanks, guys. We'll see you tonight."

FOURTEEN

ON THE way to lunch, Bruce had organized the list of potential suspects, for the lack of a better word, by the areas of the city in which they lived. The first name on the list was in New Orleans East, about thirty minutes from downtown, which would give him and Auggie a little time to talk, although Auggie had been silent since they got in the car.

"Aug?"

Auggie didn't take his eyes off of the road. "I don't want to talk about it."

Bruce exhaled. "We have to talk about it."

"Not now we don't."

"Come on, Auggie. Tell me what you're thinking."

"Fine!" Auggie said. "You wanna know what I'm thinking. I'm thinking *my* best friend thought it was okay to tell his ex-lover and his boyfriend he was in love and moving to another country before he told me. I'm sure you remember Jenny and I were the only friends who stood by you through the earthquake you caused that ripped my two best friends apart and left a tsunami in its wake. There. You happy now?"

"No! I'm not happy at all," Bruce replied. "Bastien and I hadn't planned on telling anyone until we were all together and we could tell you all at the same time, but after the crap at the parade last night, we just got a little emotional and spilled our beans."

"Fuck you, Jenkins."

"I'm sorry, Aug. You are my best friend, and you're right—I should have told you first."

Auggie was silent for a long moment. "Do you love the guy?"

Bruce didn't hesitate. "Yes. Very much."

Auggie sighed. "I can't say I didn't see this coming, but I thought you would at least have told Jenny and me as soon as you decided."

"And I should have."

"This is gonna break her heart, you know. First you and Beau break up and our lives are torn apart. Then Beau acts like the complete asshole he can be and life becomes miserable for all of us. And then Tollison comes into our lives, things start to settle down, and now Bastien takes you away from us."

"I wish there were another way, but Bastien's business is overseas."

"What about your job? Is he gonna be your sugar daddy?"

"No!" Bruce yelled.

"Then how are you gonna support yourself?"

"I haven't figured that out yet. Maybe I'll join the police force in Geneva. I don't know."

"Bruce. There are a lot of 'I don't knows' coming out of your mouth."

"All I know is, I'm in love with the guy, and I want to be happy. Is it too much to ask for a little support from my best friend?"

"You mean me or Beau?"

"That's not fair."

Auggie ignored the comment. "Beau's probably all for this," he said sarcastically.

"I meant you, asshole. And you know it."

"Now I've gotta fucking break in a new partner."

"So that's what all this is about?" Bruce asked. "Breaking in a new partner?"

"Shit!" Auggie said. "It's about losing my best friend. Okay!"

"Come on, Aug. You know I love you and Jenny. But after the hell I've been through for the last few years, don't you think I deserve a chance to be happy?"

"When you put it that way, I guess I'm taking a page out of Beau's book and making this all about me."

"You are being a bit of an asshole."

"Fine. You have my support," Auggie conceded with a slight smile. "But the next time there is a major development in your life and you tell anyone else before you tell me, we're through. Do I make myself perfectly clear? And that includes you getting pregnant!"

"Yes, sir. Although I doubt the pregnancy thing is an option. I'm already going through early man-o-pause."

"TMI, Bruce. TMI. All kidding aside, I'm happy for you. And don't worry about Jenny. I'll break it to her tonight, and she'll deal with it."

"And what's this crap about something coming up tonight?"

"Oh, nothing. I think our calendar opened up again."

Bruce laughed. "You're such a baby."

"Fuck you, Jenkins."

THEIR FIRST suspect turned out to be a bit of a catfish. He was a four-hundred-pound shut-in. His only outlet was social media, and he lived on it. However, his profile picture looked nothing like him, and he wasn't on Grindr. That ruled him out completely.

Their next suspect took them back to the Faubourg Marigny, a little area east of the French Quarter. They banged on the front door of the left side of a shotgun double, named because of the way the interior and exterior doors were lined up. You could shoot a shotgun through the front door and it would go right out of the back door.

"Whaddya want?"

"This is the NOPD. Open the door?"

The door opened about four inches, stopping when the backup chain caught. "Let me see some ID, please," the man said.

Auggie flashed his badge. "Wade Duffourc?"

"I'm Wade Duffourc."

"Can you open the door, sir? We have a few questions for you."

Wade closed the door, and the sound of the chain sliding out of its cradle was apparent. When the door opened again, a good-looking, well-built man in his late thirties or early forties appeared in the doorway in nothing but gym shorts. He looked at them without saying a word.

Bruce held up a photograph. "Do you know a Jacob Chaps?"

Wade looked at the photo. "Not off the top of my head."

Bruce held up the other two pictures. "What about these guys?"

"That guy looks somewhat familiar."

"His name is Stuart Cole," Bruce said. "Ring a bell?"

Wade cocked his head to the side. "Maybe. Why?"

"Because he's dead. And so are the other two guys," Bruce said. "Murdered. In cold blood."

Wade's voice got a little shaky. "What does that have to do with me?"

Auggie took over again. "That's what I want you to tell me. You are friends with all three of these guys on Facebook."

"I have a lot of friends on Facebook," Wade said, referencing an open laptop on the coffee table with a nod.

"Tell me, Mr. Duffourc, are you on Grindr?"

The guy blushed a little bit. "Yes," he responded.

"What is your profile name?" Auggie asked.

This time, Duffourc's face got extremely red. "Why is that important?"

"Just answer the question, sir."

"If you must know, it's Gutter."

Auggie had to hold back a smile. "Gutter?"

Wade shook his head. "It seemed like a good idea at the time."

"Mr. Duffourc. Were you at the Krewe of Athena parade?"

"No."

"Are you sure?"

"Look. I absolutely love Mardi Gras, and I used to go to as many parades as I could, but now the noises and the crowds get to me, and I can't take it."

"What about the Krewe of Adonis and the Krewe of Carrollton?"

"Did you not hear me? I told you I can't go to any more parades."

"Yeah. Sorry. One more thing, Mr. Duffourc. Do you own a gun?"

Wade hesitated, then said, "Yes."

"May I ask what kind?"

"An M24."

"A sniper rifle!" Bruce said looking at Auggie.

"It's licensed. I'm a former Marine!" Wade said sounding defensive.

"What do you do now, Mr. Duffourc?"

Wade sat down on his couch and covered his face with his hands. When he looked up, there were tears in his eyes. "Nothing," he said.

"Nothing?" Bruce repeated.

"I'm on disability, all right. I suffer from PTSD."

"I'm sorry to hear that," Auggie said. "What did you do in the Marines?"

"I was a lance corporal and a… scout sniper."

Auggie and Bruce exchanged glances. "Order a warrant for the weapon and the laptop," Auggie said.

"No need for a warrant," Wade volunteered. "I'll give you the damn rifle, and you can check my laptop too. The gun hasn't been shot in over seven years, and I'm damn happy to get rid of it. My laptop is clean too. Other than some porn, you're not going to find anything illegal on that thing. Nowadays, it's my only link to the outside world. I can't seem to drag myself out of this apartment anymore."

"Get the rifle while I make a call," Auggie said.

Bruce followed Wade into a bedroom where an old trunk sat at the end of a bed. Bruce stepped back and placed his hand on his own gun when Wade opened the trunk. The guy removed a pair of combat boots, a stack of uniforms, a helmet, and finally the rifle. His hands were trembling as he laid the rifle on the foot of the bed. He closed his eyes, took a deep breath, and then put everything else back in the trunk. "You're gonna have to carry it," Wade pleaded. "I don't want to touch that thing again."

When Bruce and Wade walked back to the living room, Bruce was holding the rifle with his handkerchief. Auggie was finishing up a call and Bruce knew instinctively Auggie had been on the phone with Danny Paris in the IT department to have him do a thorough report on Mr. Duffourc's background.

"Mr. Duffourc, I'm afraid we're gonna have to ask you to accompany us to the station for more questioning," Auggie said. "And bring your laptop."

"You're arresting me? For what?"

"We're not arresting you. We're asking you to come down to the station with us. If you refuse, then we'll have no choice but to arrest you."

"On what charges?" Wade asked.

"Murder," Bruce said.

"Jesus! I didn't kill anyone. I can't even leave my apartment. Not to mention go anywhere near that rifle without breaking into a cold sweat."

"Then you have nothing to hide and no reason to not come with us."

AN HOUR later Auggie and Bruce were at the station watching Wade Duffourc through a two-way mirror. He was nervously pacing back and forth in the interrogation room.

Wade had been in there alone for almost an hour while Auggie waited for Danny's report and the forensics report on the gun, but no one was in any rush. It was normal protocol to allow a suspect to be alone for up to two hours to give them time to contemplate what was at stake. On rare occasions in the deafening silence, the suspect might even confess to a crime out loud before the interrogation even started, making everyone's job a lot easier. But no such luck with this guy; he was as tightlipped as a mafia wife.

He was getting increasingly agitated and was sweating profusely, but he seemed to be doing some type of mantra or mental exercise to try and calm himself down.

When Danny's report finally showed up, Auggie read through it, shook his head, and then gave the report to Bruce. Bruce scanned it, and it was pretty clean. The guy was indeed an ex-Marine, highly awarded and discharged honorably seven years ago. Except for one arrest for assault and battery in a French Quarter bar at three in the morning, his record was clean. It also showed he was indeed being treated for PTSD at the VA Hospital downtown on Canal Street.

Bruce closed the file. "Doesn't mean he's not guilty. You want at him, or do you want me to handle it?"

"You go first," Auggie said. "And if there's cause, I'll go in for round two."

Bruce nodded, tucked the folder under his arm, and entered the interrogation room. Wade was standing with his back to the door, and the poor man almost jumped out of his skin when Bruce allowed the door to slam behind him. He turned quickly with an expression of desperation on his face, and Bruce almost felt bad for the guy. "It's okay. Mr. Duffourc, it's just me."

Wade flashed an uncomfortable smile. "I'm sorry. Ever since I got back from Afghanistan, I get extremely nervous when I'm confined to a small area. I get these panic attacks, and I can't help myself. I start to sweat and tremble, and I eventually lose it."

"It's okay. I understand," Bruce said. "And if you cooperate with us and all goes well, we'll have you out of here in no time. But I must tell you our conversation is being recorded. Okay?"

Wade nodded. "It's okay. And thank you for understanding my situation."

"You're welcome," Bruce said. "But, Mr. Duffourc, you have to be completely honest with me, or this just isn't going to work."

Wade nodded again and Bruce spread the photos of the three vics on the table. "Tell me everything you know about these three guys."

Wade studied the first picture closely. "I don't recognize this guy at all. We may be Facebook friends, but I have a lot of friends on social media. I accept everyone that asks. For some reason it makes me feel better. Like I'm not so alone all the time."

"Okay. I get that," Bruce said. "What about this guy?"

"I sort of recognize him. I think I commented on a few of his posts, and we may have even PM'd a couple of times."

"PM'd?" Bruce asked, knowing what the term meant but wanting to make it perfectly clear on the recording.

"PM stands for private message," Wade said. "It's a way to e-mail or chat with someone privately on Facebook after you've accepted or requested they become your Facebook friend."

"I see," Bruce said. "Do you remember what you PM'd about?"

"Not off the top of my head, but if you let me look at my laptop, I can look it up."

"All right," Bruce said. "Show me."

Wade opened his laptop. "Do you have a network here I can sign on to?"

Bruce selected the network and typed in the password. "There."

Wade opened Facebook and clicked on the message icons. "What's the guy's name?"

"Curtis Borne."

Wade scrolled down what seemed like hundreds of messages, and then he stopped. "Here he is. His profile name is CBorne."

Wade clicked on the message. There were three exchanges between them. The first was CBorne thanking Wade for accepting his friendship. The second was Wade replying he was happy to meet him. And the last one was Wade commenting on how a picture that CBorne posted of a sunny day at City Park was almost beautiful enough to want to make him venture out of his house.

"See," Wade said. "It's all just mostly protocol."

"So what about this guy?"

As Wade studied the picture, he got increasingly nervous. It seemed to inch up on him, but within a couple of minutes, he slapped his palm on the table. "Shit. I know this guy."

"How?" Bruce asked.

"He was the first guy I ever hooked up with on Grindr. It was over a year ago, and it was a disaster. I was already nervous. Add the PTSD on top of that, and what a shit show. The guy never called me back, and I don't blame him."

Bruce heard a knock on the door. "Excuse me," he said. "I'll be right back."

Bruce opened the door to see Auggie holding another piece of paper. "The forensics report?"

"Yep."

"Let me guess," Bruce said. "Wade is telling the truth."

Auggie nodded. "No residue. Nothing. Their best guest is it hasn't been shot in over five years."

"That jives with Wade's story. I don't think this is our guy, but I think we should put a tail on him just to make sure he really is a recluse. I almost feel sorry for the guy. That PTSD shit really sucks."

"Yeah. I was listening. These guys go away and fight for their country and are asked to do God knows what, and they do it willingly. Then when they finally come home, they're sometimes ruined for life. And the fucking government acts like they don't exist. Let's let him go, and we'll put a tail on him just to make sure. But tell him we need to keep his laptop for a day or two and we'll get it back to him as soon as we can."

Bruce stepped back into the room. "Okay, Mr. Duffourc, you're free to go."

"Is that guy really dead?"

"Unfortunately yes," Bruce said. "And the other two guys also took a single bullet to the head at a Mardi Gras parade."

"Jesus," Wade said. "And you think I could have done that?"

"Stranger things have happened, Mr. Duffourc. But your gun checked out. Forensics confirmed your story. We're gonna keep your laptop for a couple of days just to make sure it's clean, but for now, as I said, you are free to go. I'll get someone to drive you home."

Wade looked like he was about to collapse. "But my laptop is my lifeline. It's my only connection to the outside world."

"I know," Bruce said, feeling sincerely bad for the guy. "We'll make it as quick as we can. I promise."

Wade nodded. "Thank you."

Auggie and Bruce met back in Auggie's office to go over their notes and prepare their report.

"I don't know," Auggie said. "This whole Grindr thing sounds like a clusterfuck to me. Where do you guys come up with this shit anyway?"

"It has its purposes, I guess," Bruce responded.

"Okay! So now you've piqued my interest. Show me how this thing works."

"Seriously?" Bruce asked.

"Yeah, seriously," Auggie said. "I'd like to know what we're dealing with, and I'm certainly not downloading an app called Grindr onto my phone."

Bruce pulled out his phone, tapped the screen a couple of times, and typed in a password. He handed the phone to Auggie.

Auggie grinned. "I should have known all you mos had the damn app at your fingertips."

"Yeah, well," Bruce said, blushing a little. "Why not? I was single for a long time. But I haven't used it since we got back from Zurich."

Auggie looked at the screen. "Warehouse Hottie?" He burst into laughter.

Bruce tried to snatch his phone from Auggie, but Auggie pulled back just in time. "I wanted to be anonymous," he said.

"Sure you did. So what do all these little bubbles mean?"

"Those represent other people on the app right now," Bruce said.

"Jesus, Bruce. There's at least a dozen queers in this very building. Look. There's one just ten feet from my office." Auggie apparently did the math and smiled. "Phil Stevens is a mo?"

"Isn't Phil married?" Bruce asked.

"Yep, but I guess he gets a little action on the side."

"Who'd want *any* action with that guy?" Bruce said.

Auggie chuckled. "You just never know. Do you? I swear. You mos never cease to amaze me."

Bruce looked at his watch. "Hey, Auggie, you mind if I cut out of here?"

Auggie gave him a knowing smile. "Yeah. I'll finish the report. Go on, and Jenny and I will see you guys at Beau's."

"Thanks, man!"

FIFTEEN

BEAU AND Tollison got back to the station just before five o'clock.

Auggie looked up when Beau huffed and the two of them plopped down in seats across from Auggie's desk.

"Well?" Auggie asked.

"Get Bruce in here?" Beau said. "So we don't have to repeat ourselves."

Auggie waved him off. "No need. He just left. I'm sure you boys remember what it was like when you first fell in love."

"Hell yeah," Beau said, looking over at Tollison and winking. "That was fun, but to be honest, nothing compares to what we have now."

Tollison reached over and squeezed Beau's knee. "I feel the same way."

"Jesus!" Auggie narrowed his eyes. "Who are you and what have you done with the edgy hardass Montgomery Beaumont Bissonet we all knew and hated?"

Beau looked at Tollison and back to Auggie. "Oh! He's still in here, but somewhere along the line he forgave a few people, let go of some things, and got over himself."

Tollison smiled.

"Christ!" Auggie said. "I think I liked you both more when you hated each other's guts. At least it was more entertaining for the rest of us."

"Fuck you. Auggie," Tollison said. "Talk about hardass!"

"Aug, are we gonna chitchat about my glowing personality, or do you want to hear what we uncovered this afternoon?"

"Fine! Let me have it."

Beau looked at Tollison. "Absolutely nothing. We struck out on three—actually four—guys."

"Seriously?" Auggie asked. "Are you losing your edge, Bissonet?"

"Hell no, but you can't make fire without a spark," Beau said.

Tollison weighed in. "The first guy on our list just returned from a three-week honeymoon in Mexico. He and his husband both had airline tickets, a hotel bill, and great tans to prove it. And they've been together over two years."

"And get this," Beau said. "His husband was also one of the guys on our list."

"And that didn't send up red flags?" Auggie asked.

Beau smirked. "Of course it did. But while we were there, both guys gave us access to their Facebook pages, and although they *were* friends with the vics, there was no noticeable correspondence between them. In this case, I think Facebook suggested friends based on locations and other common friends, and they simply accepted. Neither recognized or even remembers ever corresponding with any of the vics."

"Besides their alibi, which is pretty solid," Tollison said, "my instincts tell me neither of them is our guy."

"I agree," Beau added.

"What about Grindr?" Auggie asked.

"One of the guys did have a Grindr profile, but he deactivated it two years ago when he entered into a committed relationship. Just to be certain, we requested his username and log-in information, and we checked it out. No activity. The other has never had a Grindr account."

Auggie leaned back in his chair. "At least you got to scratch two off of your list with one hit. What about the third?"

"William G. Milner. He goes by Billy and was yet another dead end," Beau said.

"Why?"

"Because he's handicapped."

"So?" Auggie replied.

"The guy is legally blind—" Tollison started.

Auggie interrupted. "That doesn't mean—"

"Let him finish," Beau snapped.

"Oh yes, it does," Tollison protested. "Billy has a progressive retina disease. He has no central vision, only peripheral, and has no real detail in his vision. There's no way he could be our man. He could never see through a scope or even aim a gun."

"And you know this for a fact?" Auggie asked.

"Yes. We know this for a fact," Beau added. "The guy has a state provided identification card with his picture on it, and he's a graduate of the Louisiana School for the Visually Impaired in Baton Rouge. He's legit, Aug."

"Does the guy work?"

Beau nodded. "Yup. He's a private mobility teacher."

"So if he's blind, how can he be on Facebook and Grindr?"

"Are visually impaired people not entitled to have a social life?" Tollison asked.

Auggie rolled his eyes. "You know what I mean."

"He's on Facebook, but not on Grindr," Beau said.

"Then how does he see to use a computer?"

"His computer and phone talk to him," Beau explained. "He showed us. It's amazing how much he can do online or on his computer with the help of specialized software."

"And besides," Tollison said, "I took an instant liking to the guy."

"Me too," Beau said. "He's smart, fit, handsome, and very funny. Hell, if Tollison and I were into ménages, we'd bring him home. Right, Tol?"

"Hell yeah," Tollison said, meeting Beau's fist bump.

"But we're not," Beau clarified.

"Oh hell!" Auggie said. "I couldn't care less what you homos do in your spare time."

"I don't know, Beau." Tollison smirked. "Maybe we should give it a try."

Auggie shook his head. "What about an alibi?" he asked, apparently ignoring the comment.

"Airtight," Beau said. "Do you remember that guy who was fired from a shipping company a few months back, and two days later emptied his .045 in the executive offices and then killed himself?"

"How can I forget?"

"Anyway, the chief financial officer took a shot to the head. It wasn't fatal, but when she regained consciousness, she was totally blind. The doctors said the bullet apparently grazed her visual cortex. No one knows if it's temporary or not, but Mr. Milner has been teaching the woman how to function with her new disability for the last three weeks."

"Twenty-four seven?" Auggie asked.

"Yup," Beau said. "Her husband brought Billy into their home full-time because his wife is so severely traumatized, she won't leave her house."

"All right. Give me number four so we can go home."

Beau looked down at his notes. "Richard M. Sabin."

"Now this one was interesting and showed some real promise in the beginning," Tollison said. "This guy is six feet two, blue eyes, blond hair, and really good-looking."

"But extremely pigeon-toed," Beau added.

"He wasn't very happy to see us and kept looking out of his window like he was waiting for someone," Tollison explained. "When we questioned his behavior, he said if we must know, he was waiting for a Grindr hookup any minute, and we were about to spoil it."

"Yeah," Beau said. "He kept bitching that it was his only day off this week, and we were going to ruin his chance at getting laid."

"Did we mention he's very promiscuous?" Tollison asked.

"Not yet," Auggie said.

Beau continued, "And get this, Aug. The guy's on the usual social media crap like Facebook, Instagram, and Grindr, but he's also on Jack'd, SCRUFF, GROWLr, BoyAhoy, Skout, and a few others. I did a little research on the way back to the station, and wow! Who knew there were so many hookup sites? Where was this shit when I was young and single?"

"Excuse me?" Tollison asked.

"You know what I mean," Beau said through a smile.

Tollison smirked, and Beau patted his leg. "Go on, Tol."

"Anyway, the guy just seemed angry. It could have been because we were ruining his hookup, but it seemed more than that. Like he was the kind of guy just waiting to explode and takes very little to detonate."

"So we went over the usual," Beau said. "Tol showed him the three vics' pictures. He did recognize Curt Borne, from Facebook by the way. We asked if he'd been to any of the parades. And then we asked where he was on the nights of the deaths."

"And that's when detonation occurred," Tollison said. "He's apparently a front-desk clerk at the Royal Sonesta Hotel on Bourbon Street, and since Mardi Gras, they've been forcing him to work twelve-hour shifts—from five o'clock in the evening until five o'clock in the morning with only one day off a week. He was livid, Auggie. So much so that Beau had to actually cuff the guy and threaten to bring him in if he didn't calm down."

"No shit?" Auggie asked.

"Eventually we got him calmed down enough to get all of his profile names so we could run a check against the vics' Grindr apps." Tollison handed Auggie a piece of paper.

"Uptown Dick? Weapon of Ass Destruction? Crescent City Dick? Dick Hound? Uncle Reamus? The Bone Ranger? Jizz Whiz? Leader of the Sack? Zipper Ripper? Are you kidding me?"

"I wish we were," Beau said.

"Don't lump us in with these guys," Tollison said. "We have no idea."

"So bottom-line it for me."

"The guy says he was working," Beau said. "Of course we have to verify that, but we'll drop by the Royal Sonesta tomorrow morning. In the meantime, have IT run the list of names and see if we get a connection."

"Shit!" Auggie said. "The list is getting shorter, and we are still no closer to solving this crime."

Beau stood and Tollison followed his lead. "We'll start on the rest of our list right after we verify his story tomorrow morning."

"Got it. What time tonight?" Auggie asked.

"Oh!" Beau said with a surprised tone to his voice. "I guess you made up with your little bitch, then?"

"Fuck you, Bissonet," Auggie cursed. "You're just jealous 'cause you're not my little bitch anymore. That's all."

Beau covered his heart with his hand, stumbled back, and fell into his seat. "Damn, Auggie. Do you have to be so cruel?"

"You guys are assholes," Tollison said.

Auggie raised his hand, and Beau high-fived him. "We've still got it, brother," he said.

"Seriously. You and Bruce are okay?" Beau asked.

"We will be. But let's just say we're in a better place."

Beau nodded. "That's good. And six o'clock will be fine."

"What can we bring?"

"Not a thing," Tollison said. "Bruce and Bastien are bringing dinner."

"Sweet! The little shit owes me."

Beau frowned. "Come on, Auggie. Be happy for the guy. He deserves a little happiness."

"You mean after the hell you put him through?"

Beau started for the door. "The hell we put each other through," he said, looking over his shoulder.

"I stand corrected."

"Of course you do," Beau said. "Let's go, Tol."

"See you at six, Aug," Tollison added.

SIXTEEN

STANDING ON the curb watching the people I care about enjoy themselves seems different somehow. As many years as I've lived in New Orleans and as many Mardi Gras as I've witnessed, none seemed to hold a candle to this one. The lights are brighter, the marching bands are louder, the floats are more spectacular, and I'm pretty sure I owe it all to the man standing next to me. Finally, after the last few years of absolute self-loathing and heartache, I finally came out on the other side, and I feel a new freedom to live. To love.

Everywhere I look people seem to be happy and joyous, celebrating the carnival season with all the gusto they can muster. And for once I want to be just like them. To be truthful the feeling almost makes me giddy.

Night after night I kept praying my time would come and happiness would once again find me, and for the longest time it eluded me. But now I know it's finally here.

The man I care the most about in this world is here. And yes—I can finally say it. He's the man I love. Hell, my ex and his boyfriend are here, and although it has been a rough road for us in the past, I think we're over the hardest part. Hopefully we can now settle into a great friendship and live our lives knowing the other is truly happy.

In the midst of all my joy, watching the news and the most recent developments have me, like so many others, continually scanning the rooftops. Paying attention to people's faces. What they are wearing. Their body language. Wondering if they could be concealing a weapon under their clothing. I jump at the sound of any loud noise. The Mardi Gras Murderer obviously has me, as well as a lot of other people, a little more than paranoid.

As another float approaches, I reach down and take my man's hand and give it a little squeeze. He turns to me with the warmest smile, winks, and returns the simple squeeze before we release and immediately throw our hands into the air, yelling for beads and trinkets like the adult children we so obviously are.

As the float passes us by, I'm still looking up when something in the distance—a reflection, maybe?—on the roof of the apartment building across St. Charles Avenue catches my eye. The building's not tall, only about four stories, and it's less than a block away, so I can clearly see the roofline from where I'm standing.

I focus all my attention on the area where I saw the reflection, or whatever it was. I watch for any sudden movements. Seconds later I don't believe my eyes. If I squint, I can barely see the outline of a person poised on the edge of the roofline. And then what I see next sends a chill down my spine. My first thought is to protect the man I love. I lunge for him, barely having time to react when I feel the shot penetrate my skull.

The jolt sends adrenaline through me, and because of it I remain conscious for a long moment. The Mardi Gras Murderer. I need to tell someone, but I can't form the words. I feel the life quickly draining out of me, and my last logical thoughts are only of the man I am leaving behind. The man I love. I try to say his name as I sink into the abyss.

BRUCE SLID his key into the elevator, and the doors closed behind him. The car jerked upward steadily, rising to the penthouse. When the doors opened again into the foyer of Bastien's suite, Bruce smiled when he heard the familiar sounds of Edith Piaf in the background. Bastien had introduced her to him, and she'd become a soothing—if not sometimes haunting—presence with her melodies.

"Bastien?" No response.

Bruce walked up the stairs to the bedroom and heard the faint sound of lapping water coming from the open door of the bathroom. He stuck his head through the doorway and stared when he saw Bastien's body leaning against the shower wall through the steamy glass. The water was beating down on his shoulders, and from his stance, Bruce thought he looked relaxed.

Maybe I can relax him a little more. Bruce slipped out of his suit coat and pulled the already loosened tie from his neck. He stripped and slipped into the shower, wrapped his arms around Bastien's waist and kissed his shoulder softly.

"I hoped you'd get here in time to join me, ma puce," Bastien said.

"I'm so glad I did."

Bastien turned around in Bruce's embrace and draped his arms over Bruce's shoulders. "I've missed you a great deal since lunch."

"Me too," Bruce said, kissing Bastien softly.

"Let me show you how much."

Without another word, Bastien slid down to his knees and took Bruce into his mouth. Bruce's head fell back, and he gripped Bastien's shoulders. His blood rushed to his groin in mere seconds, and he became instantly hard. He couldn't think, and he couldn't move, his legs damn close to crumbling beneath him. Bruce squeezed Bastien's shoulders and used Bastien's strength to steady himself.

The hot water beat on his back, and Bastien's warm mouth slid up and down his length in long, even movements. Bruce was concentrating anxiously on not shooting his load in mere seconds and was almost succeeding until Bastien slipped a finger under Bruce's balls and found his opening.

Bruce let his head fall forward and sucked in a ragged breath as Bastien slowly worked a finger inside him. He watched as Bastien's head slid along his length, tantalizing him and coaxing his release ever so masterfully. Now desperately trying to hold back, Bruce focused on the beautiful body kneeling at his feet. Bastien's eyes were closed, and drops of hot water lingered and pooled on his long, dark eyelashes as they rested against his soft olive skin. His black hair was wet and plastered to his head, and the silver at his temples glistened against the reflection of the dimly lit glass-enclosed shower.

Bastien's hands were steady and sure as he pleasured Bruce to the verge of insanity. Bruce was momentarily fascinated by Bastien's muscles—his broad, powerful shoulders and round, solid biceps and triceps—as they moved in unison with his efforts, working as a symphony, so in tune that the imagined sound was breathtaking.

Bruce was now hanging on by a thread: any sudden sensation would send him over the edge. But before he could vocalize his impending orgasm, Bastien suddenly stopped. His finger slipped from Bruce's body as he released Bruce's erection. But Bastien instantly started kissing his way up Bruce's torso, following the line of hair running from his crotch to his chest. Bruce dug his fingers into Bastien's hips as Bastien teased both of his nipples, biting just enough to smart and then licking the sting away. Then Bastien worked his way farther upward, dropping soft gentle kisses along Bruce's shoulders, the tender spot between neck and shoulder, and eventually Bruce's lips.

"I love you, ma puce," Bastien whispered, "and want us to be together in every way."

"I want that too," Bruce said. "I'm yours for the taking."

"I need to get a condom."

"No! Don't go," Bruce said. "I am safe and tested regularly."

"I too," Bastien said. "I give you my word."

"And I trust you with all my heart." Bruce closed his eyes and rested his head on Bastien's chest. Moments later when he opened them, Bastien was staring down at him with so much love in his eyes, Bruce could hardly stand it.

"I want you so badly, Bastien. Please, take me."

Stepping out of the direct line of the shower, Bruce squeezed a handful of shower gel into his palm, coated his opening, and palmed his erection. He turned, rested his hands on the shower wall, and looked over his shoulder. "I'm ready," he said.

He could feel Bastien's warm chest pressing against his back and Bastien's erection teasing him, sliding back and forth, brushing against the sensitive skin surrounding his opening. Bastien dropped slow wet kisses on Bruce's back and neck, then reached around and took Bruce into his hand as he slowly pushed into him.

Bruce tensed and swallowed the gasp that almost escaped his lips as Bastien breached him. Bastien stopped pressing forward, but never stopped stroking him. When the burn turned into a sting and the sting became a dull ache, Bruce instantly wanted more. He relaxed as Bastien's kisses turned into nips of teeth and then laps of tongue. Bruce cried out with a mixture of pain and pleasure when Bastien bit his shoulder and pushed all the way in.

Bastien stopped and waited as Bruce hung his head and caught his breath. The throb of the bite quickly vanished in the joy of being taken. No one had ever entered him like this, and the mixture of pain and pleasure, combined with the emotions, was almost too much to process. When Bastien withdrew, Bruce spread his legs wider, arched his back, and started moving with him. Within moments they were in a rhythm that seemed almost impossible for two people who had only just become physical a day ago. They moved like a couple so in tune with each other, they each knew what the other was thinking and, more importantly, feeling.

Each time Bastien withdrew, Bruce wanted him back instantly. He wanted to feel Bastien fill him almost to capacity. He wanted the stretch. Wanted the burn. Needed the man. Bruce looked over his shoulder and prayed for Bastien's kisses. Bastien answered his prayers and plastered his lips to Bruce's, his tongue plowing into Bruce's mouth in time with each thrust of his cock. Bruce was quickly reaching his limit, the sensations running through him almost too much to bear.

Bastien changed his angle and in doing so brushed repeatedly against the spot that made Bruce weak in the knees. "Oh, Bastien," Bruce cried. "I'm so close."

"Let go, ma puce. I am with you."

Bruce replaced Bastien's hand on his cock as Bastien started pumping harder into him, Bastien's hand now gripping his hips and thrusting forward and back with just the right amount of force. As his release rose from somewhere deep inside of him, Bruce closed his eyes and cried out. The first wave of his cum landed on the shower wall in front of him. The backs of his eyelids exploded with color, as if he were watching some kind of fireworks display. His spasms were jerky and rough as the second and third waves of his release escaped his body.

Bastien bit down onto his shoulder again and moaned loudly as he repeatedly emptied into Bruce, warming him from the inside out. When they both stopped moving, Bastien rested his face against Bruce's back and sighed. He extended his arms under Bruce's armpits and gripped Bruce's chest and shoulders, holding him securely in place.

Bruce craned his head around, and Bastien smiled before he covered his lips in a kiss. When the kiss ended, Bastien rested his forehead against Bruce's shoulder. "Now we are one, ma puce."

With those simple words, Bruce was suddenly overcome with emotion. He'd spent the last few years of his life in shame, believing he would never again love or be worthy of someone to love him. And for a split second, he even wondered if any of this was real. *It could all just be a wonderful dream.* But then he felt Bastien move inside of him, Bastien's soft sweet kisses on his back, and his arms holding him tightly. He dropped his head and exhaled in relief. *No, this is real.*

Fighting the urge to spin around, wrap his arms around Bastien, and never let him go, Bruce held steady. But as usual Bastien seemed to be in sync with his every need. He had to be a mind reader because the second he naturally slipped from Bruce, Bastien turned him around and pulled him close. "I love you, ma puce."

"You saved me from myself, Bastien," Bruce said. "And for that, even if you left me right now, I would still love you more than you could ever know."

The two men spent the next half hour in the shower, washing every inch of each other's bodies. It was one of the most sensual things Bruce had ever done. His relationship with Beau had been so different. No less love, exactly, but maybe rough and ready was a good way to describe it. Beau was a man's man, and he would always be. Bastien, on the other hand, *could* be rough and ready—he'd already proven that today—but his natural instinct was to be tender and sweet, and Bruce liked that side of him.

When they were both shriveled like prunes, Bastien shut off the water, opened the door, and handed Bruce a bath towel from the warmer. He kissed Bruce gently on the lips. "Thank you. I don't think I've ever been bathed before."

Bruce smiled. "And I couldn't be happier I was the first man to do it."

Before Bastien could respond, Bruce heard his pants ringing from the bathroom floor. He stepped out of the shower and retrieved his cell from his pocket, then looked at the caller ID.

"What time is it?" he asked.

Bastien stuck his head out of the bathroom and looked at the clock. "Six forty. Why?" he said.

"Because it's Beau, and we're so late."

Bruce answered the call. "I know. We're running late."

"What the fuck?" Beau said. "Auggie and Jenny have been here for over forty-five minutes. Traffic is gonna be shit, and if we don't go soon, we're not going to find a place to watch the parade."

"We're really sorry, Beau. You guys go ahead. Call me as soon as you find a spot, and we'll drop off the food at your place and then meet you there."

"Fine. But hurry."

"We will."

Bruce ended the call. "He's not too happy with us right now."

"Well, to be honest, we are invited guests to his home, and we *are* terribly late."

"I know, but he'll get over it," Bruce said. "Besides, I wouldn't have passed up what we just did for any stupid Mardi Gras parade."

Bastien chuckled. "Nor I, ma puce."

Bastien and Bruce were en route to Beau and Tollison's when Bruce's cell rang again. "Still mad at me?"

"Not if you had a good reason," Beau replied.

"The best," Bruce said, looking at Bastien's hand resting on his knee.

"I look forward to hearing about it," Beau said. "But we found a spot at the corner of Louisiana Avenue and St. Charles, so just leave your car at the house and walk over."

"Okay. We'll see you guys as soon as we can."

As Bruce maneuvered his way through the Uptown streets, he remembered how much heavier the traffic and crowds always became the closer it got to Mardi Gras. It was almost as if everyone knew Fat Tuesday was approaching, signaling the end of the Mardi Gras season, and was trying to cram every parade in they could before it was all over for another year.

After picking up a shitload of food from Taqueria Corona on Magazine Street and dropping it off at Beau's, they made their way to Louisiana and St. Charles Avenues. The parade looked to be well underway, and after twenty minutes of searching, they finally spotted Auggie standing at the back of the crowd, but Jenny, Beau, and Tollison were nowhere in sight. He and Bastien made their way over, apologized profusely for being late, and asked about the rest of the crew.

"Guess?" Auggie pointed to the very front of the crowd.

Bruce went up onto his tiptoes and craned his neck over the crowd. The three of them were on the front row, jumping up and down and waving their hands like ten-year-olds. Bruce smiled at Bastien and pointed. Bastien, who was a little taller, looked out over the crowd, returned Bruce's smile, and nodded.

"I guess I should have known," Bruce said to Auggie.

"But not you?" Bastien asked.

"Hell no!" Auggie said. "I'd rather stay back here and guard the beer."

"I agree with you there," Bastien said.

"Speaking of?" Bruce looked at Auggie and then the cooler.

"Oh yeah." Auggie reached into the cooler and retrieved two Silver Bullets, popped the tops, and handed each of them one.

Bruce took a long pull and looked at Auggie. "So how pissed is Beau that we're so late?"

"Oh hell. You know Beau," Auggie said. "If he's not in control of everyone and everything around him, he's not a happy camper. On the other hand, that's what made him a great detective. No one could manage a crime scene like old Beau could."

"Old Beau, as you call him, sounded pretty pissed off at me over the phone."

"I don't think I would lose any sleep over it."

"I'm afraid it was truly all my doing," Bastien said, winking at Bruce.

"Oh fuck no," Auggie said, covering his ears. "You both have that *just-laid* look, and I don't want any part of the details."

Bruce elbowed Auggie and laughed.

As the parade raged on and the crowds thickened, Bruce found himself constantly scanning the balconies and rooftops of the surrounding buildings. He thought the odds of him ever seeing anyone lurking in the shadows were pretty slim, but he just had this strange feeling. It had first hit him when they'd started walking down St. Charles Avenue toward Louisiana and had stayed with him. He tried to attribute it to being a cop so he could put it out of his mind and enjoy the parade. And so far he was managing that, but he found himself staying very close to Bastien's side. During any lull in the parade, and even the short minutes between floats, Bruce's eyes darted upward, scanning constantly.

Minutes later Bruce saw the three amigos working their way through the crowds. Their necks were loaded down with beads, some of them sparkling and flashing from battery operated LEDs, and their arms were full of trinkets and stuffed animals.

When Beau spotted Bruce, he smirked. "Look who finally showed up."

Bruce ignored the dig. "It's not like you to give up so soon."

"Outta beer!" Beau said, holding up his empty can.

"That makes sense."

"But I think we'll hang back just the same. There are only two more floats to go, and the kids up there are vicious."

Auggie popped a top for Jenny and tossed Beau and Tollison each a cold one. When the next float approached, the party started up again. As the float rolled by, Bruce was screaming at the people on the upper level because they had the best chance of throwing something that would reach so far to the back in the crowd. A string of beads smacked him in the chest. He caught it, slipped it over his head, and looked up again, still waving his hands in the air.

As the float pulled away, something on the rooftop across the street caught Bruce's eye. Maybe it was just a reflection, but it held his attention. The building was less than twenty yards from him, and he quickly checked all the balconies and then scanned the roofline from left to right. Nothing. He forced his mind to remember exactly where he'd seen whatever the hell it was he'd seen, and there it was.

His heart dropped to his feet, and the hairs stood up on the back of his neck. He blinked a few times to make sure he wasn't seeing things, but the figure of a person with a rifle was now very clear. "Everybody down!" he yelled. "Now!"

Beau and Auggie turned immediately with confused expressions on their faces. But when he locked eyes with each of them, Bruce saw the recognition register almost immediately. Maybe it was because they all knew the other so well, or because of the years they'd all worked together, but no questions were asked and no explanation was needed. Beau dove for Tollison and Auggie for Jenny. But before Bruce could reach Bastien, he felt the impact of the bullet as it pierced his skull.

I know who the Mardi Gras Murderer is! They are all safe. Thank God it was me!

Bruce hit the ground with a thud. For an instant he could hear people screaming, and then everything started to slowly fade away. The last thing he heard was Beau yelling his name. And then everything went black.

SEVENTEEN

BEAU HAD Tollison pinned safely under him with his face buried in Tollison's neck when he heard the shot ring through the night. He raised his head and locked eyes with Tollison. Tollison nodded and Beau breathed a sigh of relief. *Thank you, Jesus!*

Looking to his left, Beau saw Auggie and Jenny scrambling to their feet, Auggie yelling Bruce's name. Beau looked to his right and saw Bruce wobble for a moment, an expression that could only be described as a mixture of shock and fear plastered on his face. Then Bruce dropped to the ground.

Beau was on his feet and at Bruce's side in record-breaking time. "Bruce!" Beau screamed.

Blood was running down the side of Bruce's face as well as forming a puddle on the concrete below his head. "Jesus, Bruce!"

Beau looked up at Tollison, who was already on his phone apparently calling 9-1-1. Auggie was on the other side of Bruce and Bastien, and Jenny looked on in horror and disbelief.

Within seconds Bastien was on the ground at Bruce's head, wiping the blood away with his shirt.

"Don't move him," Beau commanded.

"I can't find a pulse," Auggie yelled.

"He's losing so much blood," Bastien screamed.

Beau studied Bruce's face for a short moment. *Jesus! He's bleeding to death!* Beau ripped off his jacket, dug into his jeans pocket, and retrieved his folding knife. He cut the sleeve of his jacket off and tied it as tightly around Bruce's head as he could, covering the wound. "This should help stop some of the bleeding."

In the distance Beau heard sirens wailing, but he had no idea how far away they were and how long it would take to get through the traffic and crowds. Then he remembered that multiple police cars and ambulances always followed the end of every parade.

"Stay with him!" Beau yelled. He jumped to his feet, broke through the crowd, and looked down the block. The end of the parade was no farther than a block away, but everything had stopped dead. Beau flashed his badge at the driver of the tractor pulling the last float and shouted, "Move! Now! Go!"

The driver put the big green machine in gear, and the float jerked forward and started rolling. As soon as the float had passed him, Beau started waving frantically at the ambulances and police cars, his badge still in his hand.

"NOPD!" he yelled at the ambulance. The EMT rolled down the window. "We have an officer down!" Beau said. "Gunshot wound to the head!"

The driver pulled the vehicle to the side, and he and his partner jumped out of the ambulance, opened the back doors, grabbed their bags, and followed Beau through the crowds.

When they reached Bruce, Bastien, Tollison, Auggie, and Jenny were all kneeling beside him. Bastien was stroking his face and talking to him, but Bruce wasn't responding. Everyone got to their feet except Bastien when the EMTs arrived. Beau reached for Bastien, attempting to pull him up.

"Bastien," he said. "We need to step back and allow them to do their job."

"No!" Bastien bellowed. "I'm not leaving him."

"Bastien," Beau said calmly. "Let them save his life. We won't leave him. I promise."

That must have gotten Bastien's attention because he stood and Beau wrapped an arm over his shoulder. He walked Bastien over to where Jenny, Auggie, and Tollison were standing just feet from Bruce.

"Stay with him," Beau said. "I'm going after this fucker. He took something of mine, and I'm sure as hell gonna take something of his."

"I'm coming with you," Tollison yelled.

"No! Stop!" Auggie ordered. "I have reinforcements combing every inch of that building and the surrounding blocks. They can handle this."

"Fuck that shit, Aug!" Beau looked at Tollison and then up, scanning the buildings across the street. "Whoever the fucker is, he sure as hell better hope they find him before I do."

Beau took off running, with Tollison and Auggie on his heels. And then it hit him like a ton of bricks. He stopped short, and Tollison ran smack into him. Auggie dodged them, but just barely.

"I know who the murderer is!" he shouted.

Tollison and Auggie both stared at him. "Think about it, guys!" Beau said. "We have a serial killer who is killing men he either dated briefly or had an affair with."

By the looks on their faces, the realization must have hit Auggie and Tollison simultaneously. Auggie spoke first. "The guy Bruce had the affair with."

"Exactly," Beau said.

"What's his name?" Auggie asked. "I'll have him picked up immediately."

Beau looked at Tollison. He felt the blood draining out of his face, and his heart filled with dread. He hung his head. "I don't know."

"What the fuck?" Auggie snapped. "How can you not know the guy's name?"

"It hurt too much, Aug. I told Bruce I didn't want to know anything about the guy."

Tollison rested his arm on Beau's shoulder, but Beau shrugged it off. "I was too caught up in my own self-pity to ask questions or want to know details. I'm sorry. If this guy kills again, it could very well be on me."

"Don't be an ass, Bissonet," Auggie said. "This is not your fault."

Beau turned to go after the shooter, but Tollison put both hands on his upper arms and stopped him. When Beau tried to shrug them off again, Tollison not only didn't allow him to move, but he tightened his grip, holding Beau securely in place.

Beau didn't think he deserved any comforting. Nor did he want anyone's pity. But he couldn't look Tollison in the eyes either. He looked down at his feet, his shoes covered in Bruce's blood.

"Look at me, Beau," Tollison said.

Beau didn't raise his head but instead focused on his bloodstained shoelaces.

Tollison shook him again. "I said look at me!"

Beau slowly brought his eyes up to meet Tollison's.

"This is not your fault, Beau. Let the police do their job, and let's go do whatever we can for Bruce and Bastien."

Logically, Beau knew Tollison was right. It really wasn't his fault. But maybe if he had handled things better with Bruce back then, more like an adult than a hurt puppy, they might have the guy by now. That part was undeniably on his head, but there was nothing he could do about it at the moment. This was not about him.

Beau let go, fell into Tollison's arms, and buried his face in Tollison's neck. He inhaled the comforting scent of safety and home and did all he could to hold back the tears stinging the backs of his eyes. "Let's go help Bruce," he said.

Tollison offered him a weak smile and kissed him on the cheek. "I love you, Beau, and we're all gonna get through this." He took Beau by the hand and led him back to Bruce.

When they rejoined the others, Bruce was on a stretcher, being loaded into the ambulance. Bastien and Jenny were standing on one side of him and an EMT on the other.

Auggie flashed his badge to the attending EMT. "How is he?"

"He's alive," the guy said.

Beau heard the words, but it took a second for them to sink in. Like a dash of cold water in the face, it all became very real. Bruce had been shot in the head. It was a good thing Tollison's arms were around him because Beau's knees almost buckled.

"But he's alive," he repeated, standing motionless, leaning on Tollison as the EMT continued.

"The bullet entered just behind his right temple and exited through the back of his skull. That's why there was so much blood. He came close to bleeding out. Whoever wrapped that tourniquet around his head saved his life."

"Did you hear that, Beau," Tollison whispered. "You saved his life."

"What now?" Auggie asked.

"We've done all we can do here, and he's as stable as we're gonna get him," the EMT said. "So we're gonna transport him."

"Where to?" Beau asked.

"Tulane Medical Center, for now."

Bastien was already climbing into the back of the ambulance. "Do you mind if I ride with him too?" Beau asked the EMT.

"I'm sorry," the EMT replied. "It's protocol for only one family member."

"Can't you go against protocol just this once?" Auggie asked.

The EMT looked at Auggie and then Bastien. When Bastien nodded his approval, the EMT gestured for Beau to get in.

Beau kissed Tollison and climbed into the back of the ambulance.

"We'll meet you guys at Tulane," Auggie said as they closed the doors.

Beau and Bastien shared a small seat along the wall of the ambulance at Bruce's feet. They each had a hand on Bruce's legs, but neither of them spoke. Bruce was white as a ghost, his head completely wrapped in heavy white gauze. He had an oxygen mask over his mouth and an IV in his right arm.

Beau looked at Bastien, who was almost as white as Bruce. "He's alive, man," he finally whispered. "That's more than we can say for any of the guy's other victims."

"He warned us all," Bastien said. "He must have seen the guy."

"He did warn us," Beau said. "And I think by trying to protect you, he saved his own life."

Bastien gave Beau a questioning glance. "We feel certain none of the other victims saw what was coming and were standing relatively still," he explained. "But Bruce must have seen the shooter. When he lunged for you, the shooter didn't get the shot he'd hoped for, and Bruce is still alive because of it."

Bastien offered Beau a weak smile. "I don't care how or what saved his life as long as he's alive. He just came into my life. I can't lose him."

Beau took Bastien's hand and held it tightly. "He's gonna make it, Bastien. I know him. He loves hard, and he fights even harder. He will come back to you. To us. Besides, he's the only one who can tell us who this monster is, and he knows that. He'll come through this. He has to."

Bastien took Bruce's hand in his. "Reviens-moi, mon amour."

Beau felt tears stinging the backs of his eyes again. "Yeah, Bruce. Come back to us both," he said to himself.

EIGHTEEN

BASTIEN DIDN'T know how far away the hospital was, but the ride seemed to go on forever. "How much farther?" he asked.

"Not long now," Beau said. "This parade traffic is holding everything up, but we're almost there."

When they finally reached the hospital, an array of medical professionals was waiting at the emergency entrance. The moment the ambulance stopped, the doors flew open, the gurney emerged, and the wheels made a thud when they hit the ground. The two EMTs rushed Bruce inside, leaving Beau and Bastien still in the ambulance. They both climbed out and started chasing the gurney.

"Stay in the emergency waiting room, and someone will come and find you," one of the EMTs said over his shoulder a moment before two automatic doors opened and they disappeared.

AUGGIE, TOLLISON, and Jenny ran into the emergency room and looked from side to side.

"We're here!" Beau called.

Tollison rushed Beau and took him in his arms, and Jenny ran to Bastien.

"Any changes?" Auggie asked.

"Not that they've shared with us," Beau said, releasing Tollison.

"Let's go sit down." Auggie led them all to a group of chairs.

THE SECOND hand on the large clock ticked away the minutes and hours and still no word. *Tick! Tick! Tick!*

Bastien watched as Beau paced for thirty minutes, checked with the attending nurses to demand some type of update, and then paced again.

Iona hurried into the emergency room, scanning from left to right. "Beau!" she yelled when she saw them.

"Iona! Oh God, I'm so sorry. I forgot to call you."

"Tollison phoned." Iona wiped at the tears streaming down her cheeks. "How is he?"

"We're waiting for some kind of word. It's been so long."

Iona took his hand and squeezed it tightly. "He's gonna make it, Beau."

"I know. He has to."

Iona exchanged hugs with everyone. She'd met Bastien when he'd come to New Orleans before his kidnapping, and they exchanged an extralong embrace.

Bastien was doing his best to fight back the array of emotions chipping away at and threatening his sanity. Anger, fear, and helplessness all came and went while he hugged Iona.

Jenny was also by his side. He really didn't know these people, nor did they know him, but at this moment they were all he had, and to their credit they were supporting him wholeheartedly.

After almost three hours, a tall doctor with an athletic build and graying hair walked through the double doors with a clipboard in his hand. He looked around the waiting room, and Bastien stood hesitantly. The man walked over. "Montgomery Bissonet?"

Beau stood and raised his hand, wondering how the man knew who he was. "Yes."

"Are you here for Mr. Bruce Jenkins?"

"Yes!" Bastien said without waiting for Beau to respond.

"And you are?" the doctor said.

"I am Sebastien Andros, Bruce's—Mr. Jenkins's—life partner."

"But we have Mr. Bissonet listed as the holder of Mr. Jenkins's healthcare power of attorney."

Beau looked shocked, and Bastien frowned.

"Mr. Jenkins and I were partners for quite some time, but we haven't been together in years. I guess he hasn't gotten around to changing it yet."

"Unfortunately we have HIPAA privacy laws we have to adhere to. If your power of attorney permits, you can grant us permission to share Mr. Jenkins's medical information with Mr. Andros. You will still be responsible for any decisions made, but if you choose to consult with Mr. Andros on them privately, of course, that is up to you."

"Beau?" Bastien pleaded with his eyes.

"Of course," Beau agreed. "We included provisions for that in the papers we signed on each other back then. In our line of work, it pays to keep things flexible. So consider permission granted."

"Thank you, Beau," Bastien said.

Beau nodded. "It's only right, and it's what Bruce would want." Beau referenced Auggie, Jenny, and Tollison. "And these are his best friends. His family, really. Just as I am. You have permission to share with them as well."

"Very good." The man smiled. "We will need to have a copy of the power of attorney for the record, but I'll take your word on it for now. By the way, I am Dr. John Waguespack, the hospital's neurologist."

Bastien shook the doctor's hand automatically.

"As you know," Dr. Waguespack went on, "Mr. Jenkins has experienced a severe head trauma."

"We know that," Bastien said. "We were there."

"He's out of surgery and in recovery now," Dr. Waguespack said. "He lost a lot of blood, but he's stable, and I think his chances of survival are fairly good."

"Surgery!" Beau said. "The EMTs said the bullet went through and through."

"It did," the doctor replied, "but it wasn't as neat and clean as all that. We needed to verify the internal damage and clean up the entry and exit wounds. All pretty standard procedure."

Relief filled Bastien's entire body, leaving him dizzy and weak in the knees. *He's going to pull through!* He grabbed Jenny by the arm to keep from falling over and finally released the tears he'd held at bay for what seemed like an eternity. When he looked up at the others, they were all teary-eyed as well. Beau, Tollison, and Auggie were in a bear hug, and Jenny's and Iona's arms were suddenly around him. They were all crying quietly. He wrapped them both in his arms and closed his eyes. He opened them when Beau reached out and touched his forearm.

"I told you he'd come back to us."

Before Bastien could respond, Dr. Waguespack interrupted. "Please. He's not out of the woods yet," he said.

"What?" Bastien said. "But you said—"

"I said I thought his chances of *survival* were fairly good. And they are, based on what we know right now. But we won't know how much damage, if any, was done until he regains consciousness. He may come out of this unfazed, or he may have a long recovery ahead of him. Or… anything in between. We just don't know."

"You mean possible brain damage?" Bastien asked.

"Possibly, but allow me to finish."

Bastien nodded.

"I just conferred with the radiologist who reviewed Mr. Jenkins's CT scan," the doctor explained, "and here's what we have."

Holding up his clipboard, Dr. Waguespack pointed to a graphic of the human brain. He traced the photograph with his pen as he spoke. "It appears the bullet entered here, just above the temple. It penetrated the cranium, here, grazed the frontal lobe, the parietal lobes—including Broca's area—and the hippocampus, and exited the cranium here at the cerebellum."

"That's all well and good," Beau said. "But can you speak to us in English, Doctor?"

"Sorry," Dr. Waguespack said. "Let me try to break it down to layman's terms."

"Thanks," Beau said.

The doctor continued, "The frontal lobe controls some movement, problem-solving, personality behaviors, and thinking or concentrating, while the parietal lobe controls sensation, language, perception, awareness, and attention. The hippocampus is associated with various short-term memory functions, and Broca's area controls speech. On the physical side, the cerebellum controls his posture, balance, and coordination."

"So all of this could quite possibly be affected?" Bastien asked.

"Potentially, yes," Dr. Waguespack explained. "But to be completely honest, we won't know until he regains consciousness. However, the good news is, although the bullet penetrated the cranium, it just grazed the other areas. In my opinion, Mr. Jenkins is a very lucky man. A quarter of an inch farther and we might not be having this conversation."

"Jesus!" Beau swore under his breath. "So if this is all good news, why isn't he awake yet?"

"I can't really answer that question right now for certain, but here's what we think," the doctor explained. "There is a significant amount of blood mixed in with the cerebrospinal fluid, and his ventricles are dilated, indicating some swelling of the brain."

"This story just keeps getting better!" Beau whispered, rubbing his eyes.

Dr. Waguespack held up a hand. "Please allow me to finish. The blood is not uncommon. As I mentioned, the areas of the brain were grazed, and that alone would produce some bleeding. But in addition to the gunshot wound, it appears Mr. Jenkins bumped his head pretty hard when he hit the concrete. The blood is a direct result of both traumas and will dissipate if and when the bleeding stops, but the swelling could become a problem if it doesn't rescind."

"I don't think I fully understand," Beau said. "Fluid? Swelling?"

"Well," the doctor said, "the human brain is surrounded with cerebrospinal fluid that acts like a cushion or a buffer for the cortex. For lack of a better word, the brain *floats* in the fluid, which provides a layer of basic protection inside the skull. When the skull or head experiences some type of trauma, the brain is bounced around, but the fluid protects it and keeps the cortex from coming in contact with the inside of the skull. In the case of a severe head trauma, the fluid is not thick or sufficient enough to completely protect the brain, so in many instances the brain slams against the inside of the skull case like a pinball and can become badly bruised or severely damaged. In Mr. Jenkins's case, the force of the bullet entering and exiting the cranium, in combination with the trauma when he fell, shouldn't be enough to cause long-term or extreme swelling, but it's really a waiting game right now."

"Oh my God!" Bastien said.

The doctor spoke again. "Before you jump to any conclusions, this is not an uncommon occurrence for this type of trauma. The issue only becomes more serious if the brain continues to swell and eventually fills the skull casing, causing further damage, which can result in paralysis, loss of speech and motor functions, or in extreme cases, even death."

Bastien spoke. "But again you said—"

"I said his chances for survival are fairly good," Dr. Waguespack interrupted.

"Can you can stop the swelling?" Bastien asked.

"We've already started Mr. Jenkins on anti-inflammatory drugs, and we're watching him very carefully. We've scheduled him for an MRI in a couple of hours, and if his brain is still showing signs of swelling, we can take further action."

The blood drained from Bastien's face and his hand involuntarily searched for Iona's. "Which means what exactly?"

The doctor continued, "After the MRI, if we determine there is limited to moderate swelling, we can drill a hole through the skull and insert an intraventricular catheter through the lateral ventricle, which is the area of the brain that contains the cerebrospinal fluid, and monitor the fluid levels, releasing fluid through the catheter as needed, giving the brain a little more room to expand. Or if the swelling is moderate to severe, we can do a trephination or burr-hole procedure, which means we'll temporarily remove a portion of Mr. Jenkins's skull to give the brain the room it needs to further expand until the swelling stops."

Bastien wasn't sure how to respond. Both options seemed invasive and aggressive, and neither sounded pleasant.

Dr. Waguespack held up a finger. "But my professional opinion is the more invasive procedure will not be needed. As I said, the bullet just grazed the brain, and the trauma when he fell was not drastic enough to cause severe swelling. We're just watching him closely. That's all we can do right now."

"When can we see him?" Bastien asked.

"They'll be moving him up to the neurointensive care unit shortly," Dr. Waguespack said, "but by the time we get there, he should be settled in. Come with me. I'll take you all up."

They followed Dr. Waguespack silently down the hall and waited for the elevator. When the doors reopened on the fourth floor, the doctor went up to the nurses' station, spoke quietly to the attending nurse, and waved Beau over.

"Mr. Bissonet is giving us formal permission to speak to Mr. Andros about Mr. Jenkins's condition," the doctor instructed. He looked at Beau. "He will arrange to have a copy of the healthcare power of attorney for Mr. Jenkins sent over for our files."

"Absolutely," Beau agreed. "There will be a copy in Bruce's—Mr. Jenkins's—personnel file at the NOPD, and I'll have it faxed over immediately."

The nurse wrote down their fax number and handed it to Beau. Beau took it and waved it in the air. "You're all set, Bastien. It's official."

"Thank you, Beau."

"Will you please come with me, Mr. Bissonet and Mr. Andros?"

Beau glanced at Tollison, and Tollison nodded. Beau then turned to Bastien. "As far as I'm concerned, you're the one with the right to be here. I'm just a technicality."

Bastien nodded and smiled warmly as the doctor led them through a series of halls to a set of secured double doors. He swiped his badge over the reader, and the doors opened to a very large area lined with glass-enclosed rooms. A large nurses' station sat in the center. They walked past three rooms with patients hooked up to all sorts of monitoring machines before reaching Bruce's room.

Bastien fought back tears when he saw Bruce. He walked gingerly up to the bed and stood gazing down. "How long can we stay?"

"Just a few minutes," the doctor said. "The Neuro ICU allows family members to see patients every four hours for thirty minutes at a time, and the next visitation isn't for another two hours, but it's okay for now. Take your time. In fact, I'll give you all a little privacy while I check his status reports." Bruce's head was wrapped in a white bandage, and his skin was ghostly white, but other than the IV and an assortment of monitors, he looked almost normal.

Bastien jumped when he heard a loud beeping noise. He turned to Beau, panicking.

Beau immediately looked through the glass wall to the nurse's station. He sighed. "It's okay. The nurse is on her way," he said to Bastien.

"I'm sure this looks much scarier than it is," she reassured them after checking all the monitors. "The IV is to keep him hydrated and to administer his medications. The other machines are monitoring his heart rate, breathing, blood pressure, and pulse rate, as well the amount of blood returning to the heart and the ability of the heart to pump the blood into the arterial system."

Bastien was grateful for the explanation. The professional-sounding words and the nurse's calm demeanor were somehow comforting. Beau, however, backed away and stared at the still figure lying in the bed.

"Talk to him," Beau urged. "I read somewhere a patient can sometimes hear you, even while in a comatose state. Let him know you're here and he's all right."

Bastien took a deep breath. He had to be strong.

"Ma puce," he said softly, taking Bruce's hand, "I don't know if you can hear me, but Beau and I are here. Don't worry about anything. You're going to be fine."

Bastien's voice started to crack, and he looked away, not wanting Beau to see him losing it.

When he could speak again, Bastien continued, "You're in the neurointensive care unit, and we can't stay with you all the time, but I'll be here as often as they allow me to. If you wake up and I'm not here, don't worry. You're not alone. I'll be right outside in the waiting room." Bastien cleared the lump forming in his throat.

"They are going to take you down for an MRI shortly, and as soon as we get the results, I'll hopefully be able to come back in and bring you some good news."

Bastien glanced at Beau. "Beau. Come say hello."

Beau stepped up to the bed. He took Bruce's other hand. "Hey, asshole," he said, his voice cracking just a bit. "You better wake your sorry ass up soon. I should know who did this to you, but because of my stubbornness and immaturity, I don't. You need to wake up so I can go and kick some serious ass."

Dr. Waguespack reentered the room just as Beau finished speaking.

"I'm sorry, gentlemen, but I'm afraid we'll need to take some vitals before they take him down for the MRI."

"We have to go for right now, but I'll be back as soon as they let me," Bastien said. "Remember, you're not alone," he repeated, his voice strained.

"Thanks, Doctor," Beau said. "We appreciate everything."

"I'll come and get you as soon as I get the results of the MRI."

Beau nodded as he took Bastien by the hand and led him out of the Neuro ICU.

When they reached the waiting room, Iona was distributing coffee to everyone.

They all stood with anticipation written all over their faces. They exchanged embraces, and Bastien took a seat in the corner and let Beau bring them up to speed on Bruce's condition.

"Let me get you some coffee, guys?" Iona offered.

"Thanks, but I can get it," Beau said. "Bastien?"

"Sure," Bastien said without looking up.

"Oh no, please. Let me," Iona pleaded. "I'm gonna go crazy if I don't have something to do."

NINETEEN

BASTIEN PACED while waiting for the doctor to come out with MRI results. Beau was like a caged tiger while Auggie and Tollison changed position every so often in the uncomfortable hospital chairs. Over two hours had passed and still no word.

"That's him," Beau said. Bastien turned, and everyone else rose to their feet. When Dr. Waguespack recognized the group, he walked in their direction, and they met him halfway.

"I have some news for you," the doctor said.

Bastien reached for Beau's hand, and Beau grabbed him and held on tight.

"It appears that, for now, the swelling is fairly minimal, and the blood in the cerebrospinal fluid seems to be dissipating. I don't feel either procedure I told you about earlier will be needed at this time."

Auggie smiled, draped his arms over Jenny's shoulders, and kissed her cheek. Iona sat down and made the sign of the cross.

"I knew he'd make it," Beau said, squeezing Bastien's hand and then releasing it and reaching for Tollison's.

Bastien sat down next to Iona and rested his head in his hands.

"We'll do another CT scan in about four hours and then one more tomorrow morning and watch him closely in the meantime," the doctor continued. "If the next scan shows no increased swelling, I think we'll be in pretty good shape. And if he continues to improve, he should start to regain consciousness. However," he added, "let me caution you. It will be a slow process, and he'll be confused. He may have temporary memory loss and even some paralysis. But with any luck it will all be transient. Only time will tell."

"But he'll live?" Bastien asked.

The doctor smiled. "From all indications, it looks very good. Just remember, when he does regain consciousness, he may not be the same guy he was before the shooting. At least for a little while."

Beau shook the doctor's hand. "We understand. And thank you."

"Good night. And try to get some rest," Dr. Waguespack said. "The nurse will call you if his condition changes."

Bastien took the doctor's hand and shook it so hard Beau thought he was going to break the man's hand off. "Thank you so much, doctor. Can I see him again?"

Dr. Waguespack looked at his watch. "Visiting hours are over now, but if you go in two at a time and promise not to stay too long, I'll get the head nurse to make an exception."

Bastien nodded. "Thanks again, Doctor," he said as the doctor turned and disappeared down the hall. "That's all good news, right?" Bastien asked, looking at Beau.

"It sounds like it to me," Beau agreed. "If he continues like this, he'll be home in no time."

Since Beau had already been to Bruce's room once, Auggie went with Bastien first, then Tollison and Iona, and finally Jenny. When Jenny returned she went directly to Beau. "Bastien asked if you would like to see him once more before they kick us all out."

"Really?" Beau asked.

"Hurry." She winked. "We've almost overstayed our welcome."

Beau turned to Auggie. "Before I go, don't you think we should have a guard stationed at the Neuro ICU? If the killer learns Bruce survived, he may feel threatened and come after him."

"Good idea. Let me make a call."

"Thanks."

When Beau reached Bruce's room, he stopped and watched Bastien through the glass wall. Bastien was standing by Bruce's bed, stroking his arm and talking to him softly. He felt a stab of guilt and sadness mixed with a little jealousy that it wasn't him standing at Bruce's side and comforting him. But he knew their time had passed, and for obvious reasons they'd both moved on. That still didn't squash the odd sensation of being on the outside looking in. He put the feeling out of his mind, straightened his shoulders, and tapped on the glass lightly.

"Can I come in?" Beau asked.

Bastien nodded. "Don't you think his color looks better?" he asked.

"It does," Beau said. "His cheeks are almost rosy."

Bastien smiled, leaned down, and kissed Bruce's forehead. Again Beau felt a pang of jealousy. What was going on with him? He loved Tollison deeply, and he was very happy. Bruce was happy with Bastien. Why these stupid feelings?

"It must be difficult," Bastien said, interrupting his thoughts.

"What?" Beau asked.

"Watching another man standing at Bruce's side, seemingly taking your place."

"Was it that obvious?" Beau asked.

"I would feel the same way if it were Tollison lying here and you were in my position."

"So I'm not losing my mind?"

"Absolutely not," Bastien said. "In fact, I would not consider you a good man if you weren't experiencing these feelings."

"That's a relief."

Bastien leaned over and kissed Bruce on the lips. "Why don't you spend a few minutes with him alone and I'll see you back in the waiting room."

"I don't want to impose or overstep any boundaries," Beau said.

"The only boundaries we have here are the ones set by you," Bastien replied. "I know you love Bruce and probably always will, and I feel the same about Tollison. But life had other things in store for us. Stay with him a few minutes, Beau. Make your peace. It has been long overdue for both of you."

Beau stepped up and hugged Bastien tightly. "Thank you."

Bastien broke the embrace, placed a kiss on Beau's cheek, turned, and was gone. Beau watched him walk away with new admiration.

Rolling a chair over to the side of Bruce's bed, Beau sat down, took Bruce's hand in his, and began to stroke Bruce's forearm. "Hey there," he said softly. "It's Beau."

Beau watched for any sign that Bruce was hearing him. A flutter of an eye. A squeeze of his hand. Anything. But nothing came. "Don't you think it's time you come back to us?" he asked. "If you can hear me, squeeze my hand."

He waited, but no squeeze came. "I guess you're not ready yet. Maybe you need more time to heal. Don't worry, we'll be here when you decide."

Beau cleared his throat. "While were here—you know, just the two of us—there's something I've been wanting to talk to you about. I really want you to know that… I know now I fucked up and neglected you. Don't get me wrong. I'm still pissed that you cheated on me, especially after the most recent developments, and I'm gonna kill that fucker. But at least I understand why you did what you did, and I take my share of the blame."

Again Beau stopped to look for any signs that Bruce was hearing him, but if he was, he wasn't letting on. "If you're hearing me and playing possum and I find out about it, I'm gonna kick your ass when you wake up."

Still nothing.

"Fine! Have it your way. Anyway I want you to know I still love you, and I forgive you and I hope you'll forgive me. I was just so crushed. Yeah. I know you're mocking me right now in that banged-up head of yours. 'How could anyone cheat on the almighty and powerful Montgomery Beaumont Bissonet?' And you're right to a certain extent. But not for the reasons you're thinking. My bravado has always been nothing more than something to hide my insecurities behind. I'm sure you knew that, so when you cheated on me, I just couldn't get past it. It fucking hurt, Bruce. I trusted you. It hurt like hell. I know I was childish, selfish, and immature, but I didn't know what else to do. I thought by hurting you as much as you'd hurt me, it might make me feel better. But in actuality it made me feel worse, and then the cycle began. I'm so sorry I treated you like shit for so long. And if you come back to us, I will spend my life trying to make it up to you."

Beau kissed Bruce's forehead and stood. "Well, that's all I have to say. I just wanted you to know. Rest well, and I'll see you during the next visiting hour."

When Beau turned to leave, he froze. Tollison was standing in the doorway with tears streaming down his face. Beau's first instinct was to apologize. How much had Tollison heard? And how did he feel about it?

"Tol," Beau said. "I hope—"

Tollison put a finger on Beau's lips. "Shh. You don't need to say a word. I'm sorry I interrupted, but you were taking so long I wanted to make sure you were all right. I tried to leave you alone, but I couldn't. That was exactly the right thing to say. If it's possible, I love you more now than I ever have."

Beau stepped into Tollison's open arms and felt safe and so loved. Tollison kissed him on the top of his head and Beau nuzzled against Tollison's chest, never wanting to move. He realized again how lucky he was to be loved by this man. And after the way he'd neglected Bruce, Beau made a promise to himself to never allow that to happen with Tollison.

"Beau?" a gravelly voice said.

Beau stepped back and looked at Bruce. His eyes were open, and he was staring at him and Tollison with a confused expression on his face.

"Oh God. Bruce! You're back."

"I'll get the nurse," Tollison said.

Beau ran over to Bruce's bed and took his hand. "How do you feel?"

"Groggy, and I have the worst headache."

Beau laughed. "I imagine so."

"What happened?"

"Don't you remember?" Beau asked.

Bruce looked like he was searching his memory, but his expression remained blank. "No. I don't."

Before Beau could continue, the nurse came in with Tollison on her heels. "I've called the doctor, and he's on his way. How do you feel, Mr. Jenkins?"

"Like I told Beau. Groggy, and I have a serious headache." The nurse looked at Beau and Tollison and chuckled.

"Why does everyone laugh when I say I have a headache?" Bruce asked.

"Because you were shot in the head, Bruce."

"Shot? Am I in a hospital?"

"Yes, and I don't want to push you too hard, but this is important."

"What's important?"

"Not now, Mr. Bissonet," the nurse objected.

"Just one question. Bruce, I need to know the name of the guy you had the affair with," Beau said.

"What affair? I would never cheat on you, Beau," Bruce exclaimed. "You know that."

Beau was silent, in shock. He glanced at Tollison, who had a serious expression on his face.

"And who's he? And why were you hugging him earlier?" Bruce demanded, staring at Tollison.

The doctor came in. "I'm gonna have to ask you gentlemen to give me some time to examine Mr. Jenkins. I'll come find you in the waiting room as soon as I'm done."

Hurrying Beau and Tollison out of Bruce's room and down the hall, the nurse said, "The doctor will talk to you shortly."

When they reached the waiting room, everyone was still there. "What took you so long?" Bastien asked. "Is everything all right?"

Beau looked at Tollison. "Bruce is awake."

Everyone smiled, and Auggie and Jenny high-fived.

"I must see him." Bastien pushed past Beau and Tollison.

Beau grabbed Bastien's arm. "The doctor is with him now. He said he would come out and talk to us as soon as he finishes with his examination."

"I see," Bastien said.

Beau gave Tollison a sideways glance.

"What?" Bastien asked, apparently picking up on the exchange.

"Bastien, Bruce is really confused. He doesn't remember anything about the shooting."

"It's gonna take some time to clear his head," Tollison added.

"What do you mean?" Bastien asked.

Beau hesitated.

"Tell him," Tollison said.

"Tell me what?" Bastien asked.

"Bruce thinks he and Beau are still a couple."

TWENTY

BEAU FELT horrible as he watched Bastien sitting in the corner of the waiting area, Iona rubbing his back and speaking to him softly. Bastien's elbows rested on his knees, his hands cupped his face, and he was staring blankly ahead with a forlorn expression on his face. He was evidently trying to wrap his head around everything they had just told him, but when Bastien and Iona abruptly jumped to their feet, Beau turned to see the doctor approaching. In an instant everyone was anxiously crowding around the poor man.

"Doctor?" Bastien asked. "How is he?"

"Physically?" the doctor said. "He's doing remarkably well. There seems to be no paralysis, speech, or vision issues. Everything seems to be fine in that department."

"Which leaves?" Bastien asked.

The doctor hesitated momentarily and then spoke quietly. "Mentally he seems to be very confused. He was so agitated we had to sedate him. He kept asking for Mr. Bissonet and rambling on about not cheating or having an affair or something along those lines."

"Doctor!" Beau said. "I think he's suffering from some type of short-term memory loss."

The doctor tilted his head and looked blankly at Beau. "When I examined him, he knew his name. He knew your name. He knew he was in a hospital, and he even knew he'd been shot in the line of duty."

"He wasn't shot in the line of duty," Beau said. "And he knew where he was and that he'd been shot because I told him just minutes before you came in."

"I see," Dr. Waguespack said.

"Doctor," Beau explained, "Bruce and I were together as a couple for many years, and four years ago he had a brief affair, which in turn destroyed our relationship. He is now in a relationship with Mr. Andros, but he seems to think he is still with me."

"I was unaware he'd been conscious that long and of your in-depth conversation with him," Dr. Waguespack said. "But I'm not surprised he's struggling a little. As I mentioned earlier, the hippocampus, which is the part of the brain that is associated with various memory functions, was grazed by the bullet. Additionally, his brain was shaken around quite a bit by the impact of the bullet as well as his head striking the concrete when he fell to the ground. To put it plainly, it may take a little time for the fog to clear. But in the meantime, I suggest we take it easy with him and ease him back into reality rather than force it on him if he's not ready to accept it yet."

"You mean lie to him?" Bastien asked.

"Not exactly," the doctor said. "When he wakes up again, we'll do a little experiment. I suggest Mr. Bissonet be there with him as a start. Then little by little, we bring his friends into his room. If he recognizes everyone and is still stable, we bring Mr. Andros in. Seeing Mr. Andros may or may not stimulate his memory, and he may recognize him without realizing who he is. Or… he may not recognize him at all. But once we see how he reacts, we'll be able to gauge how we proceed from there."

"What if he doesn't recognize me, Doctor?" Bastien asked.

"I would say not to force things on him too soon. He's just been conscious for under an hour. I suggest we hold off for a little while and, as I said earlier, ease him back into reality. The main thing right now is to keep him calm."

"How long will the sedative last?" Bastien asked.

"He should be out for at least four hours," Dr. Waguespack calculated. "Maybe more. I suggest you all go home and get a little rest."

"Doc," Beau said. "Bruce has a very high tolerance for sedatives and drugs in general. He always has. In fact, he normally takes double what is prescribed for him to get the minimal desired effect. I feel certain he'll be awake long before four hours."

"I'll notate that on his chart. Thank you."

"I'm not leaving," Bastien said. "You guys go ahead and I'll see you in a little while."

"It's your decision," the doctor replied. "Mr. Bissonet, if you wouldn't mind getting back in a couple of hours—as I mentioned I'd like you to be there when he wakes up."

"That'll be no problem. I'm staying too. I don't want him to be alone if he wakes up before I get back."

Beau looked at Tollison and prayed like hell Tollison understood why he had said what he'd just said. If Tollison didn't understand why Beau had to stay, or even worse objected to Beau staying, his face didn't betray him. He simply nodded.

"Thank you," Beau mouthed.

"Seriously, gentlemen. Even based on Mr. Bissonet's calculations, Mr. Jenkins is gonna be unconscious for at least two hours. Why don't you take a break? Go home and shower—"

"My mind's made up. I'm staying," Beau said.

"We're staying," Tollison added, resting his hand on Beau's shoulder.

"If they're staying, we are too," Auggie, Jenny, and Iona said simultaneously.

The doctor sighed. "Okay. It's your decision. But personally, I've been on call for thirty-two hours, so I'm gonna get a few hours' rest. I'm gonna stay in the hospital, and the nurses will call me if there is any change. In the meantime, let's all just give him a little time to recuperate and then see how it goes."

"Can Bastien and I stay with him?"

Bastien reached out and touched Beau on the arm. "No, Beau. You go. He's already seen you in an embrace with Tollison, and that upset him badly. If he wakes and sees you with me, someone else he doesn't recognize, it might just send him over the edge again."

"I'm sorry to say, but I agree with Mr. Andros," Dr. Waguespack said. "We want—no, we need him to stay as calm as possible."

"Then it's settled," Bastien said, wiping away a single tear before it slid down his face. "Go to him, Beau."

Beau looked at Tollison. "Will you be okay?"

"Sure. I'll stay here. We'll all be fine. Just let us know if anything changes."

"Thank you." Beau kissed Tollison on the cheek and whispered, "I love you," in Tollison's ear just before he pulled away.

"Me too," Tollison mouthed.

Dr. Waguespack led Beau back to the Neuro ICU. He stopped at the nurse's station to explain why Beau would be staying, and when he finally left, Beau was comfortably seated at Bruce's side, staring at him. Even with bandages wrapped around his head and a bruised cheek from where he'd hit the ground, Bruce was still an extremely handsome man. Beau hadn't allowed himself to think of Bruce in those terms, or even acknowledge such a thing, since the affair, but he saw it clearly now. He slipped his hand in Bruce's and held it tightly.

It was well after midnight, and Beau was starting to feel the familiar signs of fatigue setting in. With the adrenaline rush long ago over and nothing to distract him but the constant, rhythmic beeping of the monitoring equipment, Beau allowed himself to process the realization staring him in the face.

Bruce came close to dying tonight. And in reality he may never be the same again. And what if he doesn't remember Bastien or that I am with Tollison now? How will he handle that? Bruce will have to relive the entire breakup again. Can I do that to him? And what about Tollison? How will Tollison handle it if I have to pretend to be with Bruce for a little while?

Beau laid his forehead on top of his and Bruce's linked hands and allowed the tears to flow freely. Images of a time when he and Bruce were happy played through his mind over and over again. Playing Frisbee in Audubon Park on Sunday mornings and then standing in line at Port of Call on Esplanade Avenue for burgers afterward. Tubing down the Bogue Falaya River in the almost unbearable New Orleans summer heat with an ice chest of beer tied between them. Stealing kisses at the police station when they thought they were alone. Driving to the Gulf Coast and lying on the beach for the day playing footsie in the bright white sand. Running to the gym together and giggling like teenagers when the same old guy would fart when he exerted any energy at all.

And then his thoughts naturally drifted to Tollison. He loved Tollison with all his heart, and Tollison was his future now, but for the first time since his and Bruce's breakup, Beau allowed himself to really think about where they had gone wrong and how they'd let themselves get to this point. And damn if the finger didn't point right back at him.

If the truth be told, he'd neglected Bruce horribly. Emotionally and physically. Yeah, he'd acknowledged that already, with Tollison's help, but what he'd openly acknowledged was just the tip of the iceberg. In all fairness, Bruce was the man he'd lived with and slept with, but his career and his aspirations had become his real life partner. He'd told himself it was because he wanted a better life for him *and* Bruce, but in reality it was all his ego. He and Bruce were happy and had everything they needed. But Beau wanted the lead detective position, if simply to feed his ego.

With all this weighing heavily on his mind, Beau closed his eyes. He jumped when he heard the sound of a cell phone ringing. He felt for his phone but remembered he'd given it to Tollison earlier, and then he looked in the direction of the sound and saw a clear plastic bag holding Bruce's personal belongings. Then it hit him. *Bruce's phone. If he still has the Grindr app on his phone, he may still have the profile for the killer as well.*

He slowly released Bruce's hand and reached over for the bag, opened it, and retrieved Bruce's phone. He looked at the caller ID but didn't recognize the name, so he sent the call to voice mail. Quickly, he scrolled through the apps on the phone. *Yes!* He tapped the Grindr app and the application sprang to life. It was protected with a username and a password. *Damn!* He tried every username and password he and Bruce had used for joint accounts and the like, but nothing worked, so he ran the phone out to Auggie.

When the gang saw him, they all stood. Bastien was the first to reach him. "Is everything all right? Is he awake?"

Beau felt instantly guilty for raising their hopes, but he needed to get the phone to IT. "No. I'm sorry, nothing's changed. He's still sleeping, but I have Bruce's cell phone."

Everyone looked at Beau like he had three heads, and then Auggie's face lit up. "Is the app still on there?"

"Yep. But it's password protected."

"Fuck that shit," Auggie said. "I'll get someone in IT to break through it."

Beau handed Auggie the phone, but Auggie was already on his phone calling someone to meet him at the hospital.

Beau looked at Bastien. Jenny was on one side of him, and Iona was on the other. "I wish I had something more to tell you, but I'll come back as soon as I do."

Bastien nodded but didn't say anything.

Beau turned and headed back for the Neuro ICU, knowing Auggie had everything under control.

When Beau got back to Bruce's room, he sighed with relief. Bruce was still out like a light. He once again took Bruce's hand, laid his head down on top of their joined hands, and tried to clear his mind. Sometimes when he was struggling with a case and he shut his mind down, things naturally came to him. Like maybe a username or password he'd missed.

Minutes later Beau felt fingers running through his hair. He blinked his eyes and looked up to see Bruce staring back at him adoringly. "Hey, sleepyhead," he said.

"I wasn't sleeping," Beau said through a smile. "I was just resting my eyes."

Bruce smiled back at him and Beau's heart melted. "Then your eyes have been resting for the last thirty minutes. And making very strange noises, I might add."

Beau cleared his throat. "Enough about me. How are you feeling? Can I get you anything?"

"I have everything I need right here," Bruce said, squeezing Beau's hand, which was still linked with his. "You look exhausted, Beau. Why don't you go home and get some rest? I'll be fine."

"Not a chance," Beau said.

"What would I do without you?" Bruce asked, brushing Beau's face with the backs of his fingers.

Beau smiled weakly, certain Bruce had not regained his memory. *Shit! He still thinks we're together.* Beau hit the Call button.

"What's wrong," Bruce asked. "Am I dying?"

"No, asshole," Beau said. "I promised the doctor I would let him know when you were awake."

In literally seconds a nurse was at Bruce's bedside. "Wow. You do have a high tolerance for drugs," he said, smiling.

"Always have," Bruce grumbled.

Beau stepped back as the nurse checked Bruce's vital signs and noted them on the chart at the foot of the bed.

"Looking good," he said, winking at Beau. "Can I get you anything?"

"I'm really thirsty," Bruce said. "Maybe a bit of water."

The nurse poured a small amount of water into a cup, tore the wrapper off of a straw, and put it up to Bruce's lips. "Very slowly," he said. "And not too much."

Bruce sipped a little, and the nurse took the cup away. He looked at Bruce. "You can have more." And then he looked at Beau. "As long as he takes it easy. Can I get you anything else?"

"I think I'm okay," Bruce said.

"All righty, then. I'll let the doctor know you're awake. And by the way, you're doing great."

"Thanks," Bruce said.

"Just ring if you need anything." The nurse trotted back out to his station.

"Do you remember anything at all about the shooting?" Beau asked.

Bruce seemed to be searching his brain for the answer. "Not really," he finally said. "Tell me?"

"We were at a Mardi Gras parade…." Beau filled Bruce in on the Mardi Gras Murderer, leaving out any reference to their relationship or his affair, and explained that Bruce had been one of his victims.

"Why me?" Bruce asked.

Before Beau could answer, Dr. Waguespack stood in the doorway. "I see our patient is awake." He picked up Bruce's chart and studied it for a few seconds. "You're a very lucky man, Mr. Jenkins. And doing remarkably well for someone who was shot in the head less than six hours ago."

Bruce looked at Beau and squeezed his hand. "You don't have to tell me how lucky I am," he said.

Beau and the doctor exchanged a quick glance. The doctor then stepped to the foot of the bed and peeled back the sheets. He ran the bottom of his pen along the sole of Bruce's foot, and Bruce immediately reacted by pulling his foot back. He did the same to the other.

The doctor smiled. "That's good. At least we know your legs work. Can you wiggle your toes for me?"

Bruce wiggled his toes.

The doctor replaced the sheet again. He pressed a button, and the head of the bed started rising until Bruce was almost sitting up. "Any dizziness?"

"No," Bruce said.

The doctor held Bruce's eyes open one at a time and quickly flashed a light into each of them. "Any issues with your vision or speech?"

"Not so far."

"Good," the doctor said.

Beau listened as the doctor went on to explain to Bruce everything he'd explained to the rest of them. "So you see, it isn't unusual for your memory to be affected. It's very common, so don't be worried if people's faces don't register right away or something feels familiar but you can't quite identify it."

Bruce nodded.

"Now we'll need to do a complete examination, but before we get into that, I know there are some folks in the waiting room that really want to see you. You feel up to it?"

Bruce looked at Beau. "Auggie?"

"And Jenny and I—" Beau stopped. *No, Beau! Not Iona.*

"Sure. I'd love to see them."

"Why don't I walk with you to the waiting room so I can let you back inside the unit without going through the normal security procedures?" the doctor said.

Beau nodded. "Thanks. That'll be great." He turned to Bruce. "You okay for a few minutes?"

"Stop worrying, Beau. I'm fine. I promise. Now go and get Auggie and Jenny."

Beau waited until he and the doctor were far enough away from Bruce before he quietly spoke. "Doc, I'm worried. He doesn't remember anything about the shooting or our current lives. It seems as if the last five years were erased from his memory."

"I know it's frustrating," the doctor said, "but let's ease him back into reality a little at a time. We can start now with the friends he knows and see how that goes. Then tomorrow when he wakes, we can reevaluate. If by then he still doesn't remember, we will have to bring him up to date."

"Jesus!" Beau said. "He's gonna have to relive the affair? That's gonna kill him. He's blamed himself for years for screwing up our relationship. Not to mention reliving the breakup. And oh my God! Tollison and Bastien. Doc, this is not good."

They stepped through the waiting room doors still deep in conversation.

"He needs to know the truth in order to deal with it," Dr. Waguespack said. "And sometimes learning the truth jogs the memory back into reality and gets the entire process moving forward."

"Seriously? Is there any other way?" Beau asked.

"Not unless you're willing to go back five years and start from there again."

"That's impossible. Isn't it?" Beau asked and then answered his own question. "Of course it is. We both have different lives now. I'm in love with someone else. We have a business together, and Bruce is about to move to Geneva with Bastien. We can't go back."

"I wasn't serious," the doctor said. "I was trying to make a point."

"Oh. Sorry!"

Dr. Waguespack looked at Beau with a concerned expression on his face. "This is none of my business," he said, "and you haven't asked for my opinion, but the fact that you even considered it for a few seconds tells me you may have some unresolved issues when it comes to Mr. Jenkins."

"We were together a long time," Beau said defensively. "And I really loved him. But… that's over now."

"I'm sorry. I shouldn't have interfered."

"No. It's okay," Beau said. "Besides, there's probably some truth to what you're saying."

Beau and the doctor walked toward the area of the waiting room where the others had been hanging out. Auggie, Jenny, Iona, and Bastien all jumped to their feet, but there was no Tollison.

"Where's Tollison?" Beau asked, looking around the room.

"Here I am," Tollison said, walking from the direction of the double doors Beau and the doctor had just exited. He looked distressed.

"You okay, baby?" Beau asked.

"I'm fine. Any news?"

"He's awake," Beau said.

Bastien looked hopeful.

"And?" Auggie asked.

"He wants to see you and Jenny."

Bastien's expression changed. He dropped his head and stepped away from the group. Iona stayed with him.

"Doc?" Beau asked. "Would you mind filling them in on Bruce's condition?"

"Of course not."

Beau joined Bastien and placed his hand on Bastien's shoulder. "It's going to be okay, Bastien. The doctor just thinks he needs a little time to clear his head. He doesn't remember anything about the shooting—"

"Or me," Bastien interrupted.

Beau dropped his head. "I'm sorry, Bastien."

Bastien sat down and rested his face in his hands.

"But," Beau said sitting down next to him, "the doctor says if he doesn't remember by tomorrow morning, we'll need to start easing him back into reality."

Bastien looked at Beau. "Really?"

Beau nodded.

"At least then he'll know who I am," Bastien said. "But the real question is, will he still want me?"

"Bastien," Beau said, putting his hand on Bastien's leg, "I'm sure his memory will come back. In the meantime, maybe you focus on making him fall in love with you all over again."

"He won't fall in love with me if he thinks he's still in love with you."

"I promise you he'll know the truth," Beau said. "This can't go on indefinitely. It's not fair to him or to Tollison."

Bastien nodded but didn't reply.

Beau stood. "Come on. If you can't speak to him, at the very least you, Tollison, and Iona can see him."

TWENTY-ONE

BASTIEN, IONA, and Tollison stayed out of Bruce's line of sight, but they had a clear view of him as Beau led Auggie and Jenny into his room.

"He looks good," Bastien said. "More alert than I expected. Don't you think so, Eddy?"

Tollison nodded but didn't comment.

"Much better than I anticipated," Iona added.

Based on what they were seeing, Bruce appeared to recognize both Auggie and Jenny, which stung a little, but watching them standing around Bruce's bed, comforting him, talking to him quietly, and conversing with the doctor, Bastien wished like hell it could be him there instead of Beau.

He couldn't hold it against Beau, of course. It wasn't his fault, but it still hurt like hell. Bastien glanced at Tollison, who was standing next to him, and Tollison was fixated on Beau, who was holding Bruce's hand. He was sure Tollison must be feeling it too. How could he not be? His partner was pretending to be in love with someone else. And with the way Bruce was staring lovingly into Beau's eyes, that had to be hard to watch.

Iona eyed Tollison intently, rubbing his arm. "He's doing this for Bruce," she said. "He loves you, Tollison. You know that."

Tollison didn't respond. He just stared at Beau and Bruce.

Bastien knew how he felt. Less than twelve hours ago, Bruce had been looking at him the way he was now looking at Beau.

When the short visit was over, Auggie, Jenny, and the doctor came out of the cubicle and left Beau with Bruce. Jenny and Auggie approached Bastien. "He knows who we are," Auggie said. "But that's probably because we knew him the longest. Back when he was with Beau. Am I right, Doc?"

"Probably," Dr. Waguespack said. "But I have an idea if you're up to it." His gaze encompassed Bastien and Tollison.

"Anything if it will help," Bastien said.

Tollison nodded.

"One of you is a detective or investigator or something, right?"

"I was an insurance investigator," Tollison said. "Now Beau and I are private investigators, and we own a business together."

The doctor nodded. "Close enough. I want you both to pretend to be with the NOPD to ask a couple of questions about the shooting. I want to see if he reacts to either of you."

"I can do that," Tollison said. "Just follow my lead, Bastien."

Bastien was skeptical. He didn't want to lie to Bruce, but he went along with it. Anything if it would help Bruce remember him.

The doctor went back into the room, and Bastien heard him explain there were a couple of detectives here to question him about the shooting if he was up to it. Beau looked up in surprise until he saw Bastien and Tollison, and then he seemed to get it.

"Are you?" Beau asked.

"Sure," Bruce said. "But as I told *you*, I don't remember a thing."

"Let's just give them a minute."

"Detectives?" Dr. Waguespack called out.

Bastien and Tollison stepped into the doorway. Bastien stuck his hands in his pockets to hide the fact they were trembling terribly.

Tollison stepped up to the bed, and Bruce looked at him for a long moment. "You're the guy who was hugging Beau when I regained consciousness."

"He is," Beau said. "We work together, and he was lending a little support."

"I'm Tollison Cruz."

"Have we met?" Bruce asked.

"We have," Tollison said. "We worked together on the Royal Street heist."

"NOPD?" Bruce asked.

"Not exactly. I'm a private investigator. Detective Hebert brought us in to help solve the Mardi Gras Murderer case."

Brilliant, Bastien thought. *He's doing this without lying.*

Tollison gestured to Bastien. "And this is Sebastien Andros. He's assisting me."

Bruce cocked his head to one side and studied Bastien intently. "You look familiar. I feel like we've met somewhere before."

Bastien stepped up closer to Bruce's bed. He didn't want to lie, so he had to think quickly. He looked at Beau, who seemed to be waiting to see how this was going to go but offered no assistance.

"As a matter of fact," Bastien said, "we met on a case several months ago." Bastien sighed internally. *There. That is the truth.*

"I thought you looked familiar," Bruce said, still eyeing Bastien closely and seeming a little confused. "I'm sorry. My memory is a little jarred. But God, you smell great. What is that cologne?"

"I believe it is Versace," Bastien said.

"Beau, we need to get some of that."

"Mr. Jenkins?" Tollison interrupted.

"Call me Bruce, please."

"Okay, Bruce. Do you remember anything at all about the shooting?"

Bruce looked at Beau and smiled warmly. "Only what Beau has told me," he said. "About the serial killer and how we were at a Mardi Gras parade and I was one of the victims. That part I don't fully understand. I mean… why me?"

"Why anyone?" Tollison asked.

"True," Beau added.

Tollison continued, "Do you remember anything about being at the parade?"

"Vaguely," Bruce said. "Since Beau explained to me everything that happened, little bits and pieces, almost like short snippets, pop into my head, and then they are gone as fast as they came. But so far it's nothing I can really identify or hold on to."

"Thank you. We've taken enough of your time," Tollison said. "We'll allow you to get some rest now. But if you remember anything at all, no matter how insignificant it may seem, please let us know. Mr. Bissonet knows how to get in touch with us."

"I will. And thank you," Bruce said. "Sorry I wasn't more helpful."

Tollison nodded and turned to leave. Bastien noticed Bruce was still eyeing him oddly as if trying to figure something out internally, but if he was remembering anything at all, he didn't voice it.

Bastien should have turned to follow Tollison, but he couldn't get his feet to move. He meant to say thank you and go, but instead he placed his hand on Bruce's arm and squeezed. Bruce looked at Bastien's hand

and then followed Bastien's arm up to his face. They held each other's gaze until the sound of the doctor's voice broke their connection.

"Okay, gentlemen. I need to start my examination, and then our patient needs to have another CT scan to check the status of the swelling. And then he needs to get some rest. Mr. Bissonet, you can see him again in the morning." The doctor looked at his watch and smiled. "Or should I say, later today."

Bastien turned and left the room abruptly. His heart was so full, he feared if he had stayed any longer he would have leaned in and kissed Bruce on the lips. When he joined the others, Tollison was already explaining what had happened.

"I think that was a good sign," Jenny said, taking his hand. "He recognized you. Maybe not like you would have hoped, but he did recognize you. That's a start."

"I guess you're right," Bastien agreed. "It's better than nothing."

Moments later Beau and the doctor came out of Bruce's room.

"I think that went pretty well," Dr. Waguespack said. "Give him time to process everything that just happened, and I feel certain he will be better after his brain gets some long, uninterrupted rest. As soon as I finish my examination and he returns from the CT scan, I'll order a sedative, and he'll get some much-deserved sleep. And don't say it, Mr. Bissonet. I'll double the dosage."

"Good man," Beau said.

"I'll see him again this afternoon, but if he continues to improve, we can get him in a real room by the end of the day. Now you folks go home. I'll see you later today."

IONA TOOK Bastien back to his hotel, and Auggie and Jenny took Beau and Tollison home, all of them agreeing to meet back at the hospital later that morning. Beau linked his fingers through Tollison's, but he noticed Tollison had barely said two words since they'd been in the car. Beau squeezed, and Tollison offered him a weak smile and returned the gesture.

When Auggie pulled into their driveway, they slid out of the vehicle, and Beau stopped and tapped on Auggie's window. "Call me the minute IT goes through Bruce's phone. They've got to find something."

"Will do," Auggie said.

Beau and Tollison waved as Auggie and Jenny pulled out of the driveway and drove off.

"Those two are good people," Beau said as he slipped his key in the lock and opened the door.

Tollison nodded, but he didn't respond. He simply kicked off his shoes at the door and started up the stairs. Beau grabbed him by the hand and pulled him back down. When they were face-to-face, Beau kissed him and wrapped his arms around Tollison. "Please come sit with me for a few minutes before we go up."

Tollison nodded and Beau led him to the den. He pushed Tollison onto the couch and lifted his feet onto the leather ottoman. Beau then sat next to him, putting his feet up on the ottoman as well. He kicked off his shoes, and each one made a thumping noise that echoed through the quiet house as it hit the hardwood floors.

Beau took Tollison's hand in his. "Talk to me, Tol."

"About what?"

"About what's bothering you."

Tollison looked at him like he had two heads. "Your ex and one of my best friends was shot last night."

"I know you," Beau said. "And it's more than that."

"I need a drink," Tollison said. "Want a beer?"

"Sure."

When Tollison returned with two longnecks, he twisted the caps off and handed one to Beau. He sat next to Beau again and took a long pull off of his beer, swallowed, and sighed.

"Are you gonna talk to me now?" Beau asked.

"I'm not sure what I can say that won't make me sound like an insecure, self-absorbed asshole."

Beau took his hand. "I know you, Tol," he repeated, "and you are neither of those things."

"So why do I feel like such a dick?"

"I don't know. But I hope you'll tell me."

Tollison sighed. "When I came to find you in the Neuro ICU and you were talking to Bruce, I was so proud of the things you said to him. And then as I sat for hours in the waiting room, I started thinking."

He gazed at Beau. "You remember a long time ago when we had that conversation about when relationships end and one or both parties are so angry they can't see straight, and they seem to hate the other until... the anger subsides, and sometimes they realize what made them fall in love originally was still there?"

Beau had an idea he knew where this was going. "I remember," he said.

Tollison took another sip of his beer and swallowed. "Well. I think you finally let go of the anger when it comes to Bruce. Not just trying to coexist with it, but really letting it go. I heard it in your voice when you were talking to him. You'd really forgiven him and taken responsibility for your part in the failure. I was happy for you. I really was. And then I started wondering if by doing that, you realized you still loved him."

"Tol—" Beau interrupted.

"No. Please let me finish."

Beau nodded.

"Then Bruce woke up, and we all found out he'd lost his memory. You stepped up to the plate and became his lover again. I saw the way Bruce looked at you, and I'm an asshole, I know it, but it hurt. And to see you holding on to his hand so tightly hurt too."

"I'm sorry," Beau said. "I did—"

"And then," Tollison interrupted, "I was bending over drinking from the water fountain when you walked through the doors with the doctor, and I overheard your conversation. And I think the doctor's right. You do have some unresolved feelings where Bruce is concerned."

Beau jumped to his feet and started pacing. "Correction!" he said. "I did have some unresolved feelings. But now they are resolved. I took ownership for my part in the breakup. I stopped blaming him. I'm over it, Tollison, I swear."

Tollison looked up with tears streaming down his face. Beau sat back down next to him and took his hand again. "I will always love Bruce. But… I'm in love with you."

"Beau," Tollison whispered, "I heard the doctor say there were no other options unless you wanted to go back five years and pick up where you left off. And Beau…. You hesitated. You thought about it. Maybe just for a second, but you thought about it. I saw the look on your face."

"Shit," Beau cursed under his breath and turned away.

He didn't know how to respond. He *had* hesitated for a brief moment and even thought about it for a longer second, but Tollison was what he wanted. He knew that.

"Tol. You're right. I did hesitate for a second. But only for a second. Haven't you ever thought if you could go back and get a do-over with Bastien, you would do things differently?"

"I guess," Tollison said. "But not since I met you."

"But for me it wasn't until I met you that I even considered I was partly to blame for my relationship with Bruce falling apart. Don't you see that? I thought I was the perfect husband, so why would I need a do-over?"

Tollison didn't answer, but Beau could see he was thinking about what he was saying. So he kept going. "Until you, in my eyes, there was nothing for me to go back and do over. It was all Bruce's fault. But once I accepted I had a part to play in the breakup, I realized I could have done things differently. That's all it was, I swear to you."

Tollison looked away and wiped his tears.

"Tol. Look at me."

Tollison turned back to face him, and Beau put his finger under Tollison's chin. "I love you. And you are where I want to be. And Bruce loves Bastien whether he remembers it right now or not. But I know he will."

Tollison smiled weakly. "I told you I was a self-absorbed, insecure asshole." He took another sip of his beer.

"Not at all," Beau said. "Can you imagine what shape I would be in if the roles were reversed and it was Bastien lying in that hospital bed with you pretending to still be in love with him?"

Tollison coughed and beer came flying out of his nose. He wiped his face on his sleeve. "Good point," he said when he could finally talk.

"So we're good."

Tollison nodded. "We're good. And I'm very proud of the way you've handled this entire thing."

"A part of me will always love Bruce, just like a part of you will always love Bastien."

"Yeah, well," Tollison said, "I'm not quite to the point with Bastien you are with Bruce, but I'm taking my own advice and trying to get there."

"Good man," Beau said. "Now how about some sleep?"

TWENTY-TWO

As WAS normally the case with Bruce, his high tolerance for drugs had him awake three hours before his six-hour sedative was supposed to wear off. He felt tired and had a dull nagging headache, but other than that, he felt remarkably well. He looked through the glass walls of his room, and nurses were milling about. He wasn't in need of anything, so he let them tend to others who needed them more than he did.

For a while he lay there listening to the rhythmic sound of the monitors beeping and the occasional pumping up and releasing of air through the automatic blood-pressure cuff wrapped around his arm. But eventually it all became mundane to him, and he looked for something else to hold his attention.

With nothing else to stimulate him, he closed his eyes and let his mind wander. Since he'd regained consciousness, he been getting these little tidbits, flashbacks so to speak, of memories he guessed were just before and during the shooting. A simple image of a float at the parade. Beau pissed at them because they got there late. And then lying in the back of some type of vehicle, probably the ambulance, being driven very fast. People yelling at him to stay with them. But wait. Beau pissed because they got there late. Who was the *they*?

After thirty minutes of searching, nothing earth-shattering came forward, so the detective in Bruce focused on what Beau had told him about the Mardi Gras Murderer. Beau had said it was a guy. And he was killing off people in New Orleans he'd dated briefly or had affairs with. So Bruce wondered how he fit into the equation. But then he remembered Beau asking him the name of the guy he'd had the affair with. *Or did I dream that?* Why would Beau ask him such a question? Unless….

Bruce searched his memory for answers, but each thought only provoked more questions. The faces of the two investigators who had questioned him about the shooting popped into his mind. They both seemed familiar, but the one with the accent seemed very familiar. What was his name? Andros, maybe? He did say they had met on a case, but it felt like more than that to him. Bruce remembered the man's cologne. That smell was tugging at his senses somehow. It was like he and the man had some type of connection. But what?

Bruce searched his memory and then gasped when the image of Andros, smiling up at him tenderly, flashed before his eyes. Andros was lying under him, and Bruce was moving in and out of him. *How could this be?*

Suddenly, images of Beau's face flashed before his eyes. But it wasn't the tender and caring Beau who had held his hand just hours ago. In his mind's eye, he saw an angry Beau. Beau yelling at him. Humiliating him. Calling him names. Treating him poorly. Suddenly his heart hurt, and he had no idea why. Something was simmering just below the surface, but for the life of him he couldn't figure out what it was.

And then another image of Andros popped into his mind. But this time he and Andros were in a shower, and Andros was taking him from behind. And the strange thing was, he was enjoying it. He wanted Andros inside of him. It was almost as if he was in love with.... Bruce shook his head to try and jar the memories loose, but the movement only made his headache worse. Had he had an affair with Andros? And even worse, was he in love with him? But he would remember that. Wouldn't he? The doctor's earlier words rang through his head. "So you see, it isn't unusual for your memory to be affected. It's very common, so don't be worried if people's faces don't register right away or something feels familiar but you can't quite identify it."

"Oh shit," Bruce said to himself. Based on what Beau had told him, if he'd had an affair with Andros, then Andros must be the killer. *Am I in love with a killer? Jesus! I've got to talk to Beau.*

Bruce pressed the button and called the nurse.

IN UNDER an hour, Beau was standing at Bruce's bedside. And oddly, Investigator Cruz was with him, but he'd stayed outside the room.

"Are you okay?" Beau asked. "Are you in pain?"

"No," Bruce said. "Beau, I'm just so.… I'm so sorry."

Beau pulled the chair closer to the bed and took a seat. "Sorry for what?"

"For cheating on you."

Oddly, Beau smiled. "You remember?"

"Bit and pieces are coming back to me. But why in the hell are you smiling?"

"Jesus, Bruce. When you woke up, you were so disoriented you thought we were still together. The doctor wanted to give you time to get things straight in your head, so I went along with it. Tollison! Come in here. Bruce has his memory back."

Bruce was confused. He was trying to keep track of all Beau was saying, but he was having a tough time.

Then Investigator Cruz appeared in the doorway, walked into the room, and laid a hand on Bruce's leg. "Welcome back, stranger."

Now Bruce was really confused. "Wait!" he said, raising his voice. "You mean you and I are no longer together?"

Bruce watched the blood drain from Beau's face until he became ghostly white. "Uh… I thought you said you remembered."

"I vaguely remember you asking me about an affair, and then images started popping in my head of me and Andros doing… well, stuff."

"So you remember Bastien?" Cruz asked.

"No. Andros," Bruce said.

"*Sebastien* Andros," Cruz repeated.

"Beau, he's the Mardi Gras Murderer," Bruce said. "Andros is your killer."

"That's ridiculous," Cruz said.

"No. It's true," Bruce insisted. "Beau said the killer was targeting guys he slept with or had an affair with. I think I had an affair with him."

"No. Buddy, no," Beau said. "You've got it all wrong."

"I didn't have an affair with him?" Bruce asked.

"Oh God," Beau said, looking at Cruz. "Where do I start?"

"The beginning," Cruz replied, patting Bruce's leg. "I'll give you guys some time."

Bruce watched Investigator Cruz leave the room, then looked at Beau. "I'm so confused. Are we or are we not a couple?"

Beau sighed. "We were, but not anymore."

Bruce felt his heart drop to his stomach. He was shot, and he survived only to have his world come crashing down around him. He looked away to hide the tears now streaming down his face. "Why?" he whispered.

"Because I got caught up in my career and neglected you terribly."

Bruce didn't respond, and Beau continued, "And you turned elsewhere."

"To Sebastien Andros?"

"No—well, yes," Beau said.

"Which is it?" Bruce asked.

"You did not have the affair with Bastien. You met Bastien after we were no longer a couple. You're in a relationship with him now, and the two of you are about to move to Geneva."

"Switzerland?" Bruce asked, surprised.

"Yep."

"Then who did I have the affair with?"

"That's what I need to know. The guy you had the affair with is the Mardi Gras Murderer. I'm sure if it."

"And who is Investigator Cruz?"

"Tollison?" Beau asked. "He's my partner now."

"Oh God," Bruce said, his head now whirling with images of him and Beau when they were together and then when they were fighting. Him and Sebastien together. Everything all jumbled up.

"I know this is a lot to take in," Beau whispered. "But if you'll let me explain it all from the beginning, I'm sure you'll be happy with the ending. Trust me when I say you're really happy with Bastien. And I'm happy with Tollison. We're all happy. I promise you."

"It sure doesn't feel like that right now," Bruce said, looking away again. "But tell me everything. From the beginning."

Bruce laid his head back, closed his eyes, and listened intently as Beau retold the story of their life together. Bruce kept interrupting when Beau described parts with which he was familiar, and then Beau would skip ahead.

It seemed Bruce was pretty much up to speed until Beau's big promotion to lead detective with the NOPD. And as Beau explained, that's where things started to go wrong. Listening intently quickly became listening in disbelief as Beau explained how his new job became overwhelming and almost more than Beau could take. And how he just sank deeper and deeper into the proverbial black hole.

All through the story, Bruce could tell Beau was making sure to reassure him that Bruce had done everything in his power to try and hold them together. At least that was something. But Beau admitted the more he struggled to keep his head above water, the more Bruce started to feel like a distraction. Something taking him away from his responsibilities.

When Bruce had eventually turned to someone else for comfort and Beau had found out, he'd been livid. Especially since he had just engineered a promotion for Bruce so they could spend more time together.

Beau had put all the blame on Bruce for their breakup, for going outside of their relationship. He had crucified Bruce at every turn, which explained the images he'd seen in his head of Beau yelling at him and belittling him.

With that part over, Beau changed direction and told him about Tollison and how Tollison had helped him see Bruce wasn't the only one to blame.

"Believe it or not," Beau said. "You and Tollison have become quite good friends."

And then he moved on to Bastien, their rescue trip to Zurich, Bastien joining him in New Orleans, and Bruce's decision to quit the force and go to Switzerland with Bastien.

Beau sighed when he finally finished, and Bruce was almost speechless. After gathering his thoughts and trying to sort everything out in his head, he looked at Beau. "And you were pretending to still love me until I remembered, or at least until you were forced to tell me the truth?"

"I wasn't pretending to love you," Beau said with a weak smile. "I will always love you. As I know you will always love me. We are just *in love* with other people now."

"How can I have forgotten the last five years of my life?"

"You were shot in the head. Remember?" Beau said. "Speaking of. Can you try to recall the name of the guy you had the affair with? You are my last hope."

Bruce searched his brain but came up empty. "I can't remember."

"It's okay," Beau said. "Just concentrate on getting better."

"I'm sure it will come back to me with the rest of the train wreck I've made of our lives."

"Stop it!" Beau said. "We both made mistakes. We are both to blame. And you have Bastien now. He loves you so much, Bruce. And he's a good man."

"I want to remember, Beau. I do," Bruce said. "I remember a few things regarding Bastien, but not everything."

"You will," Beau promised. "You will."

"Do you mind if I have some time alone?" Bruce asked. "I just need to sort through all of this."

"Not at all. Tollison and I will be in the waiting room if you need us."

"Thank you, Beau. For everything. And thank Tollison as well. I'm sure it couldn't have been easy for him to watch you pretend to still be in love with me."

"He's a good guy, Bruce. And a strong one," Beau said. "He handled it just fine."

Beau stood just as the doctor was coming in the room. "How is our patient today?" Dr. Waguespack asked.

Before Bruce could answer, Beau spoke. "The little shit tricked me into telling him everything."

The doctor looked at Bruce and raised an eyebrow.

"To be perfectly truthful," Bruce said, "I remembered some things, and Beau thought I remembered everything, and typical Beau, he went spouting off at the mouth and left me with more questions than revelations."

"Hey!" Beau said. "That's not very nice. True," he acquiesced, "but not very nice."

"So how do you feel about all of this?" the doctor asked.

"A little relieved," Bruce admitted. "And a little crazy."

The doctor laughed. "I can imagine."

Bruce continued, "I've been having some flashbacks that didn't make much sense, and trying to figure them out made me jump to some incorrect conclusions. On the flip side of the coin, it's also very overwhelming and confusing that so much could have happened that I can't remember."

"Mr. Jenkins. Please, let me assure you everything you're experiencing is completely normal. It's a very good sign that you've already started regaining some of your memory, and I feel certain it won't be long before the rest of it comes back to you."

"I sure hope so," Bruce said.

"But also keep in mind that can be a little daunting as well," the doctor said. "So just take it easy."

Dr. Waguespack removed the chart from the end of the bed and started reviewing it. "It looks like the most recent CT scan and MRI shows the anti-inflammatory drugs are doing their job."

"That means no more swelling?" Beau asked.

"That's right, and the blood levels are virtually undetectable in the cerebrospinal fluid, which means the bleeding has slowed down significantly or even stopped. I think you're doing exceptionally well, Mr. Jenkins."

Bruce tried to smile, but the reality of he and Beau no longer being together was a hard pill to swallow. Not to mention the fact that, according to Beau, Bruce was in love with another man. And what about Beau and Tollison? God! It was all so overwhelming.

"Mr. Jenkins?"

"Sorry, I drifted away there for a second."

"It's okay. I know this is a lot to process. I'm gonna order another sedative so you can get some more rest. When you wake up in a few hours, I see no reason why we can't get you moved to a regular room."

"Thanks, Doc," Beau said.

Bruce laid his head back and closed his eyes.

DR. WAGUESPACK gestured with his head for Beau to follow him from Bruce's room. When they were safely out of earshot, the doctor whispered, "Now how did all this come about?"

Beau explained what had transpired between them when he and Tollison arrived, how Beau had sort of spilled the beans without really meaning to. "I'm sorry, but when he said he remembered the affair, I thought maybe he remembered the guy's name as well."

"But it was Mr. Andros he was remembering."

"Exactly," Beau said. "Did I set back his progress in any way, Doc?"

"Not really," Dr. Waguespack said. "He needed to know the truth, and we had discussed telling him today, but I was hoping some of it would come back on its own."

"Which it did," Beau said.

The doctor nodded. "Just give him some time. He's doing very well considering everything he's been through. In fact, I could actually move him now, but I want him to get a little more downtime to see if it helps him sort through all this and quite possibly stimulates more of his memory."

"I get it," Beau said. "We'll be in the waiting room. Please come get us if anything changes."

"I will."

TWENTY-THREE

BRUCE WANTED very badly to break free of the grip of the sedative, but its hold was too strong. He wanted to sit up and open his eyes—anything to stop the vivid dreams and nightmares plaguing him. But the harder he fought, the harder the damn drugs battled to pull him back under.

Bruce sensed someone else's presence very nearby, and there was a familiar scent surrounding him, but he couldn't quite put all the pieces together. It was odd sensing things but not truly recognizing them. But just knowing he wasn't alone helped a little.

Since the nurse had given him the sedative, he'd had so many images flashing through his mind, he was having trouble keeping track of what was real and what was not. Hell. He wasn't even sure he could tell the difference between the two at this point.

In one image he saw himself and Beau in their bed, watching late-night television hand in hand, and in the next he was crying, alone in that very same room packing suitcases and cardboard boxes. Just as soon as one image came and went, a new one replaced it. Next he saw himself untying Bastien's restraints in some hotel room. And then he and Bastien were making love again, like in the first dream. Bastien smiled up at him and called him some funny name. Marmaduke? Pucie? Something like that. But before he could figure it out, another vision of him, Beau, and Tollison in Beau's office at the NOPD invaded his mind. He and Beau were fighting, and Tollison was trying to calm them down. Bruce suddenly remembered how difficult it had been to work with Beau and Tollison, knowing they were sleeping together and getting closer.

Then in an instant they were all on an airplane. Bruce was watching the little plane move over the ocean, heading for Europe, on the television screen in the seatback in front of him. The images were all so vivid. Not like dreams, but like reality repeating itself.

And then just as quickly as that image came, it was gone and replaced with another. This time it was an image of him having sex with someone in a hotel room. The guy's face was not clear, but Bruce didn't feel any connection to the stranger. It was just sex. Pure and simple. The guy was bent over a chair, and Bruce—still dressed, pants puddling around his ankles, and still wearing his shoulder holster—was fucking him. The guy was begging him to fuck him harder and harder, and Bruce gave him what he asked for, taking the guy almost brutally.

When the sex was over, Bruce felt overwhelmingly guilty and instantly knew it was a mistake. He ordered the guy out and even threatened to arrest him if he ever breathed a word of this. The guy quietly got dressed and walked to the door. He smirked and said, "That's it? Just like that? Use me and send me away. Well, you take care. And cop or no cop, if I were you, I'd watch my back." Then he was gone.

Various images and flashbacks continued to torment Bruce for what seemed like forever. Some seemed as if they had just happened, while others felt like a piece of fiction he'd just read. He was so confused he wanted to scream. He wanted the flashbacks—or images, or whatever the hell they were—to stop, but he was powerless against the effects of the drugs or his own brain, which seemed to be turning on him.

When he finally woke again, he was exhausted, sweating profusely, and very disoriented. He blinked into the dimly lit room, and slowly it all came back to him. He'd been shot, and he was in a hospital. *Get it together, Bruce, or people are gonna think you're batshit crazy!*

He was alive. His brain was a jumbled mess, sure. But he was trying to come to terms with that. He slowly opened his eyes and turned to see Bastien sitting next to his bed, holding his hand. Bastien tilted his head and smiled at him, and his smile was so warm it melted Bruce's heart. The smell of Bastien's cologne filled his senses. If he was truly in love with this man, as Beau had assured him he was, he certainly knew why. Bastien had a gentle way about him, not to mention he was handsome as hell.

Bastien pulled a white linen handkerchief from his coat pocket and patted Bruce's brow, nose, face, and neck. "How are you feeling, ma puce?"

"Disoriented and tired, but otherwise okay," Bruce said. "Thirsty."

Bastien put a straw to Bruce's lips, and the cool water tasted like fine wine. He drank almost the entire cup, and then Bastien put it back on the tray.

"Just rest, and everything will be okay."

"Ma puce?" Bruce repeated, realizing what Bastien had called him. "That's what you called me in my dreams."

"It's my pet name for you—wait, were you dreaming of me?" Bastien asked with a surprised tone in his voice.

"Yes," Bruce whispered. "I dreamed I was untying you in some hotel room."

"That was no dream," Bastien said. "That actually happened in Zurich."

"And then we made love?" Bruce asked.

Bastien's expression was one of pure, undeniable lust. His blue eyes turned dark and heavy and his smile seductive. Bruce realized he could get lost in those eyes very easily.

"Eventually," Bastien said finally. "And yes, if you're wondering, it was wonderful."

"You are right. I was wondering," Bruce replied. "Beau tells me we're in love."

"We are. And as soon as you're ready, if you still want to, you're coming to Geneva with me, and we're gonna start a new life together."

"He told me that too," Bruce admitted. "I may need a little longer to process that one."

"You take all the time you need," Bastien said. "You need to get well, and besides, I can work from here and stay as long as we need to."

Bastien's eyes were warm, and his voice was soothing and kind. When he looked into Bruce's eyes, Bruce felt like they were the only two people on earth.

"Rest now, ma puce." Bastien glanced at his watch. "They will be here to move you to a room very soon."

"I don't want to rest," Bruce said. "I want to get to know the man I'm supposedly in love with. I want my life back."

"All in good time, ma puce."

"Aren't you worried I won't get my memory back?" Bruce asked.

"Not in the least," Bastien said. "If you do not remember what we shared, we will start over. You fell in love with me once. I'm confident I can make you do it again."

Bruce smiled. "I do love a confident man," he said.

"I have gotten to know your Beau very well while you've been here. And I can see what you say is true. He is a very confident man."

Bruce laughed out loud for the first time since he'd been in the hospital and it made his head smart a little. "That is a major understatement."

"What's so funny?" Beau asked as he and Tollison walked into the room.

"Speak of the devil," Bruce said.

"Really?" Beau teased. "Jokes at my expense again. Does that ever get old?"

"I might not remember much, but I do remember how fun it is to tease you, Beau."

"Touché," Tollison said. "But don't be too hard on him. He's tired, and not all of his jets are firing."

Bruce nodded. "Tollison. I'm looking forward to getting to know you. If Beau loves you, and I know he does—" He looked over at Beau and winked. "—then you've got to be a good person."

"I do believe I like this new Bruce much better than the old one," Tollison teased.

"Seriously, though," Bruce said. "I can't thank you enough for all you've done for me."

"I'm sure you would have done the same for us," Tollison replied. "We're friends—no, we're family."

"All right, gentlemen," a voice said from the door. They all turned to see a nurse standing with her hands resting on her curvy hips. "Someone is going for a little ride in about five minutes. So vamoose. All of you. We're taking Mr. Jenkins down one floor to room 359. You can wait for him there."

Bastien leaned over the bed and pressed his warm lips against Bruce's. Gunshot wound to the head or not, Bruce felt something stir in his nether regions. At that moment he knew Bastien had been right earlier. One way or the other, they were going to find their way back to each other.

A COUPLE of hours later, Bruce was comfortable in his new room. Beau was leaning against the back of the door, watching Tollison and Bastien hovering over him like nursemaids, when he heard a knock on the door.

He opened the door to see Auggie, Jenny, and Iona standing in the hall with a couple guys from the station and Bruce's guard, who had moved with him from the Neuro ICU.

Beau looked at Bruce. "You up for a little company?"

"Sure," Bruce said. "I feel like I've been sleeping for the last week."

Beau opened the door and everyone but Auggie came in. He gestured for Beau to join him in the hall.

"What's up?"

"Not a fucking thing," Auggie said. "Bruce's phone gave us nothing more than the others. Just random profile names, some with body parts for pictures, and some with no pictures at all. None that match any of the profile names on the other's phones. This guy is good. He's thorough, and he's good."

"We're gonna get him," Beau reassured Auggie. "Don't you worry. He's gonna slip up, and when he does, we're gonna be right there. But ya know what? Something's been nagging at me. All the other guys were tracked by social media. Grindr or the like. But Bruce isn't on Facebook, and he told me he hasn't been on Grindr or any other site since he and Bastien have been involved. How did the perp track him down?"

Auggie kicked a spot on the floor with the toe of his shoe. "I think that was my fault."

"What?" Beau asked. "How can that be your fault?"

"We were going over our case notes in my office, and I asked him to explain to me how Grindr worked. I certainly didn't want to download that shit on my phone. So he opened the application and showed it to me. And—"

"—he didn't close the app when he was done," Beau finished for him.

"Apparently not. It was still open when IT started working on his phone."

"Fuck!" Beau said.

"I know. I feel like a piece of shit."

"No, Aug. Don't beat yourself up. I probably would have done the same thing. I mean… who knew this was the same guy?" Beau thought for a moment. "But what I don't understand is how the guy knew Bruce was going to be at that parade and at that location. If Bruce isn't on Facebook or any other social media, and if you have to be within a certain distance to see someone's profile, it would be a huge coincidence if they were at the same place at the same time."

"Maybe the guy was tailing Bruce. I'm sure he knew Bruce was a detective with the NOPD. If Bruce didn't tell him that, any Google search would."

"Maybe," Beau said.

"Bruce needs to remember this fucker's name," Auggie said. "That's it."

"I'm pushing him as hard as I dare. His memory is coming back in bits and pieces, so I'm hoping he comes up with something before the guy kills again."

"We'll know soon enough," Auggie said. "There are six parades rolling tonight. All over the city."

"I'll talk to Bruce again before we leave. But in the meantime, go in and say hello. He's doing really well, and I'm sure he wants to see you."

THE OTHERS said their good-byes, which left Beau, Tollison, and Bastien standing around Bruce's bed. Bruce protested repeatedly as Bastien stated he was staying the night and there would be no further discussion. Eventually Bruce gave up, but even while protesting, he never let go of Bastien's hand. Beau smiled at him like a pleased parent, and Bruce blushed.

"Bruce?" Beau asked when there was a lull in the conversation. "I know I already questioned you about the guy you had the affair with, and you said you didn't remember anything about him, but if you do remember something—anything—please call me. Day or night. I don't want to put any pressure on you, but we need to get this guy before he strikes again."

Bruce hesitated before he responded, trying to remember something significant.

"What?" Beau asked.

"I'm not sure," Bruce replied. "I had such bizarre dreams earlier. But something seems to be nagging at me." He hesitated, staring straight ahead. "Oh well. If I remember anything, I promise I'll call."

Beau nodded. "Thanks. Tol, you think it's time we give these men a little time alone?"

"Absolutely."

Tollison squeezed Bruce's leg and smiled, and Bruce smiled back. "Thank you again."

Beau leaned over and kissed Bruce's cheek. "Well, you take care," he said as they turned to leave. "We'll see you tomorrow."

Bruce heard "Well, you take care" ringing through his mind over and over. But why? And then he remembered. It was what the stranger in his dream had said when Bruce sent him away. *Could that be the guy I had the affair with?*

"Wait!" Bruce said.

Beau stopped. He turned and met Bruce's gaze.

"I thought it was just a dream," Bruce said. "But maybe it was a real flashback."

"What? Tell me," Beau insisted. "What do you remember?"

"It may be nothing at all, but while I was asleep, I had a vision or flashback or whatever the hell it was, of me being intimate with…." He looked at Bastien and felt heat creep up his face.

Tollison must have anticipated what the blush meant. "Why don't we step out, Bastien, and let Beau and Bruce do a little detective work," he said.

"No need," Bruce said. "It's okay." He looked at Bastien again. "I'm sure this was before I even met you."

"It's okay, ma puce," Bastien said. "I love you, and nothing you've done or could ever do will change that."

"Thank you." Bruce squeezed Bastien's hand. "In my dream—or whatever it was—I had this image of me having rather rough sex with someone I didn't know. There was no connection at all, just sex. I remember being so frustrated and angry, and I took it out on this guy. After it was over, I was horrified that I'd even done it. I sent the guy away, and he wasn't happy about it. His exact words were—and I can hear them clearly—'Well, you take care. Cop or no cop, if I were you I'd watch my back.'" Bruce hesitated. "That's got to be the guy. Right?"

"He fucking threatened you?" Beau asked.

"Yeah. But to be fair, I had just used the guy and thrown him out."

"Can you remember his name, or do you think you could identify him from a photograph?" Beau asked.

"My dream was fuzzy," Bruce said. "And I don't remember his name. But the more I think about it, the more I feel like I'm missing something."

"It's okay," Beau said. "Just give it some time. I'm sure it'll come back to you. And when it does, just pick up the phone."

"I will," Bruce answered. Suddenly the overhead light in his hospital room flashed and went out. There was another light over his bed, so they weren't in total darkness, but the room dimmed quite a bit.

"I'll tell the nurse on my way out," Tollison said. "Good night, you two. Sleep tight. Beau, I'll see you at the elevator."

"Okay," Beau said. "Remember, anytime, day or night."

"I got it, Beau," Bruce said, rolling his eyes and smiling at Bastien.

"Okay. I'm outta here. Night, guys."

BRUCE STIRRED at the sound of metal scraping the floor. He opened his eyes to see a maintenance man positioning an aluminum ladder at the foot of his bed under the burned-out lightbulb.

"Sorry to wake you," he said when he saw Bruce looking at him. "I was trying to be as quiet as I could."

Bruce shook his head. "I was just dozing," he whispered. He looked over at Bastien, who was still asleep and seemed to be unaffected.

"It'll only take me a couple of minutes and I will be out of your hair," the man said.

The maintenance man wore a blue uniform with the name of the hospital embroidered over one pocket and his name, Charlie, over the other.

"Thanks, Charlie," Bruce said.

He watched the man closely as he climbed up the ladder and began to change the bulb. Bruce was fixated on his blue uniform. The flashback of him and his mystery man came back to him. *That's it!* His hookup had also been wearing a blue uniform.

Bruce closed his eyes and tried to recall the vision in detail. He watched the guy pull up his pants and angrily tuck his shirt in. He walked toward Bruce and then stopped. In his mind's eye, Bruce saw the uniform clearly. Over the right pocket, he read NOLA Heating & Air, and over the left he saw Zach.

"Oh my God!" Bruce shouted.

The lightbulb in Charlie's hand flew into the air. Luckily he caught it before it came crashing to the floor. Bastien jumped to his feet and rushed to Bruce's bed. "What's wrong? Are you okay?"

"I remember. Get Beau on the phone."

TWENTY-FOUR

IT WAS just past 4:00 a.m. when Beau woke up and fumbled for the telephone. Since the first parade had rolled at six o'clock the night before, he and Auggie had both been waiting for the phone to ring, alerting them to another shooting. Fortunately, no calls came. By the end of the last parade, they had attributed the lack of another incident to the fact that the news had reported that Bruce had survived the shooting but was in critical condition.

Beau had been so glad they'd put an armed guard at Bruce's door. If Beau had been the murderer, he'd have done one of two things. He would either have tried to finish the job and gotten rid of the only witness who could ID him, or lain low for a day or two and then gotten out of Dodge.

"Bissonet," Beau said curtly when he answered the phone.

At the sound of Bastien's voice, Beau elbowed Tollison. "Bastien? Is everything all right?"

"Yes," Bastien said. "Here. Talk to Bruce."

Bruce came on the line, sounding a little shaky but very sure of himself as he explained what he'd remembered.

Beau listened carefully. He had to admit it wasn't easy hearing the details of the affair he'd pleaded with Bruce to remember. He fought to hold at bay the feelings of betrayal and anger lingering just beyond his conscious thoughts, knowing if he let them in, he'd be a basket case again. *No, Beau! You've been through this. Get over it, and don't allow anything to distract you from the job at hand.* He told himself there would be plenty of time to deal with the emotional side of it later. He knew Tollison would know what to say to help him sort through it all.

As soon as Beau hung up with Bruce, he phoned Auggie and filled him in on what he now knew. They agreed to meet at the station within the hour. All they had was the perp's employment information and his first name, and they would need as much time as they could get to come up with a plan before sunrise.

When Beau and Tollison got to the station, it was nearing five o'clock, and Auggie was already at his desk tapping on his keyboard. He looked up and offered a weak smile.

"I have someone gathering info on NOLA Heating & Air, but right now I'm on their website, trying to find a list of names and/or pictures of their technicians."

"And?" Beau asked.

"Nothing so far but the services they offer, hours of operation, and contact information."

"What about an after-hours emergency telephone number?" Beau asked.

Auggie clicked his mouse a few times. "Yeah. Here we go."

"Give it to me," Beau said, picking up Auggie's office phone.

"Do you guys really think we should chance that?" Tollison said.

Beau and Auggie both gave Tollison a questioning glance.

"Come on, guys," Tollison said. "You're supposed to be the detectives here. Think. What if Zach's the one on call?"

"Oh shit!" Beau said. "Good point. Are we brain dead, Aug?"

"Likely, but we're probably just tired and not cooking on all four burners."

"Auggie, go to the About section," Tollison instructed. "Does the site say how many employees the company has?"

Auggie moved the mouse and clicked a few times. "No. Why?"

"Because if they have a lot of employees, the chances of Zach being on call are pretty slim, but if NOLA Heating & Air is a mom-and-pop operation, there could be only one or two technicians, and the chance is much greater. Hell, Zach could even own the place for all we know."

"This is a pretty pitiful website. The kind where you load your info and photos and voilà, you have a website," Auggie said.

Tollison frowned. "Which indicates mom-and-pop to me."

"Then we don't risk it," Auggie said. "I don't want to take a chance on tipping this guy off."

"Where are they located?" Beau asked.

Auggie scrolled down the page. "At 1610 Airline Highway. Near the airport."

"And what time do they open?"

"Seven o'clock."

Beau looked at his watch. "I say we leave now and stake the place out. We see how big this operation is and how many people show up for work. Then we go from there."

"If it's a big outfit," Auggie said, "we'll go in and see what we can find out."

"And if it's small with only a couple of guys," Beau added, "we rush the place."

"Hold on, Bissonet. No rushing. We need to be smart about this."

"Okay, be smart," Beau replied. "We'll have backup in place if we need them, and then we rush the place. Let's go."

THIRTY-FIVE MINUTES later, Auggie pulled his unmarked black Crown Victoria into the used-car section of a Ford dealership directly across the street from NOLA Heating & Air.

"How lucky are we that a Ford dealership was so close?" Beau asked rhetorically.

Auggie chuckled. "We look like we fit right in."

NOLA Heating & Air was in a strip mall, along with Crescent City Electric and, oddly enough, an Adam & Eve sex store.

"You mos need an extra butt plug while we're here?" Auggie asked, looking through his small binoculars.

"We're good," Beau said. "But I'm sure Jenny would love a dildo to make up for *your* shortcomings."

"But you might want to think about that before you do it, Aug," Tollison teased. "Once you go big, you can never go back."

"Good one, Tol," Beau said.

Auggie dropped his binoculars. "Hey! She's never complained before," he shot back.

"Why complain?" Tollison asked. "It's not like it will make your dick any bigger."

Auggie huffed and lifted his binoculars to his face again. "Can we just get back to the case?"

"What's the matter, Aug?" Beau asked. "Can't hold your own with the big guys?"

"Fuck you, Bissonet."

"Look, guys!" Tollison said. "A car just pulled into the parking lot."

"Yeah. It's a woman. A blonde to be exact."

Tollison watched her get out of her car and walk toward the building.

"Never mind," Auggie said when the woman slid her key into Crescent City Electric's door.

"Wait! A van just pulled in and parked next to the woman's car," Tollison said. "Can you read the writing on the side?"

"Bingo," Auggie said. NOLA Heating & Air was written in a circle surrounding a fleur-de-lis.

"Let me see those," Beau said, reaching for Auggie's binoculars.

The first thing he noticed was that the guy was very short, maybe five-five, and he walked with a waddle. He looked to be between forty-five and fifty, was balding, and had a pudgy midsection. "Nope. Not our guy."

"How do you know that?" Auggie asked.

Beau handed the binoculars back to Auggie. "Look at him."

"I'm looking. So?"

"Come on, Aug. Bruce would never sleep with a guy like that."

"He's right," Tollison agreed. "I can't even see his face clearly, but I can tell he's not Bruce's type."

Auggie dropped the binoculars again. "Maybe he's the owner. If no one else shows up in the next fifteen minutes, we'll go in."

"I don't know, Aug. The perp is smart," Beau said. "Do you think he would actually have the balls to show up for work? I would be on my way out of the country by now."

Auggie looked like he was mulling this over. "You know something? You're right," he finally said. "He is smart. But maybe too smart for his own good. I'd bet my career this guy thinks he's outsmarted us and has no reason to run."

"That *would* work in our favor," Tollison said. "But I think you both have good points."

Just then another van pulled into the parking lot with the same logo on the side. "Here we go again," Auggie said, raising the binoculars back up to his eyes.

After a moment he handed the binoculars back to Beau. "Check this guy out, Bissonet. Hell. He's so hot I'd sleep with him."

Beau focused the lenses. "Now this is more like it. In fact, this guy looks a lot like me. He's built like a brick shithouse. He's got my hair, and he's even got my complexion. I'll bet he has my eyes too." Beau looked at Tollison and winked. "I'd say he's downright gorgeous."

Auggie rolled his eyes. "Christ, Beau. Modest much?"

"Hell, Aug. If I had known you found me so attractive, we could have given it a go a long time ago."

"In your dreams, asshole."

Beau and Tollison exchanged high fives. "Nicely played," Tollison said.

"Fuck you too, Cruz."

A few minutes later another car pulled into the parking lot, and a robust woman climbed out. She dropped her cigarette to the cement, stomped it out with her foot, and shuffled to the front door. "Must be the receptionist or secretary," Beau said. "No worries. Even *you* could take her, Aug."

"Not me," Auggie replied. "Some mountains are just too big to climb."

Beau looked at his watch again. "It's almost seven thirty. I think we should give her a few minutes to get settled and then go for it. If these guys have jobs today, they are going to be pulling out very soon."

"Let's do it." Auggie tapped the screen of his phone and held it to his ear. "We're going in. Give us five minutes and then surround the place."

Auggie started the car, crossed Airline Highway, and pulled into the parking lot.

The three men entered the small storefront and saw the woman sitting behind a gray metal desk. Looking around, Beau saw a couple of chairs, a watercooler, and some filing cabinets. Besides the front door, there was one other door, but it was closed. He assumed it led to a supply room or some type of storage area.

The woman eyed the three of them and smiled. "Good morning, gentlemen," she said, batting her eyelashes.

Auggie was the first to flash his badge. "I'm Detective August Hebert with the NOPD. Can you tell me who owns this place?"

The blood drained out of the woman's face, and she stared at the badge like she wasn't sure if it was real or not.

"I assure you we're the real deal," Auggie explained. "Beau?"

Beau flashed his badge as well. "Detective Bissonet," he said.

"My husband and I own it," she finally said.

"And your name is?" Beau asked.

"Bonnie. Bonnie Boudreaux."

"And your husband's name?"

"Stanley Boudreaux. Why? Are we in some kind of trouble?"

"I don't know that yet," Auggie said. "Do you have a Zach working here?"

"Yeah."

"What is his last name?" Beau asked.

"Patton."

"Is he here?"

"I haven't seen him yet, but I assume he is. That's his truck outside next to my husband's."

Beau gave Tollison and Auggie a knowing glance. "Ms. Boudreaux, is there an intercom or PA system you can use to call him up here without actually talking to him?"

"We have an intercom system, but I need to know what this is all about before I do anything of the sort."

"Do it," Auggie said, "or I'm gonna arrest you for obstruction of justice."

The woman's eyes got as big as saucers. "You wouldn't."

Auggie reached under his suit jacket and pulled a set of handcuffs off his belt. He dangled them in front of Bonnie, and she started to visibly tremble. "You wanna try me?"

She swallowed hard.

"Now get on the intercom and tell him you need him up front. And do it casually so as not to make it sound suspicious."

Bonnie picked up the phone, but before she could speak into the receiver, the back door opened, and the man they assumed was Zach stood in the doorway. He looked at Beau, Tollison, and Auggie for a long moment, and then when it looked like it had all registered in his brain, he slammed the door shut again.

"He's running," Beau yelled.

"Got it." Auggie was on his phone in an instant.

Tollison looked at Bonnie. "Is there a back door?"

"Yes."

"Oh hell no!" Beau was at the door in a split second. He drew his gun from his shoulder holster, threw the door open, and hit the floor in one fluid movement. A shot blew right past his head and hit the front window, shattering it and sending particles of glass all over the office and Bonnie. She screamed, dropped to the floor, and crawled under her desk.

Three cars screeched to a halt in the parking lot, and Beau heard more sirens around back. Auggie's backup had arrived.

"The place is surrounded, Zach," Beau screamed. "There's no place to go."

Another shot rang out, and Auggie and Tollison hit the floor.

"Don't make this harder on yourself," Beau yelled.

"Can't get any worse," Zach yelled back. "Capital punishment is alive and well in Louisiana, and if you convict me on just one murder charge, I'll die by lethal injection. Might as well take out as many as I can. You can only kill me once."

"He has a point," Beau whispered as another shot rang out and ricocheted off the metal filing cabinet. Bonnie screamed again and called, "Stanley!"

"Can you see if her husband is back there?" Tollison asked.

"No," Beau said. "He may have run out the back at the first shot."

Bonnie stuck her head out from under the desk. "If that asshole ran and left me here to fend for myself, if you don't kill him, I will."

Another shot crossed the office, and Beau looked back to make sure no one was hit. He saw a bullet hole in the front door, but amazingly the door didn't shatter.

"We need a distraction," Beau whispered.

Auggie was on his phone. "Already on it."

Beau saw daylight when the back door swung open. Another shot was fired instantly, so he used the opportunity to crawl into the storage room and take cover behind a crated central-air-conditioning unit. He scanned the room and finally spotted Zach in the left corner behind some shelving. The barrel of his rifle was resting on one of the shelving units, and he was scanning back and forth between the two doors.

Damn! That looks like some variation of an M40. Can't be. M40 is a single-shot rifle. Think, Beau. This is important. Wait! M40A1s. I think they hold six shots. Yes!

Beau got on his phone and dialed Auggie. "He's in the back left corner about twenty feet from the door," he whispered. "Right now he's shooting blind, but if one of your guys tries to take him from outside, make sure they're behind cover."

"Got it."

Beau assumed Auggie passed along the information because shortly thereafter two shots were fired right through the exterior prefabbed metal wall, missing Zach by a few feet.

Zach immediately returned fire with one succinct round. Beau had been trying to keep track of the rounds fired, and if he was right, that was number six.

Two more shots blasted through the walls, closer to Zach this time, but not close enough to hit him. But he didn't return fire.

He's reloading!

"Hold fire," Beau whispered into his phone. "I'm going in."

Beau ran across the room as fast as his legs would carry him, his gun drawn. He rounded the corner behind the shelving, and luckily he'd been right. Zach was reloading. When their eyes met, Zach froze and smiled. "Hello, Beau," he said. "I knew we'd meet one day."

Beau stood with his gun aimed at Zach's head, and all the hurt, anger, and despair Zach had caused him and Bruce came back with a vengeance.

"Aren't you gonna shoot?" Zach said calmly.

"You're not worth it," Beau replied.

"But I fucked your husband. Hard. And you know what? He loved it. He said I was way better than you. The best he's ever had. He begged me for more."

Unable to stop himself, Beau tossed his gun to the side and leapt through the air. "Fuck you, asshole," he screamed as he landed on Zach. Zach went down with a thud, and the box of ammo he was holding flew into the air and landed on the ground, sending bullets in every direction.

Beau picked up a bullet and pressed it against Zach's neck. "You move and I'll run this right through your jugular."

"Go on, Beau. Do it."

Beau didn't trust himself. He tossed the bullet and wrapped his bare hands round Zach's neck. "Just so you know, you were nothing to Bruce but a onetime fuck. In fact, he's the one who fucked you. Hard, just the way you like it."

Zach bucked, and Beau tightened his grip on Zach's neck. "Oh? Didn't think I knew all of that? I know it all. And the part I love the best is how he threw you out right afterward. He fucking used your ass and tossed you aside like an old shoe. Isn't that what really happened?"

Beau saw the first chink in Zach's armor, so he went in for the kill. "As a matter of fact, you were nothing to any of the guys you killed. You were just a bad fuck to all of them."

As Beau tightened his grip on Zach's neck again, Zach gasped, "Do it. Please."

"That's enough, Beau."

Beau looked up to see Tollison standing over him. "It's over. Killing him won't change anything."

Auggie stepped up next to Tollison and put his hand on Beau's shoulder. "He's right, man. It's over. You're not a killer. Let someone else judge him. That's not your job."

Zach's face had turned several shades of blue. Beau released him, and he sucked air. After a few deep breaths, he smiled coyly. "I always knew you were a coward," he forced out. "You gave Bruce up for one stupid mistake. You didn't even fight for him."

Beau was seconds from finishing the job. "You know nothing about me or my relationship with Bruce."

"I know you tossed *him* out like yesterday's trash, just like he tossed me out," Zach said.

Beau drew back and was about to let Zach have it when Auggie caught his hand. "Enough, Beau!"

Beau looked around to see a shitload of uniformed cops watching him.

"Let these guys do their job," Auggie said.

Beau got to his feet, found his gun, and took Tollison by the hand. "Let's go see Bruce."

EPILOGUE

ZACH PATTON confessed to three counts of murder, one count of attempted murder, and one count of possessing an illegal firearm. The gun was indeed an M40A1 sniper rifle, and he'd kept it hidden behind plumbing supplies at work to make sure if he was ever suspected of the murders, the weapon would not easily be found.

Beau, Tollison, and Auggie all kept tabs as Zach's case progressed through the courts. Beau learned Zach would be on death row soon, which was where he wanted to be, but Beau had mixed emotions about it all. He hated the guy for hurting Bruce and for ruining their relationship, but he couldn't give Zach all the credit. He'd done a pretty good job of that on his own. He *had* tossed Bruce out like yesterday's trash, and he would have to live with that for the rest of his life. But he also felt sorry for Zach. The guy needed psychological help, but his self-hatred ran so deep he couldn't see any way out. That didn't excuse what he had done, of course. If he had ever found someone to love, his story might have had a different ending. Beau could relate to that and thanked his lucky stars every day for Tollison.

Zach also confessed he *had* been stalking Bruce and his other victims for quite some time. He was fine as long as they were as miserable as he was. But what pushed him over the edge was when a couple of the guys started dating other men or were seemingly happy in their lives, Bruce being one of them. His rationale was, why should any of these guys be happy when he never would be? And the ball started rolling from there.

And lastly, as suspected, in addition to the stalking, Zach had had help from social media in pinpointing his victims' exact locations, but according to him, he had so many profiles on the various applications that he could lure most of his victims, or anyone else for that matter, anywhere he wanted them to be. He had planned a lot more murders, but without the cloak of Mardi Gras to hide behind, he would have had to wait for more opportune times. Either way, he'd been certain he would eventually be able to lure his victims exactly where he wanted them.

BEAU, TOLLISON, Auggie, Jenny, and Iona were all at the airport to wish Bruce and Bastien well as they started their new life.

Bruce's full physical and emotional recovery had taken nearly six months, but with each passing day, he'd remembered more: His life with Beau. His life without Beau. Tollison and Beau's life. His and Bastien's life and, more importantly, their love.

As the group stood outside of security, taking advantage of a last few minutes before Bruce and Bastien had to go, Bruce excused himself and disappeared into the men's room. He leaned against the wall, closed his eyes, and did everything he could to fight off an anxiety attack. He loved Bastien with all his heart, and he wanted a forever with him, but how was he going to say good-bye to his friends—no, his family?

Forcing himself to calm down, he opened his eyes again, and Beau was standing in front of him with his arms crossed over his chest.

"I know you, Jenkins." Beau unfolded his arms and grabbed Bruce by the shoulders. "If you're having second thoughts about this, you can walk right outta here, and I'll handle everything. You won't even have to talk to the guy."

"No!" Bruce said. "I'm not—I love Bastien. It's just...."

Beau smiled. "We're your family, and it's hard to leave the comforts of family for the unknown?"

"Exactly," Bruce said, surprised. "Who are you and what have you done with Beau Bissonet?"

"Don't be an ass, Bruce."

"Sorry."

"If you love the guy, it will all work out," Beau said. "And you know I'll will always be your family. Tollison and me—hell, the entire gang—will always be here for you. We may be farther away, but we're still here. All you have to do is call."

Bruce felt his heart rate starting to slow down, and he smiled. "Thank you."

"Are you sure?"

"I'm sure."

"Then let's go. You and Bastien have a plane to catch."

Beau dropped an arm over Bruce's shoulder, and together they walked back to the gate.

When they arrived, Bastien was looking around with a concerned expression on his face.

"Sorry," Bruce said. "I had to pee, and look who was working the bathroom?"

Beau punched Bruce in the arm. "Really? What did I say about being an asshole?"

Before Bruce could respond, Bastien took him by the hand. He glanced at his watch. "We have to get through security, ma puce, if we're going to make our flight."

Bruce looked at Beau and then Bastien. "I guess this is it," he said nervously.

Beau gave Bruce a reassuring smile and pulled him into a hug. "Remember," Beau whispered in his ear. "I love you, and if you ever need me, I'm here."

"I love you too," Bruce whispered back. "Thank you. For everything."

Beau nodded and stepped back. "And we'll all see you guys this summer."

Auggie wrapped Bruce in a bear hug. "If it doesn't work out, you come right back here and we pick up where we left off. You got it? Best friends and partners till the end."

As he heard these words from the big macho detective, Bruce's bottom lip began to quiver, and his eyes quickly filled with tears. Unable to speak, he simply nodded against Auggie's shoulder and stepped back, looking away briefly to get himself under control.

Everyone else exchanged hugs and well-wishes, and Bruce and Bastien showed their boarding passes and walked to the security line. Bruce stopped and turned back to see his family all standing there smiling and waving at them.

Bastien studied him. "You're not having second thoughts, are you?"

"I love them, Bastien. They are my family. And I hate to leave them."

Now Bastien's forehead wrinkled, and he tensed.

"But I love you more, and you are my future."

Bastien's frown melted into a broad smile. "I love you, ma puce," he said, and he grabbed Bruce and kissed him soundly right there in the security line.

Beau whistled, and everyone else did their best catcalls. Bruce turned back one last time and waved good-bye. Then with a swoop of excitement in his chest, he gripped Bastien's hand, and they headed into the next stage of their journey together.

BISSONET AND Cruz Investigations had settled back into a routine. Beau and Tollison were in their office, and Iona was buzzing around them like a bee around a hive. She'd sort of become a mother to all of them, and as much as it drove Beau crazy, he loved her caring and nurturing nature.

Auggie was still a little bitter about losing yet another partner and was working his way through the NOPD to find just the right one. He'd sworn up and down they would have to sign their life away in blood and promise to never leave the organization before he would even consider them as his new guy Friday.

They all planned a trip to Geneva during the summer months to see Bruce and Bastien, and Iona and Jenny were put in charge of the arrangements. From the looks of it, they were taking the job very seriously. Beau and Tollison had observed them for the last week sitting at Iona's desk at least an hour a day, looking at flights and making travel plans. Life for all of them was getting back to normal, and Beau was happy about that.

"I gotta pee," Beau said, glancing at Tollison across the desk, "and then I gotta get home. It's Friday night, and I'm making my man dinner. Then we're going to have a nice, long, quiet evening at home. Will you be along soon?"

Tollison looked up and smiled. "Actually, I'm about done here, so I'll walk out with you."

When Beau and Tollison got to the bathroom door, it was closed. But a second later, it opened, and Iona came out. She smiled sheepishly, walked past them without a word, and disappeared down the hall.

Beau picked up on the odor immediately. He quickly shoved Tollison into the bathroom, closed the door, and held the doorknob.

"Very funny, Beau," Tollison said. "I get it. Now open the door."

Beau released the door, and Tollison bolted out. They scuffled with each other to be the first to escape down the hall.

"I thought you had to pee," Tollison said.

"It can wait," Beau said. "Forever."

As they rounded the corner, the bell on the door jingled. Beau looked toward the front entrance and saw a handsome middle-aged man heading for Iona's desk. After a brief conversation with the caller, Iona looked over her shoulder at them.

"You gentlemen have a visitor," she said.

"Who is it?" Beau asked.

"His name is Collier James, and he says he requires your assistance."

Beau and Tollison stood up straight and brushed at the fronts of their suit coats.

"Ready for another round on the Ferris wheel?" Tollison asked.

"Hell yeah!"

SCOTTY CADE left Corporate America and twenty-five years of marketing and public relations in 2004 to buy an inn & restaurant on the island of Martha's Vineyard with Kell, his husband of over twenty years.

He started writing stories as soon as he could read, but only in the last five years for publication. When not at the inn, you can find him on the bow of his boat writing romance novels with his Shetland sheepdog, Mavis, at his side. Being from the South and a lover of commitment and fidelity, all of his characters find their way to long, healthy relationships, however long it takes them to get there. He believes that, in the end, the boy should always get the boy.

Scotty and Kell are avid boaters and live aboard their boat, spending the summers on Martha's Vineyard and winters in various locations down south.

Website: www.scottycade.com
Facebook: www.facebook.com/scotty.cade
Twitter: @ScottyCade
E-mail: scotty@scottycade.com

SCOTTY CADE

THE ROYAL STREET HEIST

Bissonet & Cruz Investigations: Book One

When valuable Civil War era art is stolen from a popular New Orleans gallery, NOPD Lead Detective Montgomery "Beau" Bissonet and his partner set out to solve the crime. When the gallery's insurance company sends Tollison Cruz to the Big Easy to conduct their own independent investigation, personalities clash and battle lines are definitely drawn.

The heist quickly becomes a politically driven high profile case, and Detective Bissonet is furious when he's ordered to work along side Investigator Cruz to assure a timely arrest. The heat index soars to new levels when the two investigators discover they have a lot more in common than originally thought.

With the tension between them temporarily sated, Bissonet and Cruz finally start to work together, on more than just a professional level. But everything comes to a screeching halt when Beau discovers his cohort in crime has been withholding information regarding the investigation and has been concealing a very questionable past. What happens next rivals the scorching summer heat.

www.dreamspinnerpress.com

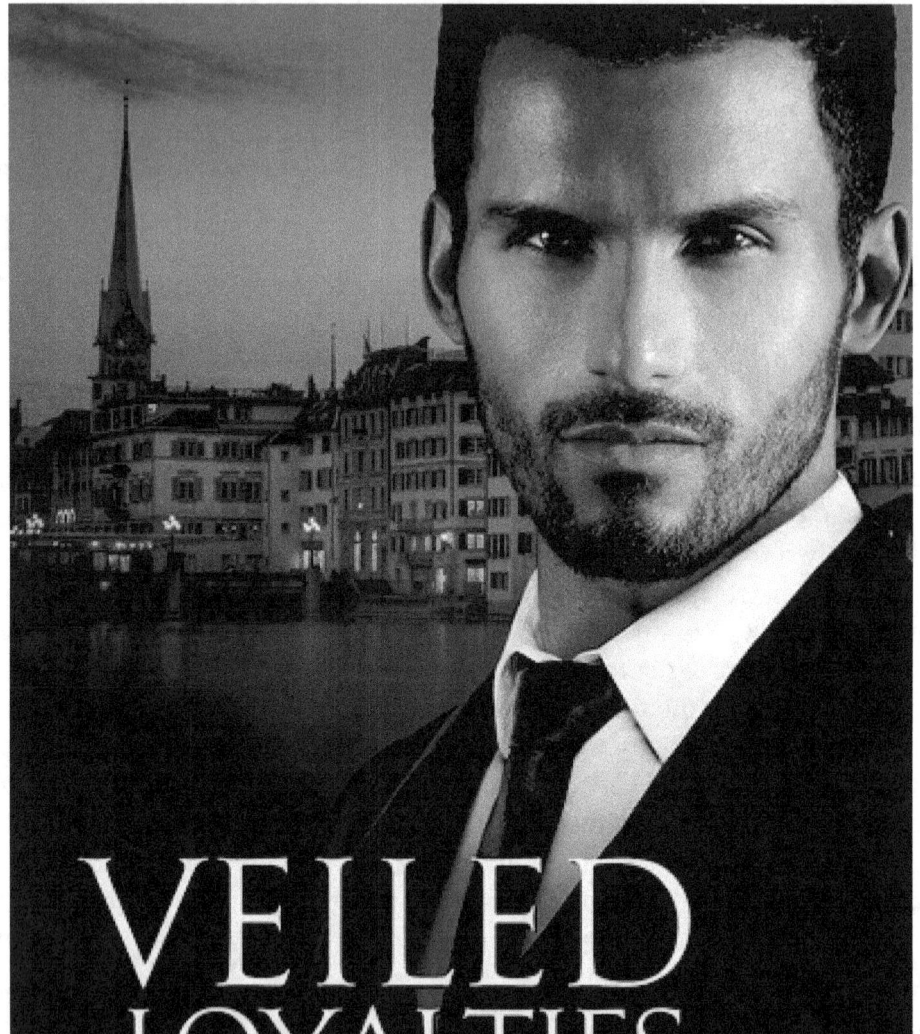

VEILED
LOYALTIES
BISSONET & CRUZ INVESTIGATIONS

SCOTTY CADE

Sequel to *The Royal Street Heist*
Bissonet & Cruz Investigations: Book Two

Halloween is Beau Bissonet's favorite holiday, from carving pumpkins to decorating his yard to donning a costume and scaring the neighborhood kids. But this year his Halloween is about to take a different turn, one that will challenge his skills as a detective and his commitment to his partner in work and love.

A year since Beau and Tollison solved *The Royal Street Heist*, found love, and formed Bissonet & Cruz Investigations, they are thriving personally and professionally. That is until Tollison's ex, Bastien Andros, shows up out of the blue. Naturally, Beau's suspicious, but two days after Bastien's arrival, he goes missing, and Tollison worries his past may catch up to him.

A mysterious package makes clear who has Bastien and what's at stake. With both Bastien and Beau's lives now at risk, Tollison has only one option: travel to Zurich, Switzerland, secure and deliver the ransom, keep both men safe, and stay true to himself at the same time.

www.dreamspinnerpress.com

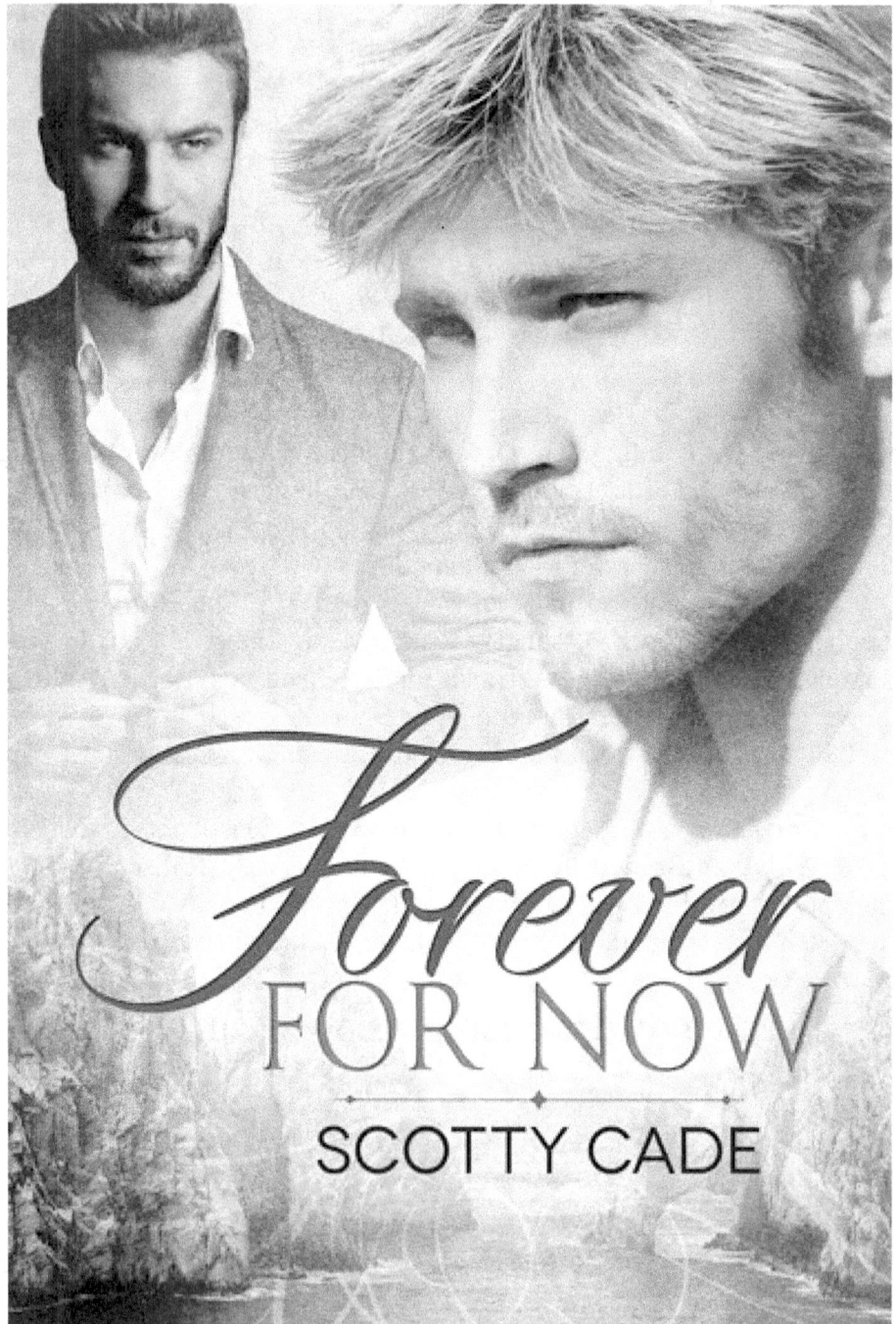

Forever
FOR NOW

SCOTTY CADE

Leeland Jeffers is a contented single man with a thriving career in Atlanta. He's had a few unsuccessful relationships over the years, but no one has even come close to his first love, Harrison Rhinehart. They met in college when a mutual friend, Suzie Garrison, introduced Harry into their close-knit group. When the supposedly "straight" Harry made a move on Lee, the two men entered into a tumultuous secret love affair. In their senior year, the relationship finally ended when Harry informed Lee he was marrying Suzie.

Since graduation, the college friends have drifted apart. However, an unexpected invitation to a destination wedding seems set to reunite them all. Lee's speculation on whether Harry and Suzie will make an appearance threatens to derail his attendance. But Lee decides the hell with it and makes plans to go, Harry Rhinehart or no Harry Rhinehart.

www.dreamspinnerpress.com

Two cadets from very different worlds.
One forbidden love.

KNOBS

SCOTTY CADE

Angus Conrad (Gus) McRae is a privileged Charlestonian following family tradition and attending the Citadel, harboring big dreams of a military career. With the infamous Hell Week behind him, he quickly realizes being a Knob (a freshman cadet) is just as tough—especially for a man like Gus who must keep his sexuality a secret. Then a sudden dorm reassignment lands him with a roommate in the form of one of the football team's top players—working-class jock Stewart Adam (Sam) Morley—and life gets increasingly complicated.

Gus can't imagine a man like Sam as gay, yet there's something between them—exchanged glances, the occasional innuendo. Sexual tensions rise, leaving them more than friends but less than lovers. Gus and Sam know there's too much to lose and they must keep their attraction hidden. If they fail, they risk destroying their hopes and dreams for a prosperous future in a military world that's not yet ready to accommodate masculine gay men.

www.dreamspinnerpress.com

Praying for answers, longing for love.

LOSING FAITH

SCOTTY CADE

Father Cullen Kiley, a gay Episcopal priest on hiatus from the church, decides to take his boat, *T-Time*, from Provincetown, Massachusetts, to Southport, North Carolina, a place that holds an abundance of bittersweet memories for him. While on a run his first day in Southport, Cullen comes upon a man sitting on a park bench staring out over the Cape Fear River with his Bible in hand. The man's body language reeks of defeat and desperation, and unable to ignore his compassion for his fellow man, Cullen stops to offer a helping hand.

Southport Baptist Church's Associate Pastor, Abel Weston, has a hard time managing his demons. When they get too overwhelming, he retreats to Southport's Historic Riverwalk with his Bible in hand and stares out over the water, praying for help and guidance that never seem to come. But Abel soon discovers that help and guidance come in many forms.

An unexpected friendship develops between the two men, and as Cullen helps Abel begin to confront his doubts and fears, he comes face-to-face with his own reality, threatening both their futures.

www.dreamspinnerpress.com

www.ingramcontent.com/pod-product-compliance
Lightning Source LLC
Chambersburg PA
CBHW070119260626
47160CB00004B/1531